THE HAVEN

Book 3, The Breeder Files

About the Author

Eliza Green tried her hand at fashion designing, massage, painting, and even ghost hunting, before finding her love of writing. She often wonders if her desire to change the ending of a particular glittery vampire story steered her in that direction (it did). After earning her degree in marketing, Eliza went on to work in everything but marketing, but swears she uses it in everyday life, or so she tells her bank manager.

Born and raised in Dublin, Ireland, she lives there with her sci-fi loving, evil genius best friend. When not working on her next amazing science fiction adventure, you can find her reading, indulging in new food at an amazing restaurant or simply singing along to something with a half decent beat.

For a list of all available books, check out:

www.elizagreenbooks.com/books

BOOK 3 IN THE BREEDER FILES

THE HAVEN

ELIZA GREEN

Copyright © 2019 Eliza Green

ISBN: 9781670799579

Copy Editor: Sara Litchfield
Cover: Deranged Doctor Design

To my wonderful readers.
Writing cliffhangers makes me feel tingly all over.
Soz, not soz.

1

Anya

Anya stared at Jason, still not convinced he was really here. They walked through the town in the valley of the Ferrous Mountains that the rebels had taken over. The afternoon sun shone bright and warmed Anya's pale skin. After so long spent underground, it breathed new life into her.

'I didn't know what had happened to you.' She shook her head. 'The last thing I remember was both of us sick in Brookfield. Then the men came.'

'I thought you were dead, Anya.' Her brother's voice cracked. 'My last memory was of you going through that machine in Arcis and there wasn't a damn thing I could do about it.' He stopped walking. 'Did it hurt?'

Anya stopped too, frowning. 'I don't remember any of it. The first memory I had was waking up in a comfortable bed. It's like the three months in Arcis never happened.' She touched her forehead. 'They

1

stole my memories. I don't have them back yet.'

Except for the one of Warren's hands on her in a bathroom; he'd tried to take something that wasn't on offer.

'They said they found you with that guy, Alex,' said Jason. 'Did you two... I mean, did anything happen between you? Did he try something?'

His question felt too personal. They weren't kids anymore. Sure, Anya had relied too much on him before and after their parents were murdered. But so much had happened to her since then. She may not remember, but she felt a change deep down.

'Not in that way, and also none of your business.'

'But we used to tell each other everything.'

'That was then. I'm not the kid I once was.'

Jason gave her a quick hug. 'I'm sorry for leaving you in Arcis. I thought you'd be safe.'

His apology meant nothing without her memories of that place. But despite her detachment from Arcis, their conversation unsettled her for reasons she couldn't explain.

'At least we're both alive.' She shifted the subject off her. 'And it looks like you found friends while I was away. Mum and Dad would be proud of you.'

'Of both of us. You're not the brat you once were.'

She thumped him in the arm, causing him to yelp. He rubbed the spot where she had hit him. 'I think you've lost some of your strength.'

She had. A week underground coupled with a mysterious, three-month absence had put a dent in her obsession with sports. She looked around at the high-fence compound, rock walls on either side. Her deceased parents came to mind. Had they ever been to this compound?

Vanessa, the librarian in Praesidium, had confirmed that Evan and Grace were rebels trying to put a stop to Praesidium's activities. Matching, something her mother had tried to force upon her, turned out to be a fake town tradition designed to keep her out of the Breeder programme. One day, Anya hoped to learn more about the real Grace and Evan Macklin.

She glanced at the building to the front of the U-shaped compound where the trucks had been parked, serving as a medical bay. It's where Dom had been taken. She still didn't remember the almost man who clearly remembered her, but she wished him well, hoped his illness had cleared up. There had been a moment when she'd thought he might not make it.

Jason's serious frown turned her stomach to butterflies. 'There's something I need to know.'

She nodded for him to go ahead, hating the probing questions.

'What happened to the copy of you? I saw it materialise when you approached the portal in Arcis' machine. Then it followed you through the same portal.'

Anya would never forget Canya. She looked away from him. 'It was weird, meeting my exact double. She didn't survive in the end.'

'She was killed?'

She looked back. 'Yeah. Turned on us, ratted us out to the guards while we were trying to escape the medical facility there.'

Jason ruffled his light brown hair. 'Jesus, that must have been weird.'

Weird only scraped the surface of her time as a prisoner in Praesidium. Not to mention her role in their Breeder programme.

'Uh, so how about you show me this place?'

She needed for Jason to be done with his questions. Her memories had been stolen from her, and to relive only parts of the journey unsettled her too much.

They stood near the entrance and Jason pointed out aspects of the compound. It had three main sections to it. A grey-bricked structure that looked to be a former community space, with stacks of chairs sitting outside, was now the medical bay. To the front of that was a grassy area with trucks parked in spaces large enough to accommodate them. Behind the medical bay were a series of streets that led back from it to another high fence.

They started for the road to the left of the makeshift trauma centre and Jason pointed out the town hall. Between it and the next building was a courtyard. They paused a moment and Anya spotted a

4

stationary exercise bike and a free weights stand in the building next to it. There was even a boxing bag at the back of the room. Some soldiers in their early twenties lifted weights while others ran through training drills in the courtyard to the front of the area. She smiled as she planned her way back to fitness.

Jason was watching her closely. 'I thought you'd like that. The tech workshop is on the other side of the exercise room. That's my playground.'

They continued their walk as he pointed out the other sections of the compound. Anya saw it was only a small part of a bigger town. In the distance, green, corrugated sheets of metal divided the rest of the former town. To their side, several ransacked buildings stood idle and unused.

They meandered down streets, past buildings without fronts, open spaces that were being used to store things the rebels must have salvaged from other towns. On one street, Anya saw a handful of businesses, if she could call the open spaces that, trading things from clothing to general purpose items like hairbrushes and soap. There was even a barber shop.

'I'm going to be working with the Inventor from Praesidium,' said Jason. 'So I can understand the Copies better. Jacob said they retain the personality traits of the Original, or human, until they're connected.'

That declaration stopped Anya cold. 'Are you saying my Copy was actually *me*, in more than just looks?'

The thought made her shiver. Could her Copy have passed as the real Anya in this world? Would Jason have noticed if Canya had turned up at the compound instead of her?

Jason nodded. 'That's what Jacob said.'

She looked away. Canya had acted in the most cruel and selfish way, passing back only the memory of Warren's attack on her. Where else would she have gotten those traits but from Anya?

She looked at Jason. 'Am I cruel? Selfish? Because that's exactly what my Copy was like.'

'Sometimes you were. But so was I. You're also kind, forgiving and loyal to your friends. Alex said that if it wasn't for you, he'd still be trapped in Praesidium. He owes you his life.' He gripped both her arms. 'Anya, you can be all of those bad things and still be a good person.'

She hoped so. But something more urgent than her behaviour bothered her.

Her stomach swirled with a new sickness. 'Is Warren here? Did he make it?'

He released her arms. 'Yeah. We found him and Jerome in Arcis. Did you want to see him?'

'No, uh, not right now.'

She'd have to see her attacker eventually, but it would be on her terms.

The thought make her palms sweat.

2

Carissa

It took three soldiers to restrain Carissa as they marched her inside a grey-walled cell. Her mind, quiet and empty of Copy or Collective voices, frightened her. She scanned the room, desperate to see a familiar face, but found no one. The Inventor had promised to look after her. Where was he?

One soldier deposited her on a single bed with just a chair in her prison cell for company, and left. Alone and against the Inventor's earlier warning, she searched for a connection to Praesidium; Quintus' voice, or one of the Copies, would do. The connection that tethered her to the city, the one that grounded her... she no longer felt it. Sat on the bed, she hugged her middle as her new reality set in. The Inventor wasn't the only one to abandon her.

At least she hadn't been terminated. Carissa laughed bitterly at that thought. Her prison, her isolation, was far worse than any punishment Quintus could order. A sharp ache spread through her chest.

Where was the Inventor? Why had he broken his promise to her?

She jumped up from the bed and paced in the area between it and the door. The pain in her mostly organic heart eased off the more she moved. She kept moving until the Inventor's betrayal of her didn't hurt as much. She would never forgive him.

The door unlocked and Carissa froze. Her damp gaze found the only person who could make this better.

'Inventor!' She pushed her anger aside and ran over to the old, stooped man, slipping her arms around his thin waist. 'Inventor,' she repeated.

He returned the hug and closed the door behind him.

'What's happening, Inventor?' She pulled away. 'Why am I here? Why have I been separated from you? Have I done something wrong?'

He stroked her hair. She leaned into his gentle touch.

'No, miss. You haven't done anything wrong. Max and the others who run this camp, they're just being cautious, like they were with Alex and my wolf.'

Carissa pulled back and frowned. 'Are they comparing me to a *Breeder* and a *beast* made of metal?'

The Inventor chuckled; the sound lifted more pain from Carissa's donated heart. 'No, miss. You're new, that's all. Max doesn't understand you like I do. I plan to change his mind about you.'

'How?'

The Inventor motioned for her to sit on the bed. She did but kept her eyes on him, fearing that if she turned her back, he'd disappear again. But to her relief, the old man sat down beside her, showing no distress from the gun blast injury to his leg when he and Carissa had escaped Praesidium. It pleased her to see he was no longer in pain.

'Max is wary of you, and for good reason,' said the Inventor. 'Nothing good has come of their interaction with the machines or Copies from Praesidium. He needs time to get to know you. I've assured him you're no longer connected to the Collective. He's carried out several scans on you, Alex and Rover and is satisfied that none of you are a threat.'

If that was the case, why was she in this room?

Carissa stood up and marched to the door. 'Okay, then let's get out of here.'

When the Inventor didn't move, the pain in her chest returned.

'Max is willing to release you, but you must promise two things.'

She nodded. 'Anything.'

'You must follow my rule. It's also now Max's main condition to your release. Never attempt to reconnect with the Collective or Praesidium's network. Your neuromorphic chip is disabled but your biogel has restorative properties. We don't know if it can revive the link. This camp is off the grid and an anti-magnetic field in the valley helps to disrupt any signals in or out.'

Carissa crossed her fingers behind her back. 'I wouldn't do that, Inventor. I don't want to be terminated.'

Starting now.

With a puff, the Inventor stood up. 'You've never been disconnected before, Carissa. Right now, you probably feel like there's a huge void in your life. That's the missing connection. You'll want to reconnect, just for a while. But you can't. You hear me?'

'I won't. I promise.'

From this point on.

'It won't be easy. You'll be tempted to try, but I promise to teach you how to live without the Collective or the Copies in your head.'

From the moment she'd started watching the last set of participants compete in Arcis, she'd wished for a simpler life, one that separated her from Quintus and the Collective. Both had the power to terminate her on a whim. During their escape from the city, Quintus had found a way to contact her offline and she still didn't know if he could terminate her remotely. But her usefulness to the Ten had kept her alive for this long. Even with the threat that accompanied reconnection, Carissa battled against her desire to return to her old life.

She nodded. 'I promise, Inventor. Can we leave now?'

'Yes, we can.' He shuffled over to the door and knocked on it. 'We're ready,' he shouted, then turned to Carissa. 'Just one more thing, miss.'

'What?'

'My name is Jacob, not Inventor. That's what you'll call me from now on. We're no longer in the city. Think of it as your first task as a new human.'

The thought made her smile. 'Human, like Anya and Dom?'

The Inventor nodded. 'Exactly like them.'

'Yes, Jacob.'

The door opened and she followed the Inventor out of the room, gripping his belt tight so he couldn't disappear again. Two female soldiers dressed in green army gear waited in the corridor. The air outside the room chilled her more than the tunnels beneath Praesidium. She let go of the Inventor and rubbed her bare arms. One of the soldiers handed her a green fatigue jacket. She slipped it on; it swamped her thirteen-year-old frame.

'Come on, miss,' said the Inventor. 'Max wants to introduce you to some people.'

She nodded, ready to follow him anywhere.

She would never be alone again.

They left the prison building, which was set at ground level, and stepped outside. The bright yellow sun stung her eyes. But she'd experienced worse pain in Praesidium, where the force field dome around the city had distorted the light and tripled the intensity of the sun's glare. Here, at least her eyes didn't water the second she saw daylight. A stiff breeze, created by something other than motion, skittered across her face. She had only felt the wind twice before, once when she'd crossed the barrier around Praesidium and again when she'd travelled in the back of a truck on her way to this camp.

She smiled and shielded her eyes, keeping close to Jacob as he crossed the compound surrounded by mountain rock to a courtyard with a high brick wall on the opposite side. They passed by an array of trucks, similar to the one they'd used to escape, parked around a grassy area. To the right of the yard stood a long, rectangular building. It resembled a warehouse. Nearing the entrance, Carissa saw it had an open side and what looked to be exercise equipment inside. The courtyard was enclosed on the left side by a large, two-storey house that had a hand painted sign erected outside. It read: "Town Hall".

The Inventor led her through the courtyard and into what looked to be a makeshift dining hall. The smell of food hit her as soon as she entered the space, about a third the size of the courtyard. She could consume human food, but the terminals in the Learning Centre fed her biogel body with enough energy to satiate her hunger. She looked around the space for the pods with the single wires hanging down from the ceiling, like in the upload room in the Learning Centre. But all she found were tables and benches, and food stations. Maybe they were in a different part of this building?

She followed the Inventor through the hall and entered a new corridor, passing by two rooms opposite each other packed with dozens of beds. The old man carried on and stopped outside a final room at the end of the corridor.

Maybe this was where they kept the terminals.

He opened the door and her heart sank. A central table dominated the space, covered with rolls of maps and several handheld computers. She recognised the basic tech that Praesidium had made especially for the towns. It was enough to satisfy their curiosity, enough to keep them from demanding more.

Quintus once said a happy town was a compliant town.

A dozen people stood inside the room. All eyes were on her as she entered. Some of the teenagers older than her wore the same type of green jacket as she did. None were from the group who had escaped Praesidium.

A man in his forties with a buzz cut, whom Carissa had learned earlier was Max, introduced himself properly. 'Carissa, we understand you are a synthetic copy, and while you are a guest in this compound it would be wise not to make an enemy of me. I assume Jacob has spoken to you about your conditions of stay here?'

Carissa nodded. Her gaze flitted to where a

group of six teenagers stood together. She recognised two of them: Warren and Jerome.

'I want to introduce you to some others we rescued from Arcis. Jacob here tells me you were watching their progress?'

Carissa nodded again but her gaze fixed on Jerome. She walked over to him, much to the unease of the dark skinned boy.

She reached out to touch his face. 'You're just like me.'

This newborn had fooled not only the Copies but the Collective too. The biogel in a newborn and Copy's body emitted a low frequency hum that she could hear. His sickness must have masked his biogel signature when he arrived at Essention's hospital. The force field surrounding Arcis may have done the same thing.

Jerome jerked away from her. 'No I'm not. *You're* from that place. I grew up in the towns.'

Her fingers grazed skin before the boy yanked his arm away. But it was long enough to sense what he was. She frowned. 'They must have erased your memories, because you were made in Praesidium. I can tell.'

'How?' said Max.

She kept her eyes on a nervous Jerome as she tapped the side of her head once. 'I can feel him. The biogel emits the same hum to mine at a low frequency, whether he's been connected or not.' She saw no NMC connection point. 'He's a newborn,

14

never connected to the Collective, never officially a Copy.' Jerome grew angry under her scrutiny. She said to him, 'You must have completed the maturation cycle by giving yourself injections of biogel.'

Jerome's anger gave way to shock. His gaze flitted around the room. 'I had a bag full of syringes. The contents made me feel better. I don't remember where I got them from.'

'Someone please explain that to me,' said Max behind her.

It was the Inventor who obliged. 'The newborns require biogel to complete the maturation process before they can be connected to the Collective's neural network. Without the biogel, the brain and organs won't fully mature and function on their own. Without the biogel, the connection point allowing a neuromorphic chip to be added won't develop. Their brains remain in a childish state. The Copies can't be controlled without it.'

'So, what you're saying is, he's technically a Copy but he was never under the Collective's command?' said Max.

Jerome squirmed under the intensity of Carissa's gaze. She knew she was frightening him, but she'd only ever met one newborn before: Canya. Anya's doppelganger, a dangerous girl who had almost ruined their plans to escape. Canya had been selfish and too focused on getting Dom at all costs— even if that meant giving up their location to the guards to get it.

Carissa had watched Jerome through the city feeds connected to Arcis. He'd come across as the most sensible of them all.

Newborns and Copies could survive on human food. But Copies needed a connection with the Collective, to make sense of the world. How could a newborn without an NMC function in the real world?

Max broke through her thoughts. 'What other clues give the Copies away, Carissa?'

She turned around, detecting Max's curiosity. Yet, his body language—arms folded tight across his body—told her he was not comfortable speaking with her.

She looked at Jerome then back at Max. 'The Originals—I mean, the humans—say it's our eyes that give us away. The Collective could never fit the right eye colour to the right Copy. The final result makes us look odd.' She narrowed her eyes when Max nodded. 'You already knew what he was, didn't you?'

Max ignored her question and spoke to the Inventor. 'We have two Copies, one of their wolf Guardians and a Breeder. And Dom Pavesi has so much tech inside him he might as well be one of them.'

'The city's medical records state that Dom has carried that tech from the age of seven,' said Carissa.

Max nodded, as if he already knew that too. 'You're the inventor for the Collective, Jacob. What do we do with them all?'

The old man shrugged. 'Let them choose what side to fight on.'

3

Anya

It was nice seeing her brother again, but their reunion didn't ground Anya or bring her the peace she'd expected. Her missing memories had left a gaping hole in her experiences; she'd sensed the absence from the moment she woke up in Alex's bed. Jason, her only remaining family member, was the last person she remembered. Growing up they'd been close. Yet, as they walked around the camp, something told her they had grown apart.

Despite her life being in turmoil, she no longer needed him.

She and Jason returned to the start of the camp to see Sheila emerging from the medical bay. She waved Anya over.

'Talk later, okay?' she said to Jason.

'Sure thing, little sis.'

'Not so little now.'

Anya flashed him a smile, pleased to have her

brother back despite her feelings, and jogged over to where Sheila waited. Tiny wings fluttered against her heart for a reason other than Warren. She didn't remember Dom, but something pushed her to ask about him.

She tried to pick up on his condition just from Sheila's mood. But Sheila's neutral expression and her casual lean against the wall made it impossible to read her.

'How is he?' she said.

Sheila nodded. 'They've reversed the infection. He's going to be okay.'

Anya released a breath she'd been holding. Why did she care so much for this stranger? She'd met him less than a day ago, and talked to him for half a second.

Sheila nodded at Jason. 'That your brother?'

Anya turned to see Jason disappear down a side street behind the training equipment room, where he said his workshop was. 'Yeah.'

She turned back to Sheila.

'It's good you two found each other.' Sheila paused, playing with the end of her braided golden-brown hair. 'Dom's asking to see you. He knows you're here.'

Sheila was the only one of the female survivors to get her memories back, courtesy of her Copy. Anya felt lost without hers. Alex was the only person she shared any connection with right now.

She shook her head. 'I don't remember him.'

'But he remembers you. Can't you just drop in? Max has called a group meeting. It begins in ten minutes. We can be in and out in a flash.' Despite her hard stance, Sheila's eyes betrayed her worry. 'I really think it would help his recovery, knowing you're okay.'

Anya nodded. If her health really mattered to a stranger, she'd do it. Besides, it was another way to distance herself from the selfish Canya. She followed Sheila inside the building.

The medical bay was a large, open-plan area with a cluster of beds and equipment at the back, including IVs and monitoring machines. Dom was sitting up in one of the beds, his right arm connected to an IV. Anya hesitated by the door. She thought of Alex, the Breeder she'd come to know in the city and for whom she'd developed feelings. Alex who she'd almost... What would he think about her being here?

She sucked in a hard breath and stepped forward. A quick visit and she could leave.

'I'll wait outside,' said Sheila, one hand on the door.

Anya nodded, grateful for the privacy, and walked towards Dom's bed.

When she neared, Dom turned his head. A pair of soft but cautious eyes trapped her in his gaze.

'Anya?'

She sensed his hesitation.

'Yeah.' She folded her arms and stood a foot away. This was close enough. 'I heard you're feeling better.'

'It's really you?'

His caution surprised her. What had transpired between him and Canya to make him doubt what he saw? Flutters of jealousy irritated her stomach. She ignored her irrational feelings for a guy she didn't even know.

Dom stood up and grabbed hold of the IV stand, his intense gaze never leaving her. His height matched that of Alex and his approach made her as nervous as Alex's had at the start.

This was a bad idea. She almost turned and walked out, but she'd made a promise to Sheila.

Anya closed her eyes, hyper aware of Dom's proximity to her. His musky scent sparked a vague recognition that made her skin hum.

'They say you still don't have your memories of Arcis. And that you don't remember me.'

His voice, deep and familiar, soothed her.

Anya opened her eyes, only to get trapped by the intensity of his deep brown gaze. His expression was different to Alex's flirty one; it was like Dom had no off switch.

She kept her arms folded to control her quivering limbs. 'I'm sorry. I really want to remember what happened there. But I don't.'

His stare unsettled her, not cruel or demanding, but too familiar to allow her to relax. She dropped her gaze to the floor.

He pulled her into a hug. The move shocked her

and she almost wriggled out of it, but she gave in to the feel of it with a sigh. With her arms still folded, she rested her head against his broad chest. It felt good. Comforting.

Right.

Wrong. She thought of Alex and pulled away.

'I'm sorry for doing that,' said a clearly nervous Dom. 'I just needed to be close to you.'

She caught the hurt in his voice and wanted to make it better. But instead she fixed her gaze on his chest, concentrating on its slow rise and fall.

'Do you remember what I said to you when you stepped through the portal in Arcis?' he said.

Anya shook her head, refusing to look up.

'I said, "Don't forget me."'

The eyes she couldn't see taunted her. She lifted her curious gaze up to meet his secret-filled one. The words sounded vaguely familiar, like they'd been uttered in a dream.

'But I did forget. I keep having these fragmented flashbacks.'

Dom lifted her chin up with one finger and pressed his lips to hers lightly. Something stirred in her core, like it had with Alex. While Alex had stoked her curiosity, this new feeling with Dom terrified her.

Her cheeks flushed and she stepped back from him. To her relief, he let go.

'I have to go. I'm glad to see you're feeling better.'

Her guilt backed her towards the door. She

turned and walked at a fast clip.

Dom shouted after her, 'I'm not giving up, Anya. I'll make you remember me.'

She stumbled outside, where she found Sheila leaning against the wall.

'How was he?'

Anya shook her head, refusing to look at her. 'Why did he affect me like that? I don't even know him.'

'Because you were a pair of lovesick puppies in Arcis.'

Anya met her gaze. 'If we were so happy, surely I'd remember him above all else, memory wipe or no memory wipe.'

'Look, I don't know how powerful that machine is. All I know is that when my Copy touched me and gave me back my memories, it was like a floodgate opened. Before, everything was vague, unimportant. Happening to someone else. Then everything came back, clear as if it had occurred yesterday.'

'But Canya is gone, and she took my memories with her.'

Anya's eyes pricked with tears at the loss of them.

'There has to be another way to get them back,' said Sheila. 'Look, if you want to know anything, all you have to do is ask.'

Anya wasn't ready to know, but she forced a smile. 'Thanks.'

'And don't forget about Carissa. She was

watching us in Arcis.' Sheila shuddered. 'Creepy, if you ask me. But still, she might be a good person to talk to. Robot, machine, whatever the hell she is.'

Anya nodded.

'Boys are stupid,' said Sheila.

Anya grinned, feeling better. 'They are.'

'Girls are better.'

'Sometimes.'

'Trust me. I'm an expert. But Dom's a good guy, so don't give up on him.' Sheila tossed her long braid back and linked arms with her. 'Come on, Max is expecting us. Let's see what he has to say.'

Anya followed Sheila past the training courtyard to a red-bricked building that used to be a town hall, according to the hand-painted sign stuck to its exterior, and to a room at the end of a corridor. Vanessa, Jacob, Carissa, Alex and Jason were there, along with several others from Max's group whom Anya didn't know. June and Jerome stood next to each other in one corner.

Her pulse pounded in her ears when she spotted Warren in another corner. He gave her a quick nod. Her stomach tightened as she sucked in a discreet breath and tried to push past the noise in her head to hear what Max had to say.

Sheila gave her arm a squeeze and leaned in close. 'Don't worry about Warren. He won't get within a hundred feet of you. Dick.'

She wanted to say he already had, that he was in her head thanks to Canya's partial return of memories to her. But in that moment Sheila's offer gave her some comfort.

Max spoke to a couple of his soldiers and an older man in his seventies who looked like his father. He turned to the group and made quick introductions all round. The older man was called Charlie.

'I'm glad to see all of you here, and I'm even more glad that Sheila, Dom and June, our soldiers, and Vanessa, a friend of ours, were returned to us safely. As you know, we have some newcomers to our compound. Some of you are wary of the Copies among you and the wolf machine that Jacob brought. But Jacob assures me the creature is under his command.

'These people have escaped from Praesidium, the one place that is impossible to enter or leave without the city's order. But with the help of a Copy, our people were able to do just that. We never thought it possible that we would play host not only to a Copy but a newborn too, along with a Breeder *and* a mechanical wolf that Praesidium calls a Guardian.'

Charlie stepped forward. 'As my son has already mentioned, we have a rare opportunity here. There are others stuck in Praesidium who did not escape. We have the chance to rescue them, but more important than that, to take down the city and destroy the Collective, a scourge upon this land. A tyrannical ruler that none of us wanted.'

He motioned for Carissa to join him. She

hesitated and glanced at Jacob, who gave her a quick nod and a smile. Then she shuffled forward, her tight posture relaxing a little.

'Carissa has agreed to work with Jacob, Jason and Thomas to unlock the secrets of the Collective ten, a group of artificial intelligent beings that controls Praesidium and the Copies,' continued Charlie. 'We will speak to the rescued and add their knowledge to our own. It will take time to figure out our next move in this war against the machines. But in the meantime, we have a bigger problem. Praesidium will no doubt be looking for their Copy and Breeder, and possibly their wolf.'

Anya studied Carissa, so innocent in appearance, yet one of the deadliest entities alive, except for the Collective. She was a Copy. Whether she was capable of change and living outside of Praesidium's control was yet to be seen.

But all was not lost. She had witnessed change in a Copy: in her medic, who had helped her and Alex to escape.

'They will be coming,' said Max. 'We must prepare for the first wave of attack. We must be ready for the machines.'

4

Dom

'Looks like your infection has cleared up,' said the military medic.

With his gown pulled up to his neck, Dom waited for him to finish his examination of his scars. Max sat on the edge of Dom's bed. Jacob, the inventor from Praesidium, stood back and watched.

Dom looked down at the scars where Praesidium had inserted its tech, when he was seven years old. It disappointed him to see he still bore the reminders.

'I thought you might have fixed those,' he said to the medic as he fixed his gown back into place.

The medic shook his head. 'I don't have the right equipment here to remove them, only the infection. I wasn't even sure I could reverse that. Jacob helped me out.'

Jacob stepped closer to his bed. 'The Collective experimented on you in the city. The tech you carry inside you now is the newest that's available to Praesidium. But the problem with the tech is it's not compatible with the makeup of human genetics.'

The pain from the infection that had lit his bones on fire twenty-four hours ago had convinced Dom he was a dead man. 'So, what did you do to fix it?'

'Rover helped,' said Jacob with a smile.

Dom vaguely recalled the Guardian that had accompanied them when they escaped from the city. It bothered him that he'd been at the mercy of another of Praesidium's toys.

'The hound from hell came with us?'

Jacob's smile dropped away and he gave him a tight nod. 'I built him to be loyal to me, not the Collective. But, more important, he carries the same Fifth Gen tech inside him that's also in you. Difference is his organic structure has natural immunities to Praesidium's tech. It's teeming with self-repairing nanobots. I injected the artificial antibodies from his system into yours to force it to accept the new material.'

Dom glanced down at his now covered belly. 'If the tech is self-repairing, why do I still have my scars?'

They served as a daily reminder of what his worthless, piece-of-shit father had done to him.

'It repairs the metal, but not skin and muscle,' said Jacob with a shake of his head. 'We don't have anything here, but I know the city does. They have machines to repair the skin of their hybrids after they operate on them—for flawless, undetectable results.'

Dom recalled a machine in the first-aid prefab on the second floor of Arcis that did just that. He'd only used it for a short time before the supervisors had taken it away.

'When we win this war,' said Max, 'we can take all of their equipment from them. You don't ever have to look at those scars again.'

A smiling, nodding Jacob appeared to back up Max's claims.

But Dom wanted to go one better. He looked up at the Inventor. 'Can you remove this tech, give me back my humanity?'

Jacob's disappearing smile didn't fill him with confidence.

'I'm not sure it's possible. Your body has come to rely on the tech. I'm worried that if we try, your body could break down.'

He didn't care. He refused to live his life as half machine. 'But we can try?'

Jacob pursed his lips. 'Yes.'

Dom placed his feet on the floor, prompting Max and the military medic to help him stand. But despite their caution, he felt strong.

'Just because you've been given the all clear from the medic doesn't mean you can push yourself,' said Max with one hand on Dom's elbow.

Dom eased him off and stood without help. 'With the threat of the city's search hanging over our heads, I'd say you need all soldiers on duty.'

Max gripped Dom's shoulder tight. 'Charlie and I almost lost you. It's my right to worry. I order you to be careful.'

Dom looked into the eyes of the man who'd been like a father to both him and Sheila. At least Charlie wasn't here. Dom wouldn't have been able to say no to the old man.

He saluted the colonel. 'Yes, sir.'

'Now, first order of business,' said Max, relaxing his hold on Dom. 'I'd like to show you around this camp, but first you should get something to eat. Also, Sheila is waiting outside for you, so there's that.'

Sheila had barely left his side since they'd arrived at the compound.

'Yes, sir.'

Max saluted him and left. Jacob followed the colonel out.

Dom thanked the medic and strode towards the outside, alone and uneasy. Nothing was resolved. He couldn't relax, not with the city potentially out looking for them. It didn't seem likely they would let a dramatic escape slide without punishment.

Then there was Anya. He wanted to see her again, but her recent visit had left him with a bad feeling. What if their connection couldn't be repaired? What if the distance between them was too great to move past being strangers?

Yet, a flicker of recognition in her eyes had

given him hope. She knew him. She just couldn't remember him.

Dom pushed the double doors open and squinted against the soft brightness. It was nearing evening time and the light was at half strength, but it still bothered his light-deprived eyes. He'd been a prisoner beneath the city for too long.

'Hey, loser,' said Sheila.

She was leaning against the wall, oversized sunglasses on her face and her arms folded, but her thin mouth said she was barely holding it together.

'Hey, brat,' said Dom. He walked over to her and pulled her into a tight hug. In her ear, he whispered, 'I'm glad you're okay.'

A shudder ran from her body to his and he knew she was crying. He pulled her in tighter, even though she tried to squirm out of it.

'Stop fighting, Sheila. I need this as much as you do. I almost died.'

His own voice sounded close to breaking. But he kept it together.

Sheila slumped against him, the tension in her body melting away. 'I didn't know if you'd come out of it. Don't scare me like that again.'

Dom pulled back and thumbed away the tears marking her beautiful, sun-kissed face, visible below her glasses. She wore her golden brown hair in a single braid and had it draped over her shoulder.

Sheila pulled her glasses away from her face to reveal puffy, red eyes. She wiped away fresh tears with her thumb. 'You're making me look like a weepy, old woman. Stop it.'

Dom smiled at Sheila's attempt to lighten the mood. 'Looks like I might have improved your face.'

Sheila thumped him on the arm, managing a smile as she did.

'Max said I'm supposed to take you to the dining hall. But we need to make a stop first.'

'Lead the way.'

They walked along the street with the town hall and courtyard and away from the medical bay, venturing deeper into the camp. As they did, Dom kept an eye out for Anya. When he didn't see her, he took in his surroundings instead. The compound sat in a valley with mountains on either side. He noticed spotters up high, hidden in the crevices of the mountain; the setting sun reflecting off their weapons gave away their location. He'd mention that to Max later. Maybe they could camouflage the guns better to be invisible to the naked eye.

About a quarter of a mile back from the courtyard, Sheila took a right onto a smaller street with open-faced stores. A barber shop on the other side, recognisable by a red, white and blue barber's pole affixed to the wall, still had its windows. He walked up to it and cupped his hands against the glass. Inside, he saw Charlie chatting to one of the male soldiers and cutting his hair.

He knocked on the glass, startling the soldier. Dom waved when Charlie looked at him. Charlie said something to the soldier as he set the scissors down, and came outside.

Dom lunged for the smiling, old man the second he set foot outside. 'Good to see you, Charlie.'

The old man hugged him back. 'Dom, I'm so glad to see you're up and about. I checked on you when you first came, but you were out of it.'

He pulled back and frowned at Dom's curly hair, giving it a sharp tug; it had grown out since Charlie had given it a buzz cut. The cut had come right before Arcis had insisted Dom stay at the training facility.

'I think I'll put a better style in that. Come see me whenever.'

'I might be busy with other things. But I'll try.'

Charlie made a noise. 'The city will do what it has to do. But we will not stop living, my boy. Make time.'

Dom nodded. 'I promise.'

Charlie winked at Sheila then returned to his customer.

They walked back the way they came.

'He missed us,' said Sheila.

'The feeling's mutual.'

Sheila led him back to an entrance to a courtyard and an open-sided gymnasium. Dom spotted a punching bag to the rear of the limited equipment.

Sheila grinned at him. 'Thought you might notice that.'

They entered the yard and passed by soldiers dressed in black cargo pants and green T-shirts, doing push ups on the paving stones. He followed her to the left though an open door and into what looked like a dining hall with mismatching tables and chairs. It bore no resemblance to the orderly space in Arcis, or the monochromatic apartment he and Sheila had been forced to live in while in Essention. He normally hated disorder, but given the order that had been forced upon him for months, he welcomed a little chaos.

The smell of food hit him and made his stomach rumble hard. When had he last eaten? Sheila approached a serving area laid out with food items that Dom recognised from the towns and Essention. The limited spread, including loaves of stale bread, cans of beans, small blocks of slimy meat and fruit, indicated to Dom this refuge would be a temporary stop.

The server handed him a compartmentalised tray that reminded him of the food tray he'd been served while prisoner in Praesidium. Salty stew, a bread roll and bottled water had been his rations three times a day. He'd eaten what he could stomach until the salt had forced him to drink their water—water laced with a drug to knock him out. The second he had, Dom had belonged to the city.

But no longer.

He repressed a shudder and thanked the server, who wasn't much older than him. He and Sheila carried their trays over to an empty table with white plastic chairs set around it. He dug into his portion of beans—a staple in Essention—and a wedge of hard bread. He washed it down with a cup of water.

'Is this all there is to eat?' he asked Sheila.

She replied with a nod. 'It's all they could grab from the towns and Essention. Charlie and the others cleaned out the factory there before they fled the urbano. But with new mouths to feed, the supplies won't last long.'

Dom finished his untainted food, grateful to no longer be a prisoner of the Collective.

He looked around the space. His heart almost stopped when he saw Anya sat at another table. She was with Alex, the blond-haired, green-eyed boy from the city.

'Who is he?' he asked Sheila.

She didn't bother turning around. 'That's Alex. He and Anya were prisoners in the city.'

Dom pinned Sheila with his gaze. 'Together or separately?'

Sheila gave a weak smile. 'What does it matter?'

'Just answer me.'

His heart pounded as he waited for her answer.

'Together. He's what they call a Breeder.'

The title alone sent his brain into overdrive. 'What did they do together?'

Sheila shrugged as if it wasn't a big deal, but her stiff posture told a different story. 'I don't know.'

'Did you have a Breeder?'

Sheila avoided his gaze and scooped food onto her fork. She nodded as she ate.

His voice rose in anger. 'What did *you* do together?'

Sheila looked up in alarm and hushed him. 'Stop it, Dom. I'll tell you if you stay calm.'

Dom flicked his gaze over to Anya. She was looking at him now. Good. It irritated him to see how close she and Alex were sitting.

He flicked his gaze back.

'What did you do, Sheila?' he said, lower this time. He drank some water to calm down.

'Nothing, Dom. But I was supposed to have sex with him.'

Dom barely managed to swallow the water. 'Is that Alex's purpose?'

He studied the good-looking man, who was a similar age to him. He was staring at Dom, challenging him, almost.

Challenge away, Breeder. You won't win this one.

Sheila snapped her fingers in his face, breaking his attention away from Alex. He blinked and refocused on her.

'Dom, stop it. We had no choice. I don't know what they did together, but they got close. That's all I know. We were being fed drugs to heighten our attraction to each other, to make the breeding process go smoothly. Don't jump to conclusions. And she

36

doesn't belong to you, so show her some respect.'

Dom shook his head to clear the images of what he imagined they'd done. 'I can't help it. I remember her so vividly. Now it feels like she and Alex are rubbing their new connection in my face. Laughing at me.'

Sheila leaned forward. 'Anya doesn't remember you, that's all. She's not rejecting you. She doesn't know who you are. There's a difference.' She slapped his hand, hard. 'Pull yourself together. We've more important things to think about than your love life.'

Sheila was right. He was being selfish. He needed to forget about Anya and focus on recovering his fitness.

People from the city would be coming soon. Dom would work out his issues with them.

5

Carissa

Ever since her release, Carissa had noticed a couple of female soldiers showing an extra interest in her. Not just her, but Jerome and Alex's movements were being monitored too. In a compound as small as this one, she struggled to shake her escorts. Carissa missed the space Praesidium offered, but not the glaring, white brightness of the buildings there. Nor did she miss having to hide her thoughts or erase her memories before Quintus and the remaining nine Collective learned them.

Being forced to live in a place without the Collective's guidance unsettled her. Not even June, her Original's sister, could fill that void. While Carissa had been thrilled to see her in the city, their connection had faded since their escape. Now, Carissa thought only of one: Quintus.

Her NMC no longer buzzed with the daily interactions between Copies. She'd even expected a call from Quintus that morning ordering her to the Great Hall. But, the damaged she'd done to her chip a day ago had severed her last connection with the city.

Yet, still she searched.

Under the watchful eye of two female soldiers, Carissa marched through the compound. She'd already walked the perimeter several times. The pair pretended not to watch her, but she, a Copy with a synthetic brain capable of fast processing, had been created to understand human interactions. She understood what stalking was and how it indicated curiosity, but more often a lack of trust. What she didn't understand was why. Without her NMC, Carissa was no longer a danger to anyone. Plus, she'd helped the humans to escape Praesidium. Surely that counted for something?

The females kept their distance while Carissa explored what Jacob had referred to as a rebel military base. One of many, he'd said. Carissa hadn't been familiar with the term "military" before the rebels stormed Arcis. Quintus had told her the rebels were not to be trusted. It's what she'd believed, until the moment Quintus had tried to kill the Inventor, her friend.

Judging by the brick constructions in various states of repair, Carissa determined that this compound used to be a town. The mountain range protecting both sides loomed over it like the force field dome had over Praesidium.

She glanced at the cluster of houses to the front

of the compound opposite the town hall, a space she'd emerged from not that long ago. The females kept up their surveillance of her as she passed by the courtyard where soldiers trained. The camp reminded her of the business district, just a less ordered version of it. In Praesidium, there had been clothing shops and places to buy art supplies, antiques and pottery. But here, a barber shop and countless, open-sided storage areas carrying ammo and essentials, like soap and hairbrushes, gave the setup a more temporary feel.

Carissa pressed her face up to the glass of the barber shop and watched the grey-haired man inside cut the hair of a young, male soldier. He reminded her of the Inventor, just a shorter, stockier version of her lanky friend. She marvelled at the speed with which he cut the young man's hair. They chatted and laughed about something that was inaudible to Carissa. She missed the screens that allowed her to see and hear the participants in Arcis.

The old man looked up at her suddenly and she froze. His smile dropped away. His hand paused, the scissors suspended mid-air. Carissa backed away from the shop and ran down the street that led to the perimeter fence. Her part-organic heart worked overtime and forced her to gulp in air. She doubled over, worried something was seriously wrong. A new panic flared inside her. This wasn't the city. She couldn't just drop in on the Inventor for a check-up.

Carissa was alone.

She leaned against the green, corrugated-sheet fencing, waiting for her breaths to normalise. The panic passed. A quick glance behind her confirmed the female soldiers still followed.

Carissa stuck her face up to a gap in the fencing. It appeared the original town didn't stop at the perimeter. In fact, it carried on for quite some distance, widening at the middle as it followed the natural curve of the mountains. In the distance, beyond houses in similar disrepair to the ones on her side, she saw evidence of a vertical farm in tatters. It looked primitive compared to the machine-built farm in Essention, designed to feed the townspeople it housed there.

To learn more about this town, Carissa pressed the chip embedded just above her ear. She searched for a connection to the city, some familiar buzz to let her know her NMC wasn't completely dead. But no response came.

With a gasp, Carissa forced her hand to her side. How many times had she attempted to contact the city?

She lifted her hand again. What harm could trying do? It wasn't like anyone could hear her anyway.

Her action sent a sharp shiver through her, forcing her hand to her side a second time. She turned away from the fence and trotted back to the main hub of activity.

The females followed, chattier now than they'd

been all morning. She assumed they were discussing her. If this had been the city, she'd have commanded the insubordinate Originals to cease their discussion. But here, Carissa was nobody. The intrusion on her personal space filled her with dread. She wished for them to stop.

So what if this wasn't the city?

With that thought, Carissa turned on her heel and marched up to the pair, both hands balled into tight fists.

'Stop following me,' she demanded.

One female lifted her brow and smiled. 'I don't know what you mean.'

'You're not very good at hiding. I can see you following me.'

The second female shrugged. 'This is a small compound. It's easy to get turned around.'

Carissa's anger bubbled viciously inside her. She sucked in a deep breath and lifted her chin, exactly how she used to in the city when talking to an Original.

On her next exhale, she said, 'I demand you tell me what you were talking about.'

To her surprise and irritation, both females smiled and glanced at each other.

'Tell me now,' she repeated.

Both females laughed hard.

'She thinks she's still in the city,' said one.

The other said, in a measured tone, 'You have no authority here, Copy. We know what you are and we don't trust you. You have been made to destroy us.'

Carissa's body shook; she breathed hard through her nose to control the shake. 'That's a lie. Quintus—the Collective—just wanted to escape their prison. The Originals were helping them to do that.'

The second female said, 'It's true then. You *are* a machine that listens to a city run by more machines.'

She shook her head. It was more complicated than that. Carissa was more human than machine. Even the Inventor had said so.

'I don't care what you think. I still demand you tell me what you were saying about me.'

The second female folded her arms. 'No.'

A ripple of anger rushed up and came out as a yell. 'Fine! Leave me alone. Otherwise I'll...'

The female uncrossed her arms. 'You'll what?' Her pitch switched to a lower, menacing tone.

'Nothing.'

Carissa turned and ran before she said something she might regret. The females followed her, which only fuelled her irritation more. She'd made a mistake by confronting them, a move that had ignited their curiosity about her. She had no links to the city. She was not a danger.

Only one person could stop her heart from pounding.

She found the Inventor in a small workshop off an alley to the rear of the courtyard. He was talking with two young men, both with brown hair. One she recognised as Anya's brother.

'I think we should start by cataloguing everything we have, Jason.' He picked up nuts, bolts and broken panels from the desk and let them fall through his fingers. His workshop in Praesidium had been a tidier space than this. 'We'll work faster that way. I know this collection belongs to the pair of you. Okay with you, Thomas?'

The quieter and skinnier of the two men nodded. 'We're happy to have the help, Jacob. We're hoping your knowledge of the machines and Copies will help us to fight them.'

Carissa stilled by the door. Did that fight include her? Her foot scuffed a stone and alerted the trio to her presence. Both Jason and Thomas' eyes widened, but her arrival didn't startle the Inventor.

'Carissa. Would you like to meet Jason and Thomas?' he said with a smile.

She shook her head so fast her shoulder-length, blonde hair fanned around her face. She backed up until she was in the alley.

'Give me a minute with her,' said the Inventor to the pair. He joined her outside. 'Is something the matter, miss?'

'Two females are following me around the compound.'

The old man nodded, as if the news didn't surprise him. 'Max ordered them to follow you, Jerome and Alex. It's only temporary until they get to know you like I have.'

His revelation rocked Carissa and forced her farther back. 'You knew Max was having me followed?'

'Yes, but please understand I have as much say here as I did in the city.'

That didn't matter to her. 'I thought you trusted me.'

The Inventor reached for her, forcing her back another step. 'I do trust you, Carissa.' His eyes narrowed. 'You haven't tried to contact the city, have you?'

She glared at him. Was he asking or accusing?

'No!' she lied. 'I promised I wouldn't.'

The old man stared at her for longer than she could stand. 'If you say you didn't then I believe you.' He nodded behind him. 'Did you want to watch us work for a while? We're just sorting through the items from the towns, but I'd like you to share your knowledge of the Collective with the young men.'

Carissa hugged her middle. 'They don't like me.'

'They don't know you yet. But they'll like you once they do.'

Carissa looked around. 'Where's Rover?'

'Max asked that I keep him sedated for the time being. He's making the others nervous. But I'm sure he'd like a visitor?' He pointed to the end of the alley that finished with a building and a double door. 'He's in the storage shed.' He glanced back inside the workshop. 'I'm sorry, but I've got to get back to it.'

Carissa watched as the Inventor returned to the workshop. She'd expected him to make her feel better, but if anything she felt worse. It made her miss the city more.

The double door at the end of the alley was attached to a building with a partial roof. She approached it and stepped inside the half shell. Rover was in one corner, lying on the grey, stone floor, head nestled between his legs. He seemed subdued, but not decommissioned. His eyes tracked her from the moment she entered the room. A soft, metallic whimper escaped his lips.

This beast remained her only connection to the city.

She slid down to the floor next to him and patted the Guardian's head. It wasn't that long ago these beasts had terrified her. But Rover was an unusual Guardian in that he took commands from the Inventor, not the Collective.

Rover lifted his head to nuzzle her hand, but as though he lacked energy, he slumped back down to the floor. Something rattled as he did. It was then she noticed the chain around his neck.

Anger coursed through her. She shook the chain, but it was too strong and heavy for Carissa to manage alone.

Was that how the rebels treated respected Guardians of Praesidium? A Guardian was a revered creature. A Copy, with human traits no less, was far superior to the Original in whose image they were created.

What hurt her more was the Inventor had allowed this to happen.

Carissa lay next to the beast on the floor. Now she knew where she belonged.

6

Dom

A female soldier dressed in a green uniform stopped at Dom and Sheila's table. 'Max wants to see you two in the battle room when you're done.'

Dom gave her a tight nod and she left. He waited for Sheila to finish eating before collecting both trays up and dropping them back to the counter.

On his way out, he tried not to look over at Anya and Alex, still sat at their table. But he slipped and glanced over, long enough to see their joined hands. She was leaning in close to him, smiling at something he said. Dom shot his eyes forward. He made it out of the dining hall and into the corridor without making a scene.

Sheila gave him a slap on the back as she passed him. 'It'll get easier, Dom. Come on.' She walked backwards to the battle room. 'Let's hear what Max has to say.'

They entered a room that looked more like an

administration office than a battle strategy centre. The room had been cleared except for one table shoved against the window that was covered in maps and blueprints. One wall was inlaid with bookcases; some shelves still had books on them. Dom couldn't tell if the rebels had taken over this town or if Praesidium had forced the residents to leave.

Max was leaning over a map while soldiers a couple of years older than Dom stood next to him and listened. One he recognised to be Imogen, Max's first in command. The second, a male Max called Julius, was new to his group. Dom had thought he knew everyone on Max's team. He shook his head; maybe he'd been out of commission for too long. Wearing a furrowed brow, Jacob, the inventor from the city, stood off to the side with Anya's brother, Jason, and Thomas, the inventor working with Max's team. Vanessa, whom Dom vaguely remembered from the city, waited alongside Jacob. He'd been too out of it to remember much about her.

June entered the room and stood next to Sheila. Dom waited with the pair for Max to finish his discussion. When Max grunted and dipped his head suddenly, Dom knew things were not going well. Imogen glanced back at the room then tapped her leader on the shoulder.

Max turned and crossed his thick, soldier arms across his chest. He pinned Dom and Sheila with his battle-hardened gaze. 'Good, you're both here. We've been discussing strategies, trying to identify weak points between here and Praesidium, places from where we could set up and mount an attack. But the landscape is barren and flat and won't provide us with suitable cover. We're assuming the city will send out search parties to retrieve its Copy, Breeder and Guardian. What we don't know is when they'll come.'

'What defences do we have against them?' said Dom.

Max nodded to his second in command. 'Julius?'

Julius explained, 'An anti-magnetic field floods the valley from the start of the compound entrance to the mouth of the mountain range. It also runs in the opposite direction to cover the remainder of the town that was cordoned off.'

'Remainder?' said Dom.

'Yes,' said Max. 'We had to reduce the size of the compound so we could manage it better.'

'What does the anti-magnetic field do?' said Sheila.

'It should stop the machines from accessing the camp,' said Imogen. 'Anything with metal components will be repelled by the force of the anti-magnetisation. We're hoping it'll be enough to keep them away, giving us time to plan our escape.'

Dom thought about the field that encased Praesidium. 'How far up and wide does the field extend?'

Julius looked to Max.

'It has a height limit,' explained Max. 'It won't stop aerial attacks from above. But that's where our spotters will come in handy.'

For what? Dom glanced at Sheila, who shrugged. They'd been out of touch with the rebels for too long.

He looked at Max and said, 'Aerial attacks?'

'Orbs. Essention was crawling with them.'

The flying spheres with the ability to record? He remembered their patrol of the water supply and the area near the hospital and entrance. But other than that, he hadn't paid them much attention.

'Okay, what do we know about these orbs?'

Jason stepped forward. 'Thomas and I had the recent opportunity to study one up close. They're fast in the air, like hummingbirds. So that makes them almost impossible to target. But we managed to deactivate one using Thomas' Disruptor gun. The Disruptor stuns the orb by using a concentrated blast of air to disrupt its flight pattern. Then, while the orb is inactive, we can use the same gun to steal power from it, rendering it inactive. All the guns were transferred from the Glenvale camp to here.'

At least they had something that could defend the camp.

Dom nodded. 'So we've covered off on aerial attacks, and, Max, you say the anti-magnetic field will deal with ground troops. Are we sure that all of their assault personnel will have trouble with the anti-magnetism?'

Max frowned at him. 'What do you mean?'

It was Jacob who answered. 'He means the Copies, don't you, son?'

Dom nodded at the man who'd come from the city. 'Praesidium's medics and guards looked organic. What metal do they have?'

'Jacob?' said Max.

The old man introduced himself to the group. 'They called me the Inventor because I helped the Collective create its Copies and build its machines. I repaired what broke and while they were busy with their prisoners, I built a Guardian wolf that answers only to me. The machines will have difficulty, and potentially the Guardian wolves, but the Copies might not.' Jacob looked at Max. 'I'm sorry if that's not what you want to hear, but the Copies carry varying degrees of metal inside them. The newborns have none and would have no trouble with the field.'

'Vanessa?' said Max. 'You were in the city too. Anything to add?'

'Whatever he says is right,' said Vanessa. 'I don't know much about their anatomy, but Jacob is best placed to judge.'

Max dropped his concerned gaze to the floor. Dom knew the colonel well enough; this news had rattled him.

When Max looked at Jacob, his gaze had hardened. 'Jerome is a newborn, yes?'

Jacob nodded. 'Completely organic. It's only after they achieve full maturation that the Collective gives them their NMC, and replaces any weak, biogel organs with stronger, metallic ones.'

'And the Breeder? What is he?' said Max.

Jacob shrugged. 'I don't have any experience with him or others like him. I assume he is organic. Again, I would need to run tests to be sure.'

Max switched his gaze to Sheila. 'Vanessa says she found you with a Breeder. What was your take on him?'

Sheila shrugged, but given her sudden stiff posture, Dom guessed she'd rather forget her time in the city's medical facility. 'I tried not to interact with him. He was charming, cool. Made promises he thought I wanted to hear. All in all, he was a convincing human.'

Dom's stomach lurched at the thought of Anya being seduced by Alex in a similar manner.

'Why are we waiting for the city to attack us?' he said, desperate to switch focus off the topic of seduction. He nodded at the table filled with blueprints and maps. 'With all of these, we should be able to sneak back to the city and attack them when they least expect it.'

'We don't know enough about the city to make assumptions, or to predict what move the Collective will make when we get there,' said Max.

'But Carissa does,' said Jacob.

Max released a sigh. 'I don't trust her yet, so, until then, we must learn their tactics the hard way.'

But Dom wasn't satisfied. 'Your pressing

concern right now is to know what can pass through the anti-magnetic field, right?'

Max pondered it then nodded. 'I'd say so.'

'So, use me to see how far I can get. I've got their tech inside me. I'm essentially a human version of them.'

'No, that wouldn't work,' said Thomas. 'We need to know how little tech poses a resistance. It would need to be someone from the city with trace amounts of their tech.'

'You mean Carissa?' Jacob's hardened gaze fell on Thomas, forcing him to look away. 'I won't have her used in this way. She already thinks everybody here hates her. She's not happy with her female escorts. For as long as Carissa resides here, she will have my protection.'

Vanessa squeezed the old man's shoulder as if to reassure him.

The lack of plan created a palpable nervous energy in the room. Everyone mumbled to each other, forcing Max to control the conversation with a whistle.

'Everyone calm down. I haven't decided what to do yet. But one thing's for certain: I'm not prepared to use Carissa until I know I can trust her. Who knows if she's sending signals back to the Collective right now? Who knows if, with a flick of her NMC connection, she could pass on the frequency of the anti-magnetic field to the Collective just by interacting with it?'

Dom didn't see how Max could avoid using the Collective's most prized possession. To advance their knowledge of the machine minds, they had to use someone they'd once trusted.

He put the main dilemma back on Max. 'So what do you suggest we do?'

Max released another sigh. 'I have no idea, Dom. But for now, all we can do is prepare.'

Vanessa spoke up. 'We should discuss what Anya Macklin told me.'

Hearing Anya's name stiffened Dom's stance. What did she have to do with this?

'We got here because she'd overheard her parents discussing this exact location: the Ferrous Mountains. Evan and Grace told me once that they'd seen the border to the Beyond close to this camp, but they weren't able to pinpoint its location.' Jason looked equally as confused as Dom felt. 'If the border is here, we'll find it.'

'What makes you think my parents knew anything about the Beyond?' asked Jason.

'Grace and Evan were both founding members of the rebellion,' said Vanessa. Jason's eyes widened. 'Members of the rebellion crossed over in secret. We can guess who, but not where. Evan and Grace were working on trying to locate the point where the rogue rebels crossed. That's when they reported seeing a shimmering border. Grace said when they approached it, it vanished. I've been out of touch with the original group due to my time in the city. And Max, you were busy looking for your wife. I don't know if what they saw was the real border but we have to check. We're going to need a safe haven after this is all over.'

Max's nostrils flared. 'Where is it?'

'In the vicinity. That's all they told me. But we spoke a while ago, so I can't say if that information still holds true.'

'What about others from their faction?' asked Dom. 'Would the Macklins have spoken to any of them?'

Max shook his head. 'We've all been split up. Some are dead or missing. Others have possibly crossed over. Only Charlie, Vanessa and I remain of the original faction.'

'There were others more senior than us who the Macklins might have shared this information with,' suggested Vanessa.

Max nodded at Jason. 'Did your parents ever discuss the rebellion while you were around?'

Jason shook his head slowly. 'I knew they opposed Praesidium, but they were careful about what they discussed at home. But I can't be sure Anya didn't overhear something. The more our parents kept from us, the more she needed to know.'

Max gave Vanessa a tight nod. 'I'll arrange for a scout party to check the vicinity. If we're close to the edge, as the Macklin's believed, we'll find it.'

'Good,' said Vanessa. 'Let me know what your soldiers find.'

Max addressed the group again. 'I'll need all

remaining soldiers back training on guns. That includes you, Dom.'

A little training was exactly what he needed to get his mind right. He was rusty and out of shape. While his scars no longer bothered him, his left arm with the new tech in it pinched enough to remind him of his ordeal.

Sheila patted his stomach. 'Don't worry, Dom; Imogen will help shift those pounds in no time.'

7

Anya

'Where are those two going?'

Anya watched as Dom and Sheila left the dining hall a few minutes after a female soldier had spoken to them.

Eyes on Alex again, she said, 'Is there a meeting happening?'

Alex looked up from his food. He lifted both brows. 'Do you think June's gone with them?'

June this. June that. Alex had only just met her but he wouldn't shut up about her.

She sighed. 'Maybe. I don't know. Why aren't we in the meeting, though?'

She might not possess the memories of her time in Arcis, but she and Alex had first-hand experience of the medical facility in Praesidium. In fact, it had been her efforts with her medic that had convinced the Copy to help them escape. 'You and I are just as important, Alex. You're a bloody Breeder.'

Alex glanced at the two male soldiers who sat at a nearby table. All through lunch, they hadn't stopped looking over. 'Tell that to them.'

Both soldiers, who were around Jason's age, looked over once again. Alex had said they'd acted as his chaperones all day.

Their continuing intrusion angered Anya. Alex had been a prisoner in Praesidium just like her. 'Max has no right to treat you like this. I'll talk to him, explain—'

Alex's eyes widened. 'No! Leave it, Anya. If Max doesn't want to trust me, it's fine by me.'

She leaned forward. 'But it's not fine.' Alex had taken some convincing to leave the city. His life there had amounted to nothing, and the Collective had worn down whatever optimism he had. She would not see him settle for a lesser life on the outside. 'I didn't risk my life to save you so you would become a prisoner here.'

Alex glared at her. 'Save me? I chose to leave. Of my own accord.'

Anya recoiled from Alex's harsh tone. 'I didn't mean it like that... I meant I promised you freedom, not this life.'

She gestured to Alex's escorts. They looked over and smirked.

He banged his fist down on the table, startling her and attracting the other soldiers' attention. 'Leave it, Anya. I'm obviously a danger here. I told you I didn't fit in anywhere.'

'Of course you do.' She lowered her voice. 'I just asked you about a secret meeting I was not invited to attend. You're not the only one being treated differently here.'

Alex laughed hard. 'Are you comparing your life to mine right now? Because I'm starting to see your Copy's traits emerging and I don't like it.'

That stung. Her Copy, Canya, had been selfish, domineering and a bitch. She'd passed back one set of memories to Anya, of Warren attacking her in the bathroom on the fourth floor of Arcis. She hadn't told anyone.

'I'm nothing like her. Take that back.'

'If the shoe fits...' He stood up. 'Stop trying to fix my life and concentrate on your own.'

Alex stormed out and into the courtyard, leaving his tray on the table.

His accusation rocked Anya to the core. Where had that come from? The two soldiers got up and followed Alex out.

Everyone watched her. Her hands shook as she dropped both her and Alex's tray back to the counter. She fought against the blush that stained her cheeks.

'Screw this.'

She marched through the dining area nestled in a section of the town hall, to the corridor and main foyer. She faced the direction of the battle room she'd been in once, but instead of going there, she turned and left through the town hall's front door. Assuming the chances of Max letting her in were low, Anya crept to the back of the hall and searched for the window to the battle room.

She found it and saw Max stood in front of a table that had been pushed up against the window. He was speaking to the room. Anya's heart caught in her throat when she saw Dom. Sheila and June stood either side of him. His hands were stuffed into his pockets. He looked distracted, staring at the floor.

Voices carried through the window's single pane of glass. Anya turned her head, needing to hear more. That's when she saw her brother, standing with another boy around his age, with similar, brown hair.

'Why does Jason get to be in the meeting?' she muttered.

Anger caused her hands to shake harder. She balled them into fists to deal with it.

She considered storming the room, demanding that Max include her in discussions. But she tempered her impulsive thoughts and observed who else was in the room. Her heart almost jumped out of her chest at the thought of seeing one person. Worse, if that person was being given an elevated status, above her.

She released a tight breath when she couldn't see Warren. Knowing that Warren breathed the same camp air as her made her want to hide.

The talk permeated through the glass as mumbles. She caught words like machines and magnetic, but the lack of context forced her to abandon her idea to listen. She walked away. Not too far, just to the trucks parked around the grassy patch where she waited for the meeting to finish. It did, about ten minutes later.

Dom emerged first, followed by Sheila and June, who chatted to each other. Dom said something to them, then peeled off and headed for the courtyard where the soldiers trained. Others Anya didn't know came out next. Her brother emerged last with the young man who'd been standing next to him.

Anya ran to catch up with him. 'Jason.'

Jason glanced behind him, then at his companion. 'I'll meet you there, Thomas.'

Thomas nodded and strode in the direction Dom had just gone.

Anya stared after the skinny boy. 'He doesn't look like the exercise type.'

Jason smiled. 'He's not. He's in the tech workshop, in the alley behind the training room. Remember me telling you about it?'

Anya shook her head as Thomas carried on past the entrance to the courtyard. This amnesia must be affecting her short-term memory now. 'Why wasn't I in the meeting?'

Jason shrugged. 'That's up to Max, not me. Sorry.'

His dismissive reply irritated her. She folded her arms. 'So what were you talking about?'

'About how to defend this place.'

She uncrossed her arms. 'What's coming?'

She'd expected the city to come looking for the escapees. But who or what would they send?

'We don't know. But we need to prepare.'

She wanted, no, she *needed* to be of use. 'I can help.'

Jason shook his head. 'Not with my stuff. You know nothing about electronics.'

That was true. Growing up, Anya had hated anything to do with it.

'Okay, then, with attack or defence training.'

Jason lifted his palms. 'Max is the one you need to speak with.'

He walked backwards, ending their conversation.

'Okay, I will.'

She stomped off and returned to the town hall. This time she headed for the battle room where she found two soldiers chatting outside.

One put their hand out when Anya reached the door. 'Where do you think you're going?'

'I need to speak with Max.'

'About what?'

Nothing she wanted to discuss with them. 'I want to help.'

'Max has enough help. He'll come find you when he needs you.'

Anya could have kicked and screamed her way inside, but that wouldn't have helped her cause. She needed distance from Canya and she knew better than to throw a tantrum like Carissa.

'I'll find another way to talk to him.'

'Uh huh. We'll let him know you called.'

The soldiers smirked at her as though she was a nuisance. They resumed their discussion about guns and training—two things Anya knew more about than them. Her skill in school had centred on sports and training, including with guns.

What she wouldn't give to show them up at the shooting range.

She returned to the outside, angry and needing to talk to someone, anyone, to help her calm down. She settled for Alex. Anya spotted his guards first, stood close to the perimeter fence marking the boundary line between the occupied compound and the rest of the town. She startled when June appeared from behind the last building. Anya hid as she strode up to the guards. June had a quick word with the guards, who nodded at her and left. Then June disappeared out of sight.

Anya crept up to the corner of the building, hearing June's and Alex's voices the closer she got. She stopped at the corner and listened.

'That was so cool,' said Alex.

June replied, 'I'm a rebel too, so they have to listen to me. Don't worry. They won't bother you when I'm around.'

'I guess I'll have to keep you around all the time, huh?'

Anya could hear Alex's smile in his words.

June's soft laugh punched a fist-sized hole in Anya's heart. She backtracked from the scene before she made one of her own and tried to control her frantic breaths. She walked around the compound, a fraction of the size of her hometown Brookfield. While the camp's size wasn't tiny, the close quarters were already making her feel claustrophobic.

Everywhere she went, she sensed hostility from soldiers she'd never met before. Max's choice to exclude her from matters wasn't helping her transition from amnesiac to prisoner to rebel. It wasn't her fault she couldn't remember.

Not only that, but having to keep track of Warren's movements filled her with a sense of dread. It was only a matter of time before she bumped into him. Maybe he'd play it smart and stay away from her. Up until now, Alex had been her buffer; Warren might be less likely to approach her if she had company. But she'd just lost him to June.

Anya rubbed her arms as a sudden chill caught hold. Feeling vulnerable and alone, she hurried to a busier location. Her journey took her down a street with a barber shop. She touched her hair, tied back in a low ponytail. It had grown too long and lost its style. She walked up to the window, but the shop was empty, Anya turned away, disappointed.

A voice behind her startled her. 'Looking for a haircut?'

She spun round to see Charlie, Max's father, standing there and sporting a friendly smile.

'I, uh...'

Charlie opened the door to the shop and gestured for her to enter. 'I don't bite. Plus, I dispense free advice, and you look like you need some.'

Anya hesitated, but only for a moment. She needed company more than advice. Being alone right now scared her.

Charlie pointed to the only seat that was an actual barber's chair. 'Sit.'

She did and stared at her brown hair in the mirror with a crack running through its centre. The tiled floor was swept clean, in contrast to the dustiness of the counters. It must have been some time since anyone had used this space.

Charlie pulled out the band from her hair and ruffled it. The action sparked a memory.

She narrowed her eyes at him. 'I know you.'

Charlie smiled. 'We never met before you came here.'

But the memory stuck with her. Someone else was getting a haircut, someone with hair the same length as hers was now.

'No, I remember. You cut someone's hair in your kitchen. I was watching through the window. I wasn't supposed to be there.'

Charlie's hand stilled in her hair. 'What kind of hair?'

She frowned in her effort to remember. Then the image came to her. 'Dreadlocks, I think.'

Charlie laughed and picked up a comb, then ran it through her hair. 'I remember. That happened while we were in Essention.' He wagged the comb at her. 'I thought I heard someone at the back of my property.'

She held his gaze. 'Sorry, I didn't mean to spy.'

He smiled and shook his head at her through the mirror. 'I don't think you understand. That, my girl, is one of your lost memories.'

A weight lifted off her shoulders, but soon returned when she thought about what else she'd forgotten. Sadness returned to her eyes. It wasn't enough.

Charlie shook her shoulders as if to break her out of it. 'That's a good thing, Anya. It means your memories are not completely gone.'

He combed out her hair. The action felt good. She hadn't done anything with it for too long.

'I suppose. But it still feels like I'm missing so much.'

'Do you remember anything else?' Charlie got out a water bottle and sprayed her hair wet. 'Sorry, no sinks or running water in the camp. I can't wash your hair.'

She hadn't shared the memory Canya had returned to her with anyone. But it crippled her so much that she had to tell someone. 'I remember one event with one of the boys who came here.'

'Good or bad? I don't need details if you'd prefer not to say.'

She swallowed. 'Bad.'

'Do you want to say who it is?'

She shook her head. She could deal with this—she should deal with this—on her own.

'I'll figure it out.'

The water weighed her head down. Charlie sectioned out her hair until he had separated the top and side parts from the back. 'How short do you want to go?'

Anya hadn't given it much thought; she'd only wanted company. 'Have at it.'

Charlie chopped the dead weight from her head. With the loss of her hair came a lightening of her mood.

'So what else is bothering you?' Charlie pressed the scissors to his chest. 'Don't worry. My barber shop is a sacred space.'

Anya bit her lip. 'Max had a meeting in the battle room and I wasn't invited.'

'Maybe he doesn't want to put too much on your plate.'

'But I need to be useful. I need... distractions.'

'From this boy?'

Anya stared at her lap and concentrated on the sound of the scissors, metal against metal making fine snips into the ends of her hair. She looked up in alarm when she saw Charlie had cut quite a bit off.

'Don't worry,' he said when he caught her expression. 'I'm very good at what I do.'

Anya slumped in the chair. 'I need for my time in Praesidium to count for something. I need to make the Collective pay, not only for stealing my memories but for killing my parents. Above all, I need for the right individuals to escape Max's punishment. Not all the Copies are bad. One helped us to escape.'

Charlie paused with the scissors in the air. 'And you're worried Max will run in there and kill them all?'

'They were prisoners as much as I was. It's not fair to kill them when they have no control over their lives. That was Alex in there. That was me for a time.'

Charlie continued chopping with the scissors, applying speed and dexterity to his cuts. 'Your main priority is to work on restoring your memories. The fight with the Collective won't happen without you, of that I'm certain. Your time there is valuable, but Vanessa believes your parents might have inadvertently shared key information with you.'

Anya jerked her head up. 'Like what?'

Charlie snapped his scissors out of the danger zone. 'Like a place called the Beyond. A safe zone that exists outside of the control of the machines. When this is all over, or if we can't defeat the machines, we'll need to go there.'

The Beyond. Could there really be a map to a safe zone somewhere inside her head?

8

Carissa

Carissa woke to the feel of something wet on her face. A part metal tongue slathered her in saliva. She jerked awake and scooted back from her attacker.

Rover panted like a dog as he assessed her with mild curiosity. Not that long ago, she'd feared these magnificent beasts, created by the Collective to serve the Collective. She'd witnessed the same Guardians supervise the participants in Arcis when she'd watched them through the city's screens. From afar, they'd appeared to be menacing. Similar beasts that had also patrolled the business district and the perimeter in the city had kept her well away from it. Carissa hadn't been brave enough to test out how friendly they were.

Until now.

The Inventor's creation, under his command, had broken down her defences. She'd fallen asleep next to the beast with no thought for her own safety.

And the Guardian had woken her with a tongue bath.

Carissa watched Rover, who was sitting up now, looking more alert than he'd been when she'd first arrived. Maybe the wolf was just lonely. She understood loneliness. Rover had been separated from his master. Carissa had lost the only family she knew.

Despite her promise to the Inventor, she searched for her connection to Quintus and the family she'd left behind, despite her chip no longer working. Still, a deep-seated curiosity drove her to seek out a sliver of her old life.

She searched for the ringing to indicate a connection had been made. She hunted for the voices of the other Copies that had melded into a singular hum, before she'd been forced out of the city. Carissa squeezed her eyes shut and grunted with the effort to connect.

Nothing. She opened her eyes and huffed.

Rover watched her, curious in disposition. His rigid mouth indicated new tension, as though he understood what she was trying to do. She made another attempt, but the same silence greeted her.

Rover slid back down to the floor, as if he, too, had given up. He rested his metallic head on his paws once more. Defeated, Carissa sat down beside him, beside her only real connection to the city and the only living beast that truly understood her. She patted his exoskeleton, made of the strongest metal known to the Collective. The action emitted a rumble from deep inside his lungs.

Alex wasn't like her. He was a Breeder, born human, his growth and maturity accelerated so fast that years passed in months. He had no NMC, no way to communicate with the Collective. To Quintus, he'd been nothing more than a vessel with which the Ten could create their army and break free from their machine prison. The Collective had used the Originals, or humans, to learn how to interact when it gained that freedom.

Jerome was a newborn, a creation without an NMC who shouldn't have been able to survive alone. Carissa had been a newborn for a week, before she reached maturity and gained the neuromorphic chip that put her on the same network as the other Copies. She had no memory of her time as a newborn, no experience of living without voices in her head.

But Jerome did.

She got up, prompting a similar reaction from Rover. The Guardian wolf whined when she started for the door.

'I'll be back, boy. You and I need to stick together now.'

The wolf barked once. She hated leaving him, but he also had to get used to being alone.

Carissa stepped out into the bright sunshine, spotting her female soldier escorts straight away. They looked bored sitting on the ground, but they clambered to their feet as soon as she approached. Carissa strode past them, her chin lifted high to convey her status. Quintus had said Originals were of lesser importance than the Copies who'd been created to transcend them.

Her chest swelled upon remembering his teaching. This might be a new prison for her, but she didn't have to act like a prisoner. She searched the compound for Jerome, finding him in the building with the open front on the same street as the barber shop. The storage area was one of a few she'd seen in the compound. This one was crammed with more common items the rebels had collected, from hairbrushes to soap to spare boots.

Jerome worked alongside Warren. Together, they sorted through new stock from a box on the floor.

Carissa stared at Warren, the strawberry blond haired boy with freckles who had hurt Anya and acted selfishly in Arcis. Her skin prickled with anger when Warren glanced at her then down at the box of equipment, as though she deserved only a second of his time.

Jerome, the boy with skin as dark as his hair, looked up at her and gave her a nod. 'You're Carissa, right?'

'Yeah.'

Warren's attention shifted suddenly from the box to her.

'I don't think we've met properly. I'm Jerome and this is Warren.'

She ignored Warren, not liking the intensity his look held.

She pretended she was back in Praesidium speaking to one of the Originals there. 'I require a moment of your time, Jerome.'

'She's very formal,' said Warren with a sneer. 'What's the matter, you think you're still in the city?'

Carissa ignored Warren's attempts to undermine her. She waited for Jerome's answer.

He replied with a shrug and told Warren he'd be right back.

Warren replied with a shrug of his own. 'Your funeral.'

Jerome stepped outside and onto the street. Carissa pulled him away from the storage area and the barber shop.

'I wanted to talk to you about something,' she said.

Jerome frowned at her. 'Okay.'

She took a deep breath. 'I want to know how you do it.'

'Do what?'

'Live alone.'

Jerome smiled and shook his head. 'I'm not following you.'

'You live without voices in your head, without a connection to the city. How do you cope?'

Jerome's body stiffened. He folded his arms across his chest. 'That's how humans live, Carissa. We don't have voices in our heads.'

'But you're not human. You're a newborn. You're like me.'

Jerome laughed and uncrossed his arms, but the tension didn't leave him. 'You and I are not alike. Your precious Collective trapped me in Arcis, made me perform tasks on each of their nine floors.'

'That's because they didn't know what you were.'

Jerome's eyes widened. 'Exactly. That's because I'm human.'

Carissa shook her head. 'I can see what you are, Jerome. I can see what you should have become.'

He folded his arms again and, with the gesture, his defensive wall lifted higher. 'Is this what you wanted to talk about? To remind me I'm like you? We are *not* alike.'

'I need to know I'm not alone.'

'Why don't you talk to your Inventor friend? Or his wolf. Rover, is it?' Carissa spotted Warren watching the interaction from the edge of the storage area. Jerome walked away, calling over his shoulder. 'I can't help you, Copy.'

Panic swelled inside her. 'Wait! There's nobody else. How do I live without the voices in my head?'

Jerome walked backwards and shrugged. 'Can't help you. It's always been just me.'

Their chat left Carissa with a sick feeling in her stomach. She stomped away, pressing down the hurt that made her pulse pound and her skin itch. Nobody understood what she needed. Only one other person with experience might help her.

Her escorts followed her as she marched to the

courtyard, hoping to find Alex there. But before she made it a hundred feet, Max's second in command, Julius, appeared from a side street and stopped both females in their tracks. He said something to them, to which they responded with a shrug. Carissa watched them leave. Had her word with the Inventor earlier convinced Max enough that she could be trusted?

With a lighter load, she carried on to the courtyard to see Alex stood at the entrance, watching the soldiers train. He wore a small smile on his face. Carissa looked inside the yard to see June and Sheila training in a group led by a commanding female, while Dom ran solo laps of the yard's perimeter.

Breeders were just as capable as naturally born humans when it came to physical exertion. Why hadn't he joined in with the others?

She stopped beside him. 'Why do you not train with the humans?'

Alex glanced at her, his smile dropping away. 'I can help in other ways.'

'Like what?'

He shrugged. 'I can fix trucks. I'm not a soldier.'

He must have learned that skill when he'd escaped from the city that one time. The Collective kept records of all their insubordinate creations. She shuddered to think her name could be on that list too. Keeping the city away might be the best solution for now.

Carissa looked up at him. 'Shouldn't everyone

train in case we are attacked?'

Alex glanced at her again. He nodded at the rebel humans. 'I know the Collective better than they do. Physical fighting is just one way to combat them.'

Carissa studied the young man grown by the Collective to become a Breeder. 'Do you miss Praesidium?'

Alex pinned her with his glare, his eyes growing large. He shook his head, as if he couldn't believe her question. 'Only a Copy would ask such a thing. Do you have any idea what they did to me in there?' He looked ahead. 'Of course you do.'

Carissa nodded.

'Yes,' she squeaked when he didn't see her reaction.

'And you think I want to go back to that?'

It wasn't what she'd meant. 'No. I meant... the city was the only life you knew. Do you miss it?'

Alex huffed out a breath. 'Do *you*?'

His anger set Carissa's heartbeat to gallop in her chest. She switched her attention to the less aggressive training session instead. 'Sometimes. I don't know how to function out here. Alone.'

'We're all alone, Carissa. The sooner you realise that, the better.'

She frowned at him. 'But I wasn't alone in the city. I was connected.'

Why couldn't anyone see that? Her situation differed from theirs, her experience of the outside stranger than most.

Alex scoffed. 'To a bunch of psycho AI minds who forced you into servitude.'

'It wasn't like that. It wasn't all that bad.'

It had been an honour to serve the Collective.

'Bad?' Alex laughed. 'It was a frigging nightmare. Seriously, Carissa. When are you going to realise you dodged a bullet by getting out of there?'

He stormed off, leaving Carissa to watch the session alone. It was easy for him to tell her to grow up. He'd been through puberty already thanks to a fast-acting growth machine that sped up not only his body's development, but his mind's too. Thanks to the machine, Alex had lived a lifetime in just a handful of months.

But Carissa was only thirteen and she still needed guidance more than eighteen-year-old Alex did.

She pushed down the hurt that nobody here could understand. Even Rover's company didn't satiate her. How was she supposed to grow up without guidance? Her eyes travelled up to the ledge where the spotters with guns watched over the valley.

Maybe she'd find answers up there.

9

Anya

Charlie put down the scissors and stood back with a finger on his lip. Anya admired her new haircut in the cracked mirror. He had styled it into a long bob. The ends had been layered and feathered slightly to frame her face. She even had a fringe.

Anya hadn't seen her hair that short since... well, before she lost her memories.

Charlie used a second mirror to show her the back, which had a similar subtle set of layers running through it.

He watched her in the main mirror and put his wrinkled face next to hers. 'Well, what do you think?'

A smile crept onto Anya's face, prompting the old man to smile himself. 'I love it. It feels so...'

'Light?'

He pulled back and straightened up.

She nodded and turned her head both ways. Her hair followed the movement with ease. Before the cut, it had sat like a lump on her head.

Anya swivelled round in the chair. 'What do I owe you?'

It felt appropriate to offer payment for such a beautiful cut.

Charlie's eyes hardened to black diamonds. 'How much money do you have on you?'

Anya blushed and patted her pockets. She didn't know why. She had nothing to her name. 'I, uh, don't have...'

The expression on Charlie's face softened and he erupted into laughter. 'Your lovely company was my reward, dear Anya Macklin.'

Anya swatted Charlie's arm, then hopped out of her chair to plant a kiss on his cheek. 'That was mean, but I'll definitely be back.'

A grinning Charlie tipped his hand to her as she left.

Anya's step felt lighter. She couldn't keep her hands off her hair. It felt so soft, even though Charlie had only dampened it with a spray bottle, not washed it.

Something more important than a cut had happened to her while she sat in the chair. She'd remembered something from her erased past, a person with dreadlocks who had gotten a haircut from Charlie. She could have asked Charlie who that person had been, but the detail wasn't as important as the recollection itself. It gave her hope that her memories were still a part of her, not locked away in the machine in Arcis.

As she strolled beneath the sunshine, her desire to test out her theory grew more. She considered asking Sheila and Dom, both of whom had been in Arcis with her. But Dom had never lost his memories and Sheila's Copy had returned hers. Anya worried their enthusiasm for her to remember could confuse what might be her memory with their recollection.

She thought of June, but the petite, blonde girl with fire in her eyes was in a similar amnesiac position to her. Not to mention June's newfound connection with Alex; Anya wasn't ready to let go of her connection with him just yet. If she spoke to June, it would be the end.

What about Jerome, a boy who she didn't remember, but who Jason and the others had rescued from Arcis after she disappeared? Maybe he could help in a more impartial way.

Anya walked the full perimeter of the compound. She found him in a storage area she'd not yet seen, in a building butting up against the fence dividing old from new. The open-sided property had been cleared of everything. A trestle table stood in the middle of the space with an assortment of guns on it, some smooth and sleek like the Electro Guns they'd stolen from the guards in Praesidium, others boxy and homemade, with fat, metal barrels soldered crudely to the front. Then there were revolvers, simple and easy for first-timers to try. A male and female soldier cleaned all the weapons.

One corner held a ball of tangled rope and a selection of badly rusted blades. Jerome was holding up one end of the rope in his hand and rubbing his chin, trying to work out what to do next. She stepped up into the property, a move that drew the attention of the two soldiers. Both of them did a double-take. Jerome looked up from his task and let out a "wow" when he saw her.

'Your hair looks great, Anya. Who cut it?'

'Charlie over at the barber shop. Max's father.'

Jerome's expression darkened at the mention of —who was it—Charlie or Max? Max probably. He'd been less than welcoming to him since his arrival. Anya still couldn't believe Jerome was a newborn— grown not born. She might not remember him, but she saw nothing to indicate he differed from anyone else.

Jerome's stare hardened. 'Why are you looking at me like I'm some freak in a show? So what if I came from the city?' He tossed the rope away in anger. 'I don't remember it.'

Anya adopted a lighter expression. 'I'm sorry, Jerome. I was just thinking about my time there, that's all.'

'But you think I'm to be avoided? I can see it on your face. Didn't our friendship in Arcis count for anything?' He stared down at the discarded rope. 'Even Dom, Sheila and June are being weird with me since they learned what I am.'

'I don't remember you.' It was the truth. 'But I

just spent a week with a Breeder who was born and grown at a fast rate and for a specific purpose. He's my friend too. I have no issues with what you are.'

Jerome appeared to relax at her admission. But then he frowned at her. 'So why *are* you here?'

'I'm starting to remember things from my time in Arcis. I... was hoping to test out a few scenarios on you.'

'Like what?' He snapped his fingers suddenly as if he remembered something. 'Hey, what happened to Yasmin? She was with you on the ninth floor, wasn't she?'

Anya nodded and swallowed. 'She was killed in the city for resisting.'

The soldiers, she noticed, were pretending not to listen in on their conversation.

Jerome pursed his lips. 'I'm sorry. It was a crap time for all of us.'

He closed his eyes and sighed.

'Okay,' he said, opening them, 'what do you want to know?'

Her mood lightened. She returned to her discussion with Charlie. 'Did someone in our group have dreadlocks?'

Jerome nodded. 'That would have been Dom. But he wasn't in our group yet. He was ahead of us.'

Hearing his name sent a surprise shiver through her. 'When did he cut it?'

Jerome gave it some thought. 'That was a while ago now... about five minutes after we met you?' He nodded, as though it all became clear. 'That's right. The first time I saw him was on the first floor walkway. He wore his hair longer then. Then like the next day or the one after that—I can't remember—it was gone.'

'How do you remember that time if you never met him?'

Jerome flashed his white teeth. 'Because you two knew each other. I think you used to be friends before rotation separated you.'

Anya frowned. She didn't remember the friendship between her and Dom, yet she recalled a boring hair cut? At least her odd memory tallied with Jerome's recollection of events.

Jerome asked her a question next. 'Other than the haircut, what else do you remember?'

Anya froze as the memory her bitch Copy had passed back to her came to the fore. 'I remember... I think it was the fourth floor...'

Jerome grinned and nodded. 'Oh yeah, the sexes had to compete against each other. Do you remember being my slave?'

Anya stared at him. 'Your what?'

His smile faded fast. Jerome put his hands up. 'Sorry, poor choice of words. I meant you had to complete tasks with me to earn points.'

Anya remembered none of that. 'Did any of it take place in the bathroom?'

'Like cleaning?' He frowned. 'I don't think so.'

A new voice froze the blood in her veins. 'Hey,

Jerome. I got some cleaning fluid that should make light work of the rust on those blades...' Warren paused when he saw Anya. 'Oh, hi.'

Her mouth puckered with terror at seeing her attacker.

'Hey, I like the new haircut.' His eyes flitted between Jerome and Anya. 'Are you two catching up?'

She sensed his curiosity—and possibly dread— over what she might have discussed with Jerome. That meant Warren and Jerome were still friends. She couldn't trust Jerome with this truth.

'I've got to go.'

She stepped down from the storage area to the street and walked away, fighting the wobble in her legs that threatened to ground her.

Warren called after her. 'Hey, Anya, did you get your memories back yet?'

She caught the tremor in his voice.

She stopped and turned, pinning him with her best glare. 'I remember *some* things.'

Warren's eyes widened almost imperceptibly, but he replied with a friendly, 'Glad to hear.'

Anya stalked away, but not before she saw Warren pat Jerome on the back—a sign that their friendship would not be so easily soured. Her heart hardened as a new mission to destroy Warren took hold.

The thrum of her heart never let up, even when she made it back to the start of the camp where the trucks were parked. She leaned against the gable of a house that had once been someone's home. A fallen rock lodged in its heart had laid it open to the elements.

Her fast breaths made her chest hurt. She slowed them down to control her rising panic. Anya hadn't expected Warren to affect her so deeply. Some of it had to do with her lack of context; no before or after memories. But an attack was an attack. And Warren had gone too far that night in the bathroom. What sickened her more was his lack of contrition for almost raping her.

She cursed Canya and her attempts to hurt her. Well, this one had worked.

'Consider me hurt, you bitch,' she muttered to the sky.

A couple of soldiers walking past gave her a strange look. Anya focused on the ground and hurried on. It didn't matter where she went, as long as there were people present. Knowing exactly where Warren was relaxed the tension in her muscles.

She crossed the grassy area and weaved through parked trucks to arrive at the crowded courtyard where most of the soldiers were training. She'd been good at sport once. But time away had set her body and mind back. She needed to find her centre again.

Anya approached the entrance, preparing to join the training. Carissa was watching the activity, but as soon as she reached her the Copy stormed off.

What was her problem?

Some soldiers did warm-up exercises in the yard, while others used the stationary bike and free weights. She caught sight of Dom in the back of the weights room, punching a boxing bag that hung from a reinforced hook in the ceiling. Anya shook her head as a new recollection of a similar scene surfaced. But it remained unclear like every other damn thought she had.

Anya turned back to see Max standing next to her. His presence startled her. She shook off her surprise and glanced up at his strong features, hardened by this fight with the machines. Anya wanted to ask him why he'd left her out of the strategy meeting.

But before she could, he stepped forward and announced to the yard, 'Tonight, we'll hold a celebration dinner in the town hall. All are welcome. The Collective will be coming soon but rebel reinforcements are on the way. We don't know how long we have before the city finds us, so let's take a moment to breathe, take stock and prepare mentally for their arrival. Seven pm sharp.'

Max glanced at Anya. 'Nice hairdo. Charlie?'

Anya nodded and went to speak, but Max walked away, giving her no chance to reply or ask her burning question.

Irritated, she jogged inside the courtyard and ran laps for the first time in a long time. The burn in her lungs and legs came too fast to deal with her anger and stopped her midway through her second lap. She looked around at the others. They paid her no mind and seemed happy just to be doing something. Her eyes darted around the space in fear that Warren had followed her.

She unclenched when she saw no sign of him, but the damage was done. No amount of exercise would set her mind right.

Let it go, Anya.

Just give it time.

Problem was, she didn't think time was on anyone's side.

10

Carissa

Her heated conversation with Alex in the minutes before Anya showed up drove Carissa past the trucks parked at an angle to the main gates and the front of the camp. Two guards with guns patrolled a foot bridge set along the top of the high-perimeter wall. Her group had arrived by truck via an access road set above the camp. They had used a service elevator to reach the valley floor. Carissa planned to use the same elevator, carved out of a weaker section of the rock, to go back up.

But the presence of gun-toting rebels giving her odd glances set her nerves on edge. She couldn't see how to get past the heavily patrolled front gate. Discouraged, she turned back to the compound with its half structures and uneven roads, both in surface and width. It was so different to Praesidium with its concentric pattern and equidistant roads that made it efficient to navigate the city.

Carissa hated how disjointed the property shapes were, and that everyone wore mismatched clothes to add to the disharmony. She enjoyed order. It made her place in society clear.

Her thoughts went to Rover. An imposing force like him would surely make the guards open the gate for her. But she didn't want to get the wolf into trouble. Who she needed to talk to wasn't in the compound. She would do this alone and in secret.

Without her escorts, Carissa explored the camp with a new freedom. Taking strides meant for longer legs than hers, she passed by the trio of houses next to the gate; the first teemed with a rebel presence. She carried on past the town hall and the courtyard to the back perimeter fence.

Carissa stuck her face up to the corrugated, green panelling that was too smooth and too high to climb. At a point where the fence met the rock race, she noticed it did not meet correctly. The tiny gap would give the adults trouble, but her smaller size could work to her advantage.

She squeezed her way inside the old part of the town, feeling a strange sensation push her back to the fence. This part looked as dilapidated as the front section. The only things that differed were the width and types of properties. She considered returning later to explore the new section further, but what she needed to see wasn't at eye level.

A crumbling set of stairs carved out of the rock stood off to the left. It led up to the lookout point above the town. Judging from their state of disrepair, she guessed the rebels didn't use this route to reach the mountain shelf.

The force, which she assumed was an additional anti-magnetic field, gave her enough leeway to access to the stairs. She took care in her climb, so as not to put her foot through gaps where pieces of the steps had broken away. If she fell in this under-visited section of the town, who would know about it? Her part organic heart was thumping wildly by the time she reached the same level from which the spotters watched. Closer to the front of the compound and with their backs turned to her, they paid her no attention.

Carissa caught her breath a little. Then she noticed a new set of steps leading even higher. She used them to reach a different shelf and pulled herself up to a grassy area perched above the level of the spotters. She sat on the shelf, with her legs dangling over the side. Up this high, she could see the length of the valley to the front of the camp. Fallen rocks dotted the barren valley floor. In the distance, she saw the bright mouth marking the start of the open landscape beyond it. If the Collective came, she guessed its troops would arrive at that point.

A group of soldiers she'd seen leave through the front gate a while ago, clearly on a scouting mission, returned to the camp. What they searched for she didn't know.

Up high, it was easy for her to forget the people

below. She would not be treated like an irritation. She would not be cast aside. She had been useful once. As soon as she received new assurances of that fact, Carissa would accept her new life.

The opinion of only one person mattered to her now. What harm could it do to speak to him one last time? High up, her neuromorphic chip tickled the skin where her disc had been embedded. Carissa scratched the surface, but it did little to relieve the itch. The itch persisted and a voice sounded in the distance.

'Hello?' she said without thinking.

Chatter reached her from the camp below. A flurry of voices came through, from the radio equipment in the main house, she assumed. Her partly operational NMC relayed their communications back to her. She listened for a while, finding the flurry of voices soothing as soldiers spoke to camps in the area. Glenvale, Oakenfield and Halforth were all mentioned. The rebels checked the status of the towns and asked how supplies were faring. Supplies were low. Someone confirmed a team from Halforth was on its way.

A new voice underpinned the main chatter. 'Hello?'

It was a male voice separate to the ones she'd just heard. The voice was so feeble, so distant; she couldn't quite make it out.

'Who is this?' she whispered.

'It's me. I've been waiting for you.'

Carissa frowned at her legs, wondering if she'd

stumbled upon a crossed connection.

'I'm sorry, I don't know who—'

'173-C, the Collective is not angry with you.'

Carissa almost slipped from her ledge. She grabbed clumps of grass to steady herself when her rapid pulse threatened to knock her loose.

'Who... What?'

'We are glad you are safe, but you must tell us where you are. We have been searching for you.'

Carissa shook her head and with it Quintus' voice faded into the background. Chatter from the rebel communications filled her head with noise.

A flurry of breaths escaped her. She slid down from the ledge and stumbled down the stone steps to the camp once more. By the time she set foot on flat ground, winded and doubled over, all the voices had vanished.

11

Anya

Her failed attempts to return to exercise irritated Anya. Her mind, too clustered with recent events, shot her concentration to hell. Her behaviour that evening only solidified her case in point. She'd shown up at the town hall early to stake out the dining hall and find a spot well away from Warren.

The furniture in the room had been rearranged into one long table with chairs around it. Whatever food could be spared had been set down on the table. There was even fresh bread. Anya spotted a drinks station set up next to where the servers usually handed out food.

Sheila and June were there with Alex. Her annoyance with him earlier had faded into the background. Meeting Warren again had brought her recent childish actions into sharp focus. She'd been unfairly using Alex as a shield to protect her from Warren. The only person who could do that was her.

Alex left June's side and walked around the table to meet her.

With a sheepish smile he said, 'Hey, I was looking for you all day. I just wanted to say sorry about our fight earlier. Friends?'

He stuck his hand out.

Anya flashed a smile at him and shook it. 'Friends.'

Trouble was, they hadn't defined what they were. While trapped in Alex's room in the medical facility, they'd come close to having sex. Their attraction to each other had been off the charts, thanks to a drug called Rapture that had boosted their libidos. Anya admitted to missing the bond they shared, but away from the city and the drug, Alex had barely shown an interest in her. In fact, they'd argued as much as she used to with Jason.

Were they supposed to be together, or not? She had no handbook for this confusing new life of hers. And without her memories, she didn't feel qualified to make important decisions about it.

'Love the hair, by the way.'

Alex flashed the sexy smile that had almost broken down her defences a few times. They'd shared things about their pasts. In their short time together, they'd become close. Now, the connection wavered, leaving a giant hole in her heart where Alex had been ripped away.

Sheila moved over to the drinks station and poured herself a drink.

'Thanks,' Anya muttered to Alex, not sure what else to say. 'Excuse me, I just need to speak to Sheila.'

Anya left him alone and joined Sheila, tapping her lightly on the shoulder as she watched Alex return to June. Sheila spun round and glared at her. But her look softened when she took in Anya's appearance.

'Oh my God.' She ran her fingers over the top of Anya's new style. 'I love it. Is this Charlie's work?'

Anya smiled and nodded. The old man was growing on her. 'He's very good at what he does.'

Sheila smirked as if she knew that already. 'Not only that, but he's scarily accurate at reading your deepest, darkest secrets.'

She twirled her hand in the air.

Her words surprised Anya. She reined in her look of shock when Sheila's eyes widened suddenly.

'I only meant he's intuitive. But don't worry; he keeps everything to himself.'

She laughed it off but her gaze, still on Anya, flicked from playful to hard in a flash. Anya wondered if Charlie wasn't the only one with good intuition.

Sheila's eyes became two slits. 'Something else is wrong. I can tell. You look like you've been kicked in the gut.'

'Feels like it.' Anya sighed, grateful for Sheila's sixth sense. Keeping secrets was hard work. 'I went to talk to Jerome because I remembered something...'

'That's great!' interrupted Sheila.

'... but then Warren showed up.'

Sheila's pupils contracted to fine points. 'That ass? I hope you told him where to shove his apology.'

'He didn't apologise.'

'That dick...' Sheila crushed the cup in her hand, spilling whatever it contained. 'Wait until I get my hands on him. Even better, I've a good mind to tell someone about him.'

Anya gripped the hand holding the cup and Sheila's grip loosened.

'Please don't. And it's okay. I had to see him at some point.' She pulled her hand back. 'I just wish I had more context around the event itself. Right now, it feels like a stranger attacked me.' Anya broke her rule for the second time that day to not ask about things she couldn't remember. 'Did Warren and I know each other before that happened?'

Sheila gave her a look. 'Are you sure you want to ask?'

Anya nodded.

'Yes. You two were friends, I think. I didn't know either of you very well, but both of you, plus Jerome, June, Tahlia and Frank all hung out together.'

Two of those names were new. 'Tahlia and Frank?'

'Yeah.' Sheila shrugged. 'They didn't make it.'

'Like Yasmin?'

Sheila nodded and stared at the crushed cup in her hand. She swapped it for an undamaged one. 'I think I need some alcohol.' She opened all the bottles and sniffed the contents, then said to the room, 'Hey, I thought this was supposed to be a party. Where's the booze?'

Nobody answered her, but the others looked equally disappointed. Charlie and Vanessa appeared at the entrance to the hall and walked over to them.

'When you're old enough to drink, young lady,' said Charlie. He nodded at Anya. 'The cut looks good on you.'

Anya fluffed the bottom of her hair with her hand. 'I'm getting a lot of compliments for it.'

'Hey, Charlie,' said Sheila, draping an arm around the old man's shoulders, like they were friends. 'I'm next. I need you to do something with this hair of mine.' She let go of him and pulled round a section of her golden brown mane. It hung loose around her shoulders. 'The usual, darling?'

Charlie laughed and said to Anya, 'That means a trim, nothing more. She won't let me cut her hair properly.'

Sheila's eyes rounded at the suggestion. She tossed her mane over one shoulder. 'Why would I, when it's *this* fabulous?'

Max strode into the room next, with Dom. Charlie excused himself and went over to meet them.

Vanessa stayed with them for a moment longer. She touched Anya's arm. 'Max and I were discussing your parents' limited knowledge of the coordinates to the Beyond. We sent a party out to locate the border they claimed to have seen, but the soldiers couldn't find anything out there. That sets us back. I was sure the border would be here, but maybe it was a trick of the eyes. Our only hope is they found it, or discovered someone else who found it, before they died. It's possible you may have overheard them talking about it.'

Anya frowned. 'I don't know anything...'

'Still, we should try. But not tonight. I want you to enjoy the party.' She paused. 'I saw you training today. From now on, you won't be part of the team. Your role will be to help us locate the coordinates or someone who might have them. That's the priority— to fill in the missing gaps.'

The latter was her priority too, except to do with her own life.

Vanessa left to join Max, Dom and Charlie.

When she was gone, Sheila said, 'Stick close to me tonight. Warren won't come within ten feet of you if he sees me.'

Anya hung back while everyone took their seats. Jason stuck with Thomas, Max and Vanessa at the top of the table while Charlie and Jacob, the inventor from Praesidium, sat next to each other. A subdued Carissa took the seat beside Jacob. She barely made eye contact with anyone.

Anya slid into a free seat. Sheila took the one next to her and pushed June into the chair the other side of Anya. Alex followed and sat beside June, naturally. On the table was water and a little wine, but not much else. Not much of a celebration in the traditional sense, but she'd take this place over the medical facility any day. From across the table, Jason raised an empty glass to her. She lifted hers, filled with water, and smiled at her brother.

Sat next to June instead of Alex unsettled Anya. In this confusing time of her life, only familiarity could calm the butterflies in her stomach. She didn't remember June from Arcis, but she *had* turned up to help her after Warren's attack. Anya hated not remembering more about her.

Dom approached the table. She watched him deliberate as to where to sit. Anya thought he'd join Sheila, but he chose a spot nearer the top of the table, next to Max and Charlie. He glanced at Anya as he settled in his chair.

Sheila elbowed her. 'He's trying to give you your space.'

Anya knew he was. 'I appreciate it.'

She decided against telling Sheila what she'd remembered about Dom's haircut from Charlie. To do so would make Sheila happy, and Anya couldn't give her hope when her feelings for Alex still confused her.

Dom stood up suddenly making Anya think he was going to leave. But then he walked over to an upright piano that she hadn't seen before, set behind the food counter. He sat down and started playing.

The melody had a haunting feel to it and gave Anya goosebumps. The scene played out like a dream. If she and Dom were supposed to be friends like Jerome had said, why couldn't she remember his piano skills?

She leaned back towards Sheila. 'Did I know this about him?'

Sheila smiled, her head caught in a dreamy, bopping motion. 'Not unless there was a piano in Arcis, which there was not. I haven't heard him play since we were both in the towns.'

Her admission made Anya feel better. She sat up straighter and absorbed the melody that cut a valley through her sadness and lifted her to a new plain. She looked around the room. Others were smiling. Ahead of her, June bopped along to the beat. Alex leaned on his arms. On occasion, he'd glance back and smile at June. Anya looked away from the interaction. It still squeezed her heart too tight and trapped a breath in her throat.

Then Jerome and Warren walked in. They sat in the two chairs opposite Anya. She swallowed and averted her gaze from Warren.

Dom finished playing and the room erupted into clapping and shouts of *Encore!* He played another song, something more lifting.

Sheila leaned close to Anya's shoulder, pretending she hadn't seen Warren. 'This one was his mother's favourite.'

Anya stared at the piano-playing man with the ability to make her forget, and tried to picture him with dreadlocks. But his abundance of soft, curly hair made it hard to imagine him with any other style. She wanted to stand next to him, to examine how his fingers caressed the piano keys. But with a room filled with rebels scrutinising everyone's move, she stayed put.

Dom finished his song. Next, one of the soldiers produced a guitar and played a new melody, while Dom returned to his seat. Anya kept her eyes on the new entertainer despite Warren's gaze burning a hole in her skin.

After dinner, some of the soldiers pushed the tables back for dancing. Dom maintained his distance while Anya stuck with her group: Sheila, June and Alex.

She had her back turned to the room when someone tapped her on the shoulder. She turned, half expecting it to be Jason or Dom. Her blood turned to ice when she saw it was Warren.

'Hey, that was some song, huh.'

Her throat closed over turning her into a mute. Anya had thought she could forget what he did. But speaking to him again scattered her rational thoughts to the wind. Her focus shifted to revenge.

Sheila stepped forward and snapped her out of her frozen fear.

'Stay the hell back, Warren. I won't warn you again.'

'Shut up, Kouris.' He had a hateful look in his eye. 'I'll talk to whoever I want.'

In her shock, Anya didn't notice an angry Dom

walk over.

He grabbed Warren by the shirt collar and pushed him back. 'You lay a finger on anyone in this room, I'll kill you.'

Warren wriggled beneath his grip. 'Take your hands off me, asshole.'

'Dom,' snapped Max. 'Let him go.'

Dom looked back at the colonel and released Warren, who coughed and rubbed his throat.

Warren glared at Anya. 'I was only trying to be nice. I won't make that mistake twice.'

Anya wrapped her arms around her waist. All eyes were on her and she hated it. Jason frowned at her from where he stood with Thomas.

He mouthed at her, 'What the hell was that?'

She replied with a shake of her head, but the attention didn't lessen.

To make her embarrassment worse, Dom cupped her face.

'Are you okay?' he said.

Her cheeks burned hotter and she shoved him away.

Sheila answered for her. 'She was fine until you went all cave man on Warren's ass. Just give her a minute.'

But Dom refused to leave. His intense stare made Anya want to run and hide.

A look of concern dominated his expression.

Max grabbed his shoulder, his thick brows drawn forward. 'Dom, what's going on?'

He shucked him off. 'Nothing.'

All Anya could hear was whispers. '*What was that about?*' She heard June and Alex wondering too, and it became too much to handle.

'Everyone, mind your own business,' she yelled to the room, then rounded on Dom. 'And I don't need you to fight my battles, okay?'

Dom looked hurt. 'Sorry. I was only trying to help...'

'Yeah? Well, you only made things worse.' Anya strode away, calling over her shoulder, 'Thanks for turning me into the local gossip.'

12

Carissa

Carissa stretched in her bed, a piece of green canopy covering layers of soft bedding. She looked around the female dorm to find it empty. Her bed last night had started out next to one of the soldiers on the floor, but that morning it had been moved to a new location near the bathroom.

She shoved her blanket aside, annoyed at being singled out by the other females. Sitting up, she touched the round, metal disc on the side of her head, the one that connected to her NMC, the one she had used in the city to upload and download information. The one she'd used the day before to pick up a familiar voice.

The usual silent echo filled her head, a white noise that sounded like emptiness and rejection. Hearing Quintus and the chatter from the rebels' communications, if only for a few seconds, had filled the empty space and given her a sense of peace. But the experience had passed and taken her peace with it.

Last night's celebration dinner had been a weird event. Warren and Anya's fight had topped the discussion in the female dorm after. Some women had branded Anya a drama queen. Probably unfair. Without her memories, Anya's disconnect from reality must be similar to how Carissa felt without her connection. One of the women had remarked that Anya had lost her memories, but it hadn't mattered to those ready to side with Warren.

'He was only trying to talk to her,' one had said.

Another female nodded. 'Max said she doesn't remember the last three months, which sounds farfetched if you ask me. I think she's putting on an act, looking for attention. Dom should just forget about her.'

'Yeah, what's their deal anyway? Are they a couple?' said a third, who sounded like an interested party.

'Dunno,' said the first. 'I heard Dom had two girlfriends back in Halforth. Kaylie's on her way here with her team.'

The second female laughed. 'You'd better hurry and get your hooks into Dom before she does. Kaylie's a beauty like Sheila.'

Carissa had pretended to be asleep during their chat. When the room fell silent, she knew Anya had arrived. She opened her eyes to see Sheila with her. The new amnesiac had looked around the space, her eyes flitting from one gossiping woman to the next, before she sat down on her bed.

Sheila had hissed, 'What are you all looking at?'

One responded in a whisper to another, 'I think you're right about Anya. Just looking for attention.'

Carissa had turned her back to the group, thinking about what she'd seen on the screens showing Arcis. While she hadn't seen what Warren had done to Anya—there'd been no cameras in the bathroom—she'd witnessed the reaction to the event afterwards. A traumatised Anya had tried to avoid Warren. And while he'd attempted to speak to her twice after, either Dom, June or Sheila had stopped him.

That morning, Carissa rose from her bed and left the empty dorm. Her rash decision to contact Quintus the day before didn't seem so bad after rest. Quintus—if the voice had even been his—had admitted to not being able to locate her. That thought filled her with relief as she headed to the only place where she felt safe.

She crept inside the storage shed to discover a sleeping Rover on the ground. He still wore the collar around his neck. A heavy chain connected that collar to the wall. The Guardian wolf lifted his head and whined, before setting his head to rest on his metal paws again.

How often did the Inventor check on his creation?

She sat cross-legged in front of Rover, but her presence did not lift the passive beast's mood. Carissa could relate to his crippling loneliness; this Guardian might not be connected to the Collective, but he shared a connection with Jacob, his absent creator.

The floor dirtied her clothes. She wore the same green trousers and white top from the day before, stained with grass from a banned location. At least the grass stains blended in with the colour of her trousers. She had to search hard to find them. And they weren't too noticeable on her sleeves either. Had this been the city, Carissa would have worn her usual white dress. But in the rebel camp, without a protective environmental bubble, she needed the extra layers.

Rover shifted his gaze from her to the side. Then, he closed his eyes again.

The silence bothered her. 'Hey.'

She snapped her fingers to get the wolf's attention. He opened his eyes and looked lazily at her.

'Play with me.'

She used to play with her orb in the grounds of Praesidium. And while she'd never engaged with a Guardian before, she had little choice for a playmate.

But the wolf never stirred past an apathetic state. She huffed out a breath and got to her feet. Whatever connection she thought she had with Rover must have been in her head. Her thoughts returned to the grassy ledge above the compound. Her skin tingled at the thought of reconnecting with a like-minded individual.

He tried to kill you and your friends, Carissa.

But the rebels' hostility towards her didn't make them feel like friends. She returned to the alleyway and stopped outside the workshop. A discussion permeated through the wooden door. Her hand paused on the iron handle. Carissa went to turn it, but stopped. She didn't feel like another lecture from the Inventor about how she should forget her past.

Easier said than done.

The connection point to her NMC irritated her skin. She relieved the itch, but only temporarily before it returned twofold. Another reason not to speak to the Inventor. He would punish her for doing the one thing she'd promised not to do.

Noise from the courtyard drew her attention away from the workshop. She followed the sound of a male soldier shouting commands inside the space. Carissa crept up to the edge of the wall that hid the courtyard. Shuffling closer to the opening, she saw Max commanding a group of males and females. In his group were Dom, Sheila and June, as well as Jerome.

Max pushed the recruits hard, shouting orders at them. Every so often, he told them to drop and give him twenty. Some jogged around the yard; others did press ups.

Max shouted more commands and most of the team ended up running laps, except for one. Jerome was doing sit-ups while Max hovered over him.

Carissa observed the newborn's attempts to fit in with the Originals he claimed to be like. It was clear Max didn't trust Jerome. So, why was Jerome trying so hard to impress him?

Her fingers grazed the smooth, metal disc on the side of her head. She wanted to be good, to serve a purpose here. She wanted to hear Quintus' voice again, if only for a second, to hear him tell her she'd surpassed her original purpose as a Copy. To remind her of her superior status to the Originals from whose DNA she had been created. The Inventor told her once that she had a conscience. She'd proved that by helping to free the teenagers from Praesidium.

But here in this camp, nobody cared about what she'd done. Nobody had thanked her. Nobody had inquired after her state of mind. Instead, they treated her like she was invisible. Carissa had not been created to be a nobody.

She looked up to the ledge where the spotters were.

13

Anya

From the entrance to the dining hall, Anya watched the training session happen without her. Her body ached from a lack of exercise over the last few months and she'd done too little here to make it count. Before Arcis, before the time that had set a major change in her life in motion, she'd been active and strong. Her mind and her body had been in tune with each other. But now, they sung off key.

As the soldiers continued to train, she longed for a better distraction from last night's disaster. Warren's attempt to talk to her was bad enough. She knew Dom had only been trying to help, but what she needed was to sort this mess out for herself. Not only Warren, but the thing between her and Alex. Did she really want him or just the protection he offered her?

He'd suggested they be friends. Would that be enough for her?

She folded her arms tight, pretending not to

notice Dom's glances as Max issued commands to the gathering of around twenty. The group included June, Sheila and Jerome, but not Jason. Her brother's absence didn't surprise her. Jason had always shunned anything to do with exercise.

Anya looked over at Carissa standing by the entrance to the courtyard, looking shy and awkward as she watched the session. What was going through her mind? The camp must be a strange place for a Copy from Praesidium. Carissa had spent her short life in the city learning about humanity. To be thrust into the reality must have come as a shock. The Copy who'd watched their time in Arcis remained Anya's best link to her missing memories. But for now, she trusted her memories would return on their own.

Her eyes blurred the session as her thoughts combed over her fragmented memories. Their slow rate of return frustrated her, but it was a start. For the first time since waking up in Alex's bedroom, she could see her future was not lost to a machine. But for all her hope, the city and its planned retribution never strayed far from her thoughts. If they sent forces to their location, who or what would they send first?

Carissa turned and left, but when Alex appeared in her place, all thoughts about her memories and the city drifted away. The beat of Anya's heart thundered in her ears like a runaway train. She caught the look Dom flashed Alex, the Breeder Anya had convinced to leave the city.

A tap on her shoulder surprised her. She spun

round to see a tentative Vanessa stood there, finger poised in the air.

'I'm sorry to startle you. I thought we could chat about what you remember of home.'

Her timing couldn't have been worse.

Vanessa was another person with a link to her —or rather her parents'—past. She had no time to reminisce about her old life, not while her head was still a mess. But she hadn't ruled out the idea that a chat with the librarian might help to knock her other memories loose.

Alex disappeared from sight. The soldiers started running laps of the courtyard.

It's now or never.

Anya mumbled to Vanessa, 'I'm sorry. I have to go.'

'Anya, we need to talk!'

She crossed the courtyard, narrowly avoiding the running group whose path she crossed, and followed him. He appeared to be headed for the perimeter fence. But he took a detour down the street behind the medical bay, where a row of roofless buildings lay open to the elements. Parked outside one property, she saw the truck they'd used to escape the city.

Alex ran his fingers over the rusted hood. He'd attempted to hotwire the car, but the battery had been dead. In the end, Rover's power supply had delivered enough juice to start it. Now, the battered truck lay idle once more, as though it had reached the end of its life.

Anya slowed her approach. Alex looked deep in thought.

'Hey,' she said, her heart pounding for the guy she'd barely known a week.

A startled Alex spun round to face her. His expression softened when he saw her. 'Oh, hey. How are you after last night?'

To any onlookers, the scene must have been confusing. She'd overheard the girls talking in the dorm about how she was a drama queen. Alex had every right to think the same. She hadn't told him the exact memory Canya had returned to her.

She shrugged. 'Fine, I suppose.'

As if he could read her thoughts, he said, 'Did it have to do with what Canya returned to you? Was Warren in your memory?'

His astuteness unsettled her; she crossed her arms in defence. She wanted to confide in Alex so bad about what Canya had shared with her—they had shared some secrets in his bedroom—but now he was like a stranger to her.

With a smile, she said, 'It was nothing. I just wanted to talk. We agreed to be friends, but there's still tension between us.'

'Yeah, I know. I've been thinking about it a lot.'

Her nerves flared at his admission. It made what she had to say next all the more difficult.

Alex concentrated on the truck once more. In

the new light, in this new setting, she didn't recognise the almost man from the city.

'It feels... weird.'

Alex looked at her. 'What does? This place?'

Anya shook her head. 'No, this, between us.'

He nodded and glanced back at the truck. 'I know.'

'So, what do we do about it?'

His eyes on her, Alex shrugged. 'What do you want to do?'

'Can we talk a little?'

He dragged his top lip through his teeth. 'Okay. What do you want to talk about?'

'We almost had sex in the city.'

He leaned against the truck and folded his arms, looking uncomfortable. 'I remember.'

'But now, it's like all of those feelings are gone.'

'Yeah.'

She uncrossed her arms and picked at her fingers. 'Were our feelings for each other just to do with the chemicals?'

Alex dipped his chin and sighed. 'I don't know. I mean, I like you.' He lifted his gaze to her. 'I liked talking to you in my room, but after we left, a switch sort of flipped in my brain.'

Anya knew what he meant. But she still had feelings for Alex, which indicated some of what she'd felt had been real. The fade just hadn't happened quite as fast for her.

'Gee, thanks.'

She rolled her eyes to break the tension, but Alex straightened up in alarm. He dropped his arms to his sides.

'You know what I mean.'

Anya smiled at him. 'I do. I'm only teasing.' She joined him at the truck and leaned against it. 'I get what you're saying, but the feelings haven't faded as fast for me.'

'So what now?' he said. 'Do we carry on as before? I meant it when I said I'd like to be friends.'

She smiled at the ground. 'I'd like that.'

Alex elbowed her lightly. 'Friends it is.'

Her smiled dropped away. A twinge of jealousy took hold as she pondered her next question.

She pinned him with her gaze, needing to see his reaction. 'So, are you and June an item?'

'What?' Alex blushed and scuffed the ground with his foot. 'No. We're just friends. I mean, I like her, but I haven't known her that long.'

His reaction told her everything. Something special was happening between the pair.

'If there's something there, you should go for it.'

Alex shifted his position. 'Problem is, I don't know what real feels like.'

He'd been a prisoner in the city, a slave to a drug called Rapture that heightened his most basic desires. But getting to know a person required digging deeper than the physical.

'If it helps, we already know what real doesn't feel like: you and me. You've got to trust your gut.'

'I'm sorry for leading you on.' Alex sighed. 'You helped me in the city. I'm grateful to you for getting me out of there.'

Anya waved away the thanks; right now, it sounded too much like a consolation prize. 'All I want to do is retrieve my missing memories.'

He turned to face her, his expression softer. 'Of course. Are they coming back?'

'A little. Too slow for my liking.'

'Give them time.'

She nodded, but she wanted them back now, not later. Her sporting endeavours had required discipline and taught her patience. But this half life, this excessive fear she felt towards her attacker, put her in a vulnerable position. Her memories were vague at best and her connection with Alex was gone.

'You should watch the training session again,' said Anya, keen to shift away from this topic. 'I think it will make your transition here go more smoothly if you show an active interest in the group events. The more you isolate yourself, the more Max and the others will continue to treat you differently.'

'They already treat me differently, but okay.' Alex gave the hood of the car one final pat. 'You coming?'

'In a little while.'

Alex stayed by the truck.

She forced a smile and pushed him on. 'Go.'

He nodded and left. Anya watched the only friend she remembered go. While her attraction to him was false, the hole in her heart his departure caused was not.

14

Dom

Max's commands blurred into nonsense the second Anya crossed the courtyard to follow Alex. Dom's mind raced with the possibilities of what that might mean. His left arm, the one with Praesidium's tech in it, pinched. So much, it almost stopped him mid run. But Max's voice, sharp and gruff, dragged his focus back to the present. He shook off the distraction.

Sheila, who ran beside him, puffed, 'I don't know why I'm doing this. I hate exercise.'

He caught enough of her complaint to reply. 'Max's orders. Unless you're coming up with creative ways to take down the Collective, you're needed here.'

Sheila breathed hard. 'So why doesn't Alex or Anya have to do this?'

Why indeed. Maybe he had different plans for them.

Them.

The word scrambled his thoughts again. From the way Anya chased after Alex, it was clear something had happened between them in the city. Dom had been too out of it to notice. Alex hadn't been selected to be a Breeder for nothing.

'Dom, pick up the pace!' shouted Max.

Several people passed him and Sheila. Sheila wasn't complaining about the slower pace. In fact, they'd almost come to a stop.

'Screw this,' said Dom, breaking off from the run. 'I need to speak to her, to apologise about last night.'

He abandoned his training, despite Max's irritated yells to come back. Sheila shouted at him to stop. Ignoring them both, he strode out of the courtyard. He got as far as the trucks before Sheila caught up with him.

'Dom, stop. You already apologised.'

She grabbed his left shoulder, an action that sent a ripple of pain through his left arm. He used his annoyance to hide his discomfort from her.

'I just need to speak to her.'

'Leave her alone,' she warned. 'She doesn't remember you. Whatever she has with Alex, they need to figure it out together.'

He shucked her off and glared at her. 'I don't know what else to do, Sheila.' He pulled at clumps of his hair. The length was starting to annoy him now. 'I remember everything. It's like... what happened never did.'

Sheila pushed him back against the truck. As tall as him, she looked into his eyes and said in a measured tone, 'Listen to me. My Copy gave me back my memories and the first person I remembered was Yasmin. It hurt when she didn't remember me. Then I saw one of the medic guards shoot her as though her life meant nothing.' Her voice wobbled. 'I watched a woman with whom I'd shared a connection die before me. But what hurt worse was she died not knowing she had a friend beside her.'

Dom relaxed his tense posture. With all the drama, he'd forgotten that Sheila had been in the same boat. 'I'm sorry. I'm being a dick.'

'At least Anya's still here.'

That was something, but he wondered if it might be better if she wasn't.

He sighed, but the tension kept his posture rigid. 'I'm trying to concentrate on what matters—protecting this compound—but with things weird between me and Anya, and the thing with Warren, I just don't care.'

Sheila punched him in the arm. His left arm. He clenched his teeth as a ripple of pain tore through it, right up to the shoulder.

She frowned. 'I didn't hit you that hard, you baby. Look, Warren will get what's coming to him. Trust me on that. You need to stop feeling sorry for yourself. Our lives are in danger. We were lucky to escape the city. You and I need to move on from our pasts. Me from Yasmin and you from Anya.' She gripped the sides of his arms, unaware of his recent surgery there. 'Whatever happens, you always have me.'

More pain blossomed in his arm. He eased his limbs out of her iron grip and stared at the girl who'd had his back for years, whom he'd die to protect. 'Thanks, Sheila. I needed that kick up the butt.'

He ruffled his long, curly mop using the fingers of his good hand.

She nodded at him. 'Maybe it's time you get that cut. Charlie should be free while the training is going on.'

Dom agreed, not ready to return to the yard. 'Tell Max I'll be back later.'

He left her alone by the truck and walked down the street leading to the back perimeter fence. Passing by the first street, he glanced down it to see their escape car. The sight of Anya leaning against it halted his next step. Her eyes were downcast as though she were deep in thought. Dom lingered by the corner, his skin pricking with a hot desire to speak to her. But instead of giving in to his impulses, he walked on. As though on autopilot, he made it to the street with the barber shop and entered the building. Charlie was inside sweeping the floor.

Dom hesitated by the door, to temper his anger and claw back control. Charlie saw more than people wanted to share; Dom wasn't ready for his failures to be brought into light. The last time Charlie had cut his hair, it had been to snip off his dreadlocks. He'd left the cottage in Essention with a short, tight haircut and a swell of anger. His chat with Charlie had reignited old feelings about his dead father.

'Dom,' said a smiling Charlie. He pointed to the only chair in the place.

Dom sat in the chair, which had pieces of tape holding the torn, cream leather in place, and stared at the cracked mirror before him.

'Seven years of bad luck,' he muttered.

Charlie chuckled and shook his head. 'To the person who cracked it before me, perhaps. But it sometimes feels like we've all broken mirrors or walked under ladders, or had black cats cross our paths. Like our entire lives are a walking nightmare.'

Dom sighed. His summation of their lives hit too close to the bone. 'Do you think we'll ever get out of this mess? Find the place called the Beyond?'

Last night over dinner, Max had told him the soldiers had found no evidence of a shimmering border, as the Macklins had described to Vanessa.

He couldn't remember a time when the machines hadn't controlled the towns. If there was a place that existed beyond their control, they had to find it.

Charlie worked his fingers through Dom's hair, damp from sweat. If it grossed him out, he didn't show it. He picked up a spray bottle and doused his hair in water.

'I don't know, son, but my Max is good at what he does. And you kids are good at what you do.'

Charlie combed Dom's hair until the wet curls had flattened. Then he sectioned the hair into four parts, front, back and two sides, and deftly worked the scissors through Dom's hair.

While he worked, he chatted. 'I haven't really spoken to you since you arrived here. How are your wounds?'

Dom idly touched his belly. 'Fine. I barely notice them. I still have the scars, you know.'

The left arm that still blazed hot from Sheila's earlier punch was a different matter.

'The scars should serve as a reminder of how special you are.'

Special? Dom made a face in the mirror. 'I don't want Praesidium's tech inside me.'

He rubbed his left arm.

Charlie continued to cut. 'That tech has been a part of you for so long. To remove it would be to remove a part of you.'

Dom had never told Charlie how he'd come by the tech. 'My father sold my seven-year-old self to Praesidium as a test subject, so the city could stick their tech in me.'

Charlie paused with the scissors in Dom's hair. 'Did your mother know?'

'No. She thought I was sick and the surgeries were my only hope. But my father had been making me sick at the city's request so nobody would question the surgeries.'

Charlie resumed cutting. The snipping sounds

124

got louder. 'Then it's best your father is dead, because I would have killed him for putting you through that. You are like a grandson to me. Max thinks of you and Sheila as his family too.'

A lump rose in Dom's throat. Charlie's words about family reminded Dom of what was important. And it wasn't the drama surrounding his on-off relationship with Anya.

Charlie continued to cut his hair. 'Anya was in here yesterday. We had a nice chat.'

So much for Dom forgetting about her. 'That's... nice.'

'You two don't seem to be talking much.'

He shrugged. 'It's what she wants. She doesn't remember me.'

'Hmm.'

Charlie worked the scissors at an angle.

'What?'

Charlie put a hold on the cut. 'Oh, it's just something she said to me.'

Dom's heart pounded. 'What did she say?'

The old man rested his hands on Dom's shoulders. 'Remember when I cut your dreadlocks off?'

'I do.'

How could he forget?

'Well, she asked me about it, said she remembered someone getting their dreadlocks cut off.'

Dom's hope sank to the pit of his stomach.

'You probably mentioned it to her, that's all.'

Charlie squeezed his shoulders. With a glint in his eye, he said, 'That's just the thing. She brought it up, not me.'

He resumed cutting. Dom's heart lightened a little. Anya was remembering on her own.

Twenty minutes later, after Charlie finished off the back and sides with a hand razor, Dom stared at his new hairstyle. Gone was the curly mop on his head, replaced by a short back and sides and a stylish length of curl on the top.

Dom admired his new cut. 'You should do this for a living.'

Charlie barked a laugh. 'You mean, I should charge you kids for my services.' He waved away the idea. 'I get payment enough from your company. Now, out of my chair. Someone's waiting outside.'

Dom looked out the window to see one of the soldiers leaning against the wall opposite the barber shop. He pushed off and walked forward as soon as Dom headed for the door.

'Thanks, Charlie.'

'Anytime.'

Dom left Charlie with a lighter head and more perspective. Anya would remember. She could remember. He just needed to give her time.

On his way back to training, a deep scream silenced his thoughts and made his blood run cold. It came from the courtyard.

15

Carissa

Carissa sat on the ledge overlooking the camp. Nobody had witnessed her return to this place. The second she got high enough, the chatter from the radios reached her.

Her fingers curled into the long grass growing out of the mountain ledge. The chatter increased as the relief team, coming from Halforth, got in touch to say they were almost there. She sucked in a breath to calm the butterflies in her stomach, waiting for her elevation to bring another voice to her.

She didn't have to wait long. The disc for her NMC irritated her skin and a familiar buzz indicating her connection invaded her mind.

'173-C? I can feel you again.' *Quintus*. 'Why did you break our earlier connection?'

His voice had a flat tone to it—a common trait among the Collective ten. But their spokesperson's voice rose every now and again, hinting at emotion.

'I... I'm not supposed to talk to you.'

Her disc continued to bother her. She imagined her NMC attempting to repair itself further.

'Why, 173-C? What harm can talking do?' Quintus paused. 'I meant it before when I said the Collective is not angry with you. But you must tell the Ten where you are.'

Her hands shook at her betrayal of the Inventor. She'd promised to stay away from her old life. How could she when the only person who cared about her was back in the city?

'I can't, Quintus. I don't know where I am.'

It was partly true. Apart from being stuck in a camp with no discernible features, she could be in any of the ranges. But she had heard Anya reveal the name of this one: Ferrous Mountain.

'Try to remember, 173-C,' urged Quintus. 'The Collective is worried about you, and about the others who were stolen from the city. We just want to bring our family home.'

Quintus was more sentimental than she'd ever heard him sound. Except for that one time before their escape, when he'd tried to talk her out of helping the others. What harm could it do to tell him?

'I don't know, Quintus.'

She trusted her instinct. Her betrayal would surely send the Inventor, the Breeder or Rover back to the city. What would the Ten do to her when she returned? She'd betrayed them in the worst way. Punishment would be on their machine minds.

'173-C, think. The Collective cannot help you if you do not tell me.'

She had thought about it, about returning to the city, but something stopped her.

'If I tell you, what will happen to the others?'

'The Originals that escaped with you will be punished. The Collective has no interest in anyone else.'

That answer didn't satisfy Carissa. 'What will you do to them exactly?'

Quintus paused. 'They will return to the city and work there until the Collective has no further use for them.'

She knew what happened to Originals who had outlived their usefulness to the Collective.

If Carissa was to go back, she wouldn't want to return without the Inventor. Yet, the thought of him being locked up in the workshop again left her feeling cold. She imagined the Inventor's voice in her head: *Why would we make the effort to leave, only to return to that prison?*

She gripped the grass tighter. 'I can't, Quintus. I'm sorry.'

Carissa slid down from the edge to the crumbling, stone steps and navigated them to the bottom.

Quintus shouted in her head, 'We have not finished our discussion, 173-C. You do not have permis—'

His voice cut off when she dropped low enough

for the signal to break. She huffed with relief, but what Quintus had said to her lingered in her mind.

A scream in the distance jolted her out of her thoughts as her foot landed on the valley floor. She squeezed through the perimeter fence and back to a deserted camp. It had been a female scream and it had sounded like it had come from the courtyard area. Carissa returned there to see a crowd had gathered by the stone wall entrance. Whatever was happening had everyone murmuring.

She squeezed through the onlookers to see Alex, Anya, Dom and Vanessa crowded around a distressed June. She was clutching at her stomach.

'Are you okay, June?' asked Vanessa.

June straightened up slowly. 'I think so. It's a stomach cramp, that's all. I must have trained too fast after eating this morning.'

'Even so, I think you should lie down.' Vanessa turned to Max. 'I'm taking her to the medical bay.'

'Good idea,' said a worried looking Max.

June grumbled when Alex took her other arm and helped her to walk.

'I'm fine,' she said with a flush of embarrassment. 'Everyone's fussing for no reason.'

'The camp medics will be the judge of that,' said Alex.

Carissa followed the pair helping June to the grey-bricked building. Her fading connection with Quintus drew her attention back to the camp and her Original's sister.

Vanessa and Alex brought her inside. Carissa kept close on their heels. As the pair eased her onto a bed under the watchful eye of a military medic, Carissa approached the girl who she hadn't spoken to properly since escaping the city. She'd been so excited to meet June, but their connection hadn't endured past that initial meeting. Carissa was, after all, only a Copy of June's sister.

'Are you okay, June?'

She approached her on the bed.

June turned and screamed into Alex's T-shirt as another stomach spasm hit her.

She pulled in air through gritted teeth and flashed Carissa a guarded gaze. 'It's just a stomach ache. I'll be fine.'

One of the medics buzzed around her, connecting dots to her skin attached to a monitoring machine. The machines here were more basic than the ones in Praesidium.

Carissa lingered by the bed. Yet the longer she stood there, the more uncomfortable June appeared to be with her presence.

June looked at Alex and whispered, 'Make her leave, please.'

Alex put his hands on Carissa's shoulders, earning him a glare.

'What are you doing, Breeder?' Alex flinched when she used his formal title. She lifted her chin up in defiance. 'I wish to stay.'

An angry Alex steered her to the door, but

Carissa pushed back. 'Get your hands off me.'

Who did this Breeder think he was?

'Look, Carissa. She doesn't want to see you. Respect her privacy. And don't call me by a name the Collective gave me.'

Her anger made her blood pump faster. 'If the name fits... You cannot stop me from seeing her. I'm her sister.'

Alex's eyes flashed with hatred. He lowered his voice. 'You are not her sister. Her sister died, thanks to you. That's right, I overheard one of the Copies in the medical facility talking about it.'

Carissa stared up at him in shock. What had happened to her Original in the days after Carissa became a Copy had not been her fault. Every human emotion had been stripped from her. She'd only been following the Collective's directive: to protect the city. Plus, her actions *had* saved the Inventor from the same fate as the others.

She pushed past Alex and made it back to June, who was doubled over on the bed in pain. One of the medics had pulled her top up to reveal her stomach. She was trying to examine it with an ultra sound wand, but the monitoring machine only beeped and flashed *error* in red.

June turned her sweaty, pasty face in her direction. 'Get her out... I don't want her here. She's a reminder of that place.'

Alex grabbed Carissa's shoulder and pulled her back. 'You heard her.'

A flare of anger shook her to the core. 'You are not my senior, Breeder.'

'Maybe not in the city,' said Alex, steering her to the door and outside, 'but in this camp, I'm older than you.'

Carissa had no comeback. She was only six months in existence. Even with Alex's accelerated growth, he was still older than her by fourteen months.

She shrugged Alex's hands off her and stumbled outside into the dazzling sun. Onlookers had gathered outside. They gave her a wide berth when she staggered towards them. Why had she left the city for this? Quintus wanted her back. Her former mentor considered her to be a valuable commodity. Out here, she was an outcast who got in everyone's way.

Maybe she should tell him the location of the camp.

Carissa ran past the onlookers and returned to the only place where she felt safe and wanted. She sat on the floor of the storage shed next to Rover. The mechanical whine of his breathing soothed her. She pressed her ear up to his chest and listened.

'There you are, miss.'

She startled, not having heard the Inventor come in.

'I've been looking for you. I heard June fell ill. Is she okay?'

She nodded. The Inventor's gaze raked over her. 'When did you and Rover become friends?'

He nodded to the wolf, who had draped a paw across her leg. In her shock, she hadn't even noticed the extra weight.

'I saw him yesterday. He was lonely.'

Rover whined as if to agree with her.

'What were you doing just now? I saw you come though the gap in the fence for the sectioned off area of the town. What did you need in there?'

Carissa averted her gaze. 'I was just exploring.' She looked up at him. 'Am I in trouble?'

'Depends on what you were doing. You weren't attempting to contact the Collective, were you? We talked about it. It's very dangerous. We need to stay off the city's radar.'

The Inventor didn't placate her in the camp like he would have in the city. That irritated her more than she let on.

With a violent shake of her head, she said, 'I wasn't, I swear.' She changed the subject. 'Why is Rover locked up?'

The Inventor moved nearer, prompting the wolf to sit up. Rover kept his head low in the presence of his master. The old man bent down and patted the creature's head. He responded by licking his outstretched hand.

'Max doesn't trust him,' he said with a sigh. 'He makes him nervous.'

Carissa patted the passive wolf's head. 'I used to be frightened of the Guardians. But that was because the Collective commanded them. Rover is nicer than the ones that patrolled the border in Praesidium.'

'That's because he's free, miss.' The Inventor straightened up. 'Like you are now.'

But Carissa struggled with the price that freedom attracted.

'He's not free now. He's chained up and unhappy.'

She stroked the wolf's paw.

The Inventor cupped his chin in thought. 'You're absolutely right.'

He disappeared from the room and Carissa thought he'd gone for good. But then he returned with a chisel and hammer.

'Rover should be free. This damn dog helped us to escape.'

He wedged the chisel into the collar around the wolf's neck.

Carissa stood up, alarmed by his rebellious behaviour. 'But what will Max say?'

He hit the hammer once. 'Let me worry about Max.' Rover scrambled to his feet and shuffled back from the Inventor's efforts to free him. 'Now help me to steady him.'

Carissa used her weight to steady the wolf's large body when he tried to pull away from the Inventor again. He weighed a ton; Carissa's small frame was no match. But she was also a Copy and Copies had strength. She applied what she had to stop the wolf from pulling too far.

The Inventor hit the top of the hammer again: once, twice, three times. On the fourth crack, the collar split apart and clattered to the stone floor.

The second the Inventor stepped away, Rover relaxed his body. Carissa stopped pushing against him.

He sniffed the floor, Carissa's clothes and the Inventor's hammer and chisel, which he still held.

'Who is your master?' said the Inventor.

Rover looked from him to Carissa. He sat in the middle between them, but his eyes settled on Carissa.

'Well, well. Looks like Rover has taken a shine to you.'

Carissa's heart swelled with love. Maybe the beast would protect her when Quintus doled out his punishment for her defiance. Or from the Inventor when he found out what she'd just done. Once was by accident. But her recent contact had been deliberate.

The Inventor walked to the door. 'Well, I've got work to do.' He paused and turned. 'You didn't answer me earlier. What were you doing past the perimeter fence?'

Carissa drew in a discreet breath. The wolf nudged her hand, as if to encourage her. 'I was just curious. I wanted to see what was back there.'

'Nothing but abandoned buildings now. You won't get far with the second anti-magnetic field anyway. The town used to be whole. But this place is too big for the spotters to watch over.' The Inventor opened the door and left, calling over his shoulder,

'Stay in the camp from now on.'

Carissa nodded, even though he could no longer see her. She turned to Rover. 'Our secret. Okay, boy?'

The wolf whined and nuzzled her hand.

16

Anya

Word spread fast around the camp that June had fallen ill. Anya put aside losing Alex as more than a friend and went to visit her. She entered the medical bay that she'd visited Dom in a couple of days ago. June was sitting upright on a bed near the door. She looked pale, but was smiling and chatting with Alex, who was keeping her company.

Feeling like she was intruding on a private moment, Anya slowed her walk until Alex saw her. He nodded to her, then whispered something to June. June looked over as Alex got to his feet and headed Anya's way.

'Hey,' he said, offering her a smile as he passed her.

She smiled back, even though her heart wasn't in it. 'Hey.'

Anya approached June, who looked paler than she'd ever seen her. Her skin glistened with sweat.

138

She flashed a nervous smile at Anya and rolled her eyes. 'Everyone is fussing over me. It's getting old.'

Anya sat down beside her. 'How do you feel?'

'Okay. The medic isn't sure what's wrong—the ultrasound machine is on the blink—but the pain seems to have settled now.'

June placed her hands outside the covers, one over the other. Anya caught the tension and worry in her eyes.

'So,' said Anya, sensing the uneasiness between them. 'You and Alex seem to have hit it off.'

June bit her lip. 'He's been a friend since we got out.'

'Is that all?' said Anya.

June shrugged. 'I don't know. I know you two were close in the city. He was your Breeder and I don't want to step on any toes.'

'What did Alex say?'

'That you two were just friends.'

Anya smarted at hearing it, even though it was true. 'We felt things for each other in the city.'

June nodded and dropped her gaze to her lap. 'He mentioned it. I'm sorry. I won't talk to him again.'

'No,' said Anya with a shake of her head. 'It was because of the Rapture they gave us. I wanted him so bad, and he me.' A blush stained June's pale and pasty face. 'But when we got out and the Rapture left our system, we sort of drifted apart.'

June looked up at her. 'So you don't feel anything for him now?'

Anya shrugged. 'I have residual feelings, sure.'

'Is that why you two are being weird with each other?'

'I think I miss the friendship we used to have.' She smiled as she remembered. 'We weren't together long, but it was intense and we got to know each other on a personal level. Seeing him with you, well, I'm like the friend who got shoved aside.'

'I didn't want that to happen, believe me,' said June, shifting in the bed so she was sitting straighter. 'It took me by surprise, if I'm being honest.'

Anya hadn't come to make June feel guilty about it. 'I wanted to check on you and to tell you I don't want to get in your way.'

'Thank you.' June touched her hand. 'Hey, I wanted to ask, what do you remember from Arcis? What memory did your Copy return to you?'

Anya shuddered. 'The one of Warren and what he did to me in the bathroom.'

'Was I there? I don't remember anything.'

Only Sheila had been lucky to receive all her memories back from her Copy.

While painful to relieve the event, she also recalled that June had been a comfort to her that night. Maybe to unlock the good stuff, she had to face up to the bad. She told June about the fourth floor in Arcis, a place where the girls and boys were separated. The girls earned points if they teamed up with the boys for certain tasks.

'One task in particular guaranteed rotation. Warren attacked me in the bathroom, tried to force himself on me.'

June's eyes widened. 'That shit! What happened then?'

Anya smiled as she remembered hitting him. 'I punched him in the jaw. When he left, you and Yasmin showed up. You had been paired up with him. To help Dom you were screwing up his progress.'

'Dom mentioned that, but not details.' She rolled her eyes a second time. 'Apparently, you and I are like delicate china. Everyone's tiptoeing around the subject of Arcis, afraid that if they tell us stuff we'll shatter into pieces.' Curiosity flashed in her eyes. 'Are you remembering anything on your own?'

Anya nodded. 'I remember someone with dreadlocks. Jerome confirmed it was Dom.'

'Yeah, I remember those dreadlocks too, from before Arcis.' June grinned at something. 'Sheila told me he wouldn't stop touching his hair after. He said it felt like they were still there.'

Anya smiled too, but it dropped away when June winced suddenly. 'Are you okay?'

She reached out for her.

'Yeah.' June settled, releasing a puff of air. 'They're phantom pains. They come and go, like spasms. But the medic can't find anything physically wrong with me.'

It relieved Anya to hear that. She patted June's hand. 'I'm glad you're okay and that we talked.'

'Me too. I don't have many friends, but Sheila said you were one.' Her eyes twinkled with an admiration that Anya didn't deserve. 'I can see that now.'

Anya left June to rest some more. Except for the odd twinge, she was no longer in pain, but June didn't look like herself. She would ask Alex to keep an eye on her. Although, she was sure he already was.

Outside, her ex-Breeder waited, chewing on his thumb and leaning against the wall. When she appeared, he straightened up, his damp thumb hovering next to his mouth.

'Is everything okay?'

Anya nodded. 'June's a great girl. I'm glad you two have found each other.'

Alex's eyes lit up; she saw the boy who'd once given her that same look. But when she pictured getting close to Alex, the same raw desire she'd felt while on Rapture no longer consumed her.

'What are you going to do now?' said Alex.

Anya knew Vanessa would try to corner her for the chat she'd been avoiding. Her aching muscles had other ideas. 'I think I need to get back into a routine. Get running again.'

Alex nodded and smiled. 'Sounds like a plan.'

He went back inside the medical bay, leaving Anya alone.

She returned to the female dorm and headed to

a closet at the back of the room. It was filled with an assortment of clothes that looked to be donations from other towns. Or maybe they'd been here when the rebels took the town over.

Anya rummaged through the assortment of clothes and shoes. She picked out a pair of trainers that fit her feet. She accompanied the look with a fitted, red T-shirt over her green combats. The ensemble gave her a boost of confidence to try exercise again. Avoiding the courtyard filled with soldiers she no longer had permission to train with, Anya exited through the main door.

The sectioned-off compound was small, but she guessed its circumference ran about a mile in length. She started with a light jog to warm up her muscles. Her joints creaked and her ankles felt like they might snap in half. It shocked her how long she'd been sedentary. It would take time to regain her lost fitness, but routine would help her to claw back control of her disjointed life.

After completing a circuit, everything felt looser. Her lungs burned. It was a good ache, as if her body were saying hello. Anya picked up the pace, passing by the open courtyard where she'd started, past the alleyway to the workshop, where she caught a fleeting glimpse of Rover with Carissa, and along the back wall perimeter fence.

By the end of her run, the act of breathing hurt. At least she hadn't seen Warren on her travels. She hit the street for another lap, but halfway around, she stopped as the exertion became too much. To her disappointment, the run hadn't revived her. Instead, it left her craving a discipline that could only come from organised group training.

Shouts and commands punctured the air inside the exclusive yard. She stood at the entrance and watched, despite the pain of her forced isolation stabbing her heart. Her brother waited next to Dom, who sported a brand new haircut. Soldiers were setting up targets on the back wall. It looked like they were about to do target practice—something she still remembered how to do, and well. But standing not far from her brother were Warren and Jerome. Her knees almost buckled. She suddenly felt grateful that Max had ordered her out of this space.

Imogen was putting Sheila through her paces. The goddess looked well able to handle it, but she, too, had lost fitness. With a threat from Praesidium sure to be arriving soon, it would be pointless trying to get the soldiers fit. Learning how to shoot would be everyone's best defence.

Anya watched the twenty or so soldiers chat with each other. She was so focused on the scene that she didn't notice Vanessa join her.

'You used to be pretty good at that,' she said.

Anya kept her eyes on the gathered group. 'Did my parents tell you that?'

Vanessa chuckled. 'You were all they talked about.'

Anya frowned at this woman with a link to her

past. 'How did you meet them?'

Vanessa met her gaze. 'We ran a rebel faction out of Halforth. Your mother and father helped to start the rebellion.'

Anya didn't understand. 'My mother never once spoke of the rebels.'

'It was a secret organisation. We didn't talk about it much. And even less when we got separated.'

But that was Anya's point. 'Neither did they, Vanessa. But you seem to think I have information to the contrary.'

Vanessa half smiled. 'You and Jason are the only remaining link to that past. Not many of the Macklins' original faction remain. In fact, Max, Charlie and I are the only ones left. You were able to tell us about this place, which confirms you overheard some things. This mountain range led us to the presumed location of the Beyond.'

'But you said you didn't find it.'

The older woman looked wistful. 'There's nothing out there except more land. What your parents claim to have seen could have been anything: a flicker of light creating a mirage in this endless, dry landscape.' She gripped Anya's shoulder. 'But we're certain others have crossed, because they never made it to the city and they're not in the rebel camps. Your parents must have located the Beyond and were able to pass the information along.'

'Or someone found it by accident.' Anya faced her fully. Vanessa released her shoulder. 'Maybe my parents told someone else. It seems odd to keep important information like that a secret.'

'It's another angle Max and I are considering, that someone preparing to cross might have hidden the coordinates somewhere safe. Your parents weren't big on trust, and for good reason. Not many knew the Beyond even existed. That was to keep others from discussing it openly.'

It was possible her parents *had* discussed this issue, but with her amnesia Anya's mind was a blank. All she remembered were stupid details like what colour their sofa was at home, what time they ate dinner at, or that Jason's electronic projects smelled like rust.

Vanessa watched her eagerly. The hope in her eyes faded when Anya shrugged. 'I'm sorry. I don't remember anything like that.'

But the older woman wasn't giving up. 'I need you to think back to someone your parents might have mentioned. A trusted friend or a colleague, perhaps? Sorry to put this on you, but you kids are our only tangible link to your parents.'

Anya looked ahead of her. She stared at her brother's back. 'What did Jason say?'

'Jason doesn't remember anything.'

She didn't see why it would be any different for her. 'I'd like to help, but I barely remember Arcis.'

'Don't give up, Anya. The time I'm asking you to remember was before Arcis. You still have those memories.' Vanessa sighed. 'We don't have much time. I'd like to work with you to see if we can jog your memory. We need to find the Beyond. We've already wasted too much time looking in the wrong place.'

Anya wanted to find this place as much as anyone. She pinned Vanessa with her gaze. 'You spent time with my Copy. What did *she* tell you?'

Vanessa pursed her lips and looked away. 'Canya was less than... cooperative.' She looked back. 'She was obsessed with Dom.'

Canya. Anya shivered at the memory of her Copy. She had looked exactly like her and had taken a name similar to hers.

She folded her arms and stared down at her boots. 'I didn't like her.'

'Why would you? She had a chance to give you back your memories. Instead she gave you one— something traumatic judging from your reaction at the time.'

Anya looked up at Vanessa. 'Did you like her?'

'I try to keep an open mind about people, but... no.' She added, 'But I like you, so don't compare yourself to her. You two were nothing alike.'

It made Anya happy to hear that. Except for the pressure to remember, Vanessa was kind. She had been an ally to her parents.

'She was the worst of me.'

'But not the complete package. Don't forget that. Can we talk later when you've had some time to think? I'd like to see what you remember.'

Anya nodded and gave her a weak smile.

Vanessa patted her on the shoulder. She entered the courtyard and walked over to Max, who was observing the training from one side of the yard. As Anya watched her whisper something to the colonel, she wondered what secrets her parents had held.

17

Dom

Dom's new haircut had attracted wolf whistles from some of the soldiers when he'd first arrived to find June doubled over in pain.

Even Max had taken a second look. 'My father is a master at cutting hair.'

And at giving advice.

With June out of danger, he enjoyed his new cut. It lightened both his head and thoughts.

Dom stood alongside others of similar fighting age to him. The group included Jason and Thomas, both of whom had been put on workshop duty. But if the machines steamrolled over everyone to get inside the compound, that skill wouldn't count for much.

Max and Vanessa stood together in front of the main group. Vanessa pulled a soft hat out of her pocket.

Max said, 'We need to split the teams up. Some of you will defend this compound. Others will go on the offensive against the machines to stop them from reaching the compound.' He glanced at his second and first in command. 'Julius will take leadership on attack and Imogen will take defence. We need everyone helping out, so that means the newbies will also need training.'

He gave Vanessa a quick nod. She pulled a piece of paper out of the hat and handed it to him.

'Vanessa and I came up with a fair system to decide who would be fighting out there or in here.' He read the piece of paper and said, 'Jerome, you're on defence.'

Dom frowned as Max called out the rest of the names. He was also on Julius' team, but why wasn't he commanding his own? Jason and Warren were with him while Thomas and Sheila joined Jerome on Imogen's team. Jason chewed on his thumb, not looking too happy about his placing.

'Okay, everyone will start off with a warm-up with their team leaders,' said Max.

Imogen and Julius stood to the front of the two groups. One smiled; the other glared. Imogen was tall like Sheila, with short, brown hair and a friendly face that would work well to calm the newbies in her group. But Julius, a blond-haired man, had a harder edge to his look and a gruffness about him. Dom hadn't met him before this camp, but something about Max's second bothered him.

Maybe he was just jealous of the position he commanded. Once, it might have been Dom stood in

Julius' place, but his recent illness and three months trapped in Arcis had knocked him off his leadership perch.

As though Max sensed his surprise, his colonel walked over to him. 'Sorry, Dom, but you're rusty. Let Julius run the group for this mission. Then, when we get out of here, I'll see about putting you back on leadership duty.'

No matter how disappointed Dom felt about it, he didn't disagree with Max. 'It was the right call. I'm still recovering and I haven't trained properly in months.'

'How do you feel?'

A twinge in Dom's left arm started, and he lied, 'I feel good. Strong, even.' He looked around the group to note the absence of two faces. 'Why aren't Anya and Alex here?'

Max folded his thick, battle-scarred arms. 'I'm not sure what to make of Alex yet, and I need Anya with Vanessa.'

Dom frowned. 'I thought Vanessa already knew where the Beyond was?'

'It's not out there. Anya is now the only one with useable knowledge of what her parents discussed. She's struggling to remember, but our goal to leave this region remains our priority after we rescue as many people as we can from the city.'

Dom had heard plenty of stories about the Beyond, but that was all it was: stories. No proof existed that the place did.

Julius called Dom over and he joined the attack group. It included soldiers of various fitness, plus Jason and Warren. Warren glared at him. Dom kept his distance from the boy with the strawberry blond hair.

They began their training with a jog around the courtyard. Despite Dom's lack of fitness, the run came easy to him as his legs rediscovered their rhythm. But both Warren and Jason struggled with the task. And this was just the warm-up. Julius switched orders to press-ups, followed by a round of sit-ups. Both newbies barely managed either task, much to Julius' irritation. By the end of the warm-up session, both Warren and Jason were panting heavily. In Imogen's group, Jerome seemed better able to cope with the pressure. A red-faced Thomas was flat on his back and breathing hard.

Next came the attack training. At the back of the courtyard, paper targets had been set up and, in teams of two, one from each team, each pair took turns to fire weapons at them. Julius and Imogen checked the results after each round and sorted the shooters into a new group.

Dom watched Warren step up next. He shot against a seasoned soldier. His technique was good, but he lacked experience. Dom wondered where he'd learned to shoot a gun. In Arcis, they'd only used the Electro Guns on the fifth floor to shoot holographic discs. And even then, Dom hadn't seen Warren shoot anything.

Jason stepped up next. His opponent? Another seasoned soldier, with at least a year of training that Dom knew of, under his belt. Dom saw a new pattern emerge. Jason steadied his firing hand with his second one. He must have had some training because his stance was confident. He fired and did a decent job of hitting the overall target, but he was no match for his opponent. Julius stuck him in a new group with just four: Warren, Jason, Thomas and Jerome. All the newbies.

Imogen whispered something to Julius.

He called Dom over. 'We can't effectively train everyone if we have to slow down for the inexperienced.' He pointed at the four. 'Take them away and show them how to shoot straight.'

That wasn't what Max had said.

He looked around for the colonel but he was gone. 'Max put you in charge of attack, Julius. That means all of them, not just the ones who look good.'

Julius strode up to him. A strange glint flashed in his eye, and his lips were drawn thin and white. But his hostile expression didn't match his words.

In a low voice, he said, 'Come on, Dom. The other soldiers are complaining about the lack of competition. We need to get the newbies up to speed and I can't do it if they're in the experienced group.'

Julius had a point.

With a nod, Dom conceded. 'Okay, but you owe me one.'

Julius slapped him on the back, a little too hard,

and handed him a piece of chalk. 'If we survive this, I'll owe you two.'

Dom picked up a weapon—a plain revolver—and motioned for his new group of four to follow him.

'Where are we going?' said Jason. 'I thought we were training with the others.'

'Change of plan. I'll be training you now. We'll practise near the back perimeter fence.'

He led the way to the corrugated fence that divided the compound from the rest of the town. On the side of the abandoned building next to the fence, Dom drew an X in chalk.

He stepped back and drew a line on the dusty ground about a metre away from the X. He waved the others behind the line, took aim and fired once. His shot grazed the edge of the centre of the X. He was out of practice.

'We're using bullets because they're useless in the fight against the machines. Jason, Thomas, Max told me it was your inventions and work that got him and the others inside Arcis. Thank you for your help.'

Jason nodded, while Thomas shrugged and blushed.

'You two are familiar with the types of guns that take down the machines, but the others are not. Please explain them now.'

Dom waited while Jason and Thomas took turns to explain the Atomiser, capable of weakening atoms, and the Disruptor gun, capable of disrupting the flying path of the scouts long enough for the same gun to drain them of energy. They also discussed the other guns on site: laser guns and guns that fired bolts of electricity. The latter were more common than specialist, but no less effective in the fight against the machines.

All the while, Dom struggled to keep from looking at Warren. Too much hate coursed through his veins, knowing what he'd done to Anya in Arcis. He'd also abandoned his teammates on the fifth floor, almost costing Sheila and Yasmin their chance to rotate.

Jason finished with a shrug and said to Dom, 'That's it.'

Dom discreetly shook away his anger and focused on the X on the back wall, imagining it was Warren's head. He knocked his new thoughts loose and handed the revolver to Jason.

'You're up. Shoot the X.'

Jason steadied himself, took aim and fired. His shot almost found the white centre.

Not bad.

'Good effort. You've had training?'

Jason handed the gun back to him. He thumbed in the direction of the courtyard. 'With some of those guys in a different camp, but not enough.'

With four bullets left, Dom handed the gun to Jerome. Jerome looked unsure, so he stepped in and steadied his firing hand, showing him how to support it with his other hand. Dom stepped back and nodded for Jerome to fire. He did and his effort was off the mark, but not a bad attempt.

Warren was up next. Dom's skin bristled as he handed him the gun.

He didn't show him anything. 'Hit the target.'

Dom chewed on his nail, hoping Warren would fail. Warren shot the target, better than he had. He turned with a smile on his face.

Dom didn't take the gun from him. 'Again.'

Warren turned back to the target. He shot it, not as good as the first time, but he was a natural.

'Again,' Dom commanded.

Warren shot the target with the last bullet in the gun.

Dom reloaded the weapon, then ordered him to fire. 'Shoot until the gun is empty.'

The noise of bullets hitting brick rang around the compound and bounced off the mountainsides as Warren's bullets hit the mark or close to it.

When he was finished, a smiling Warren looked around at his colleagues.

Dom snatched the gun from him and said, 'You need the most practice, Warren. The others are way ahead of you in skills.'

'Bullshit!' said Warren. 'I hit the target most of the time.'

'But your stance was off, your position was lazy, and you don't listen to commands.'

Warren opened and closed his mouth in shock. 'What are you talking about? You didn't show me anything! You told me to fire.'

'Watch your mouth, Hunt. I won't warn you again.'

Warren glared at him. 'Why are you being a dick?'

Dom smiled. 'I remember everything that happened in Arcis.'

Warren threw the gun on the ground and stormed off.

'That wasn't fair, Dom,' said Jerome. 'He did everything you asked.'

Not everything. Not in Arcis, when he'd told Warren to leave Anya alone. And look how that turned out? Before his attack on her, Dom had admitted to having an odd feeling about Warren Hunt.

'Rejoin the main group. I need to take a break.'

He strode away from their session. It had lasted all of twenty minutes. They could train for the rest of the day, but none of these men would be ready to fight the machines. The only thing that would win this battle was pure luck.

He returned to the male dorm and flopped down on a free bed, covering his eyes with his arm. Warren deserved his punishment. But Dom needed to get his head in the game now. This war wouldn't win itself.

Someone kicked his bed, causing Dom to jerk his arm away.

'What the hell...?' He glared up at his attacker, but his expression softened when he saw who it was. 'Anya, I didn't know it was you.'

'What was that about outside? With Warren?'

Her hands shook and she looked close to losing it with him.

Dom sat up. 'You saw that?'

'I not only saw it but I heard what you said about remembering.'

Dom tried to laugh it off. 'I was just trying to scare him.'

But a livid Anya clearly wasn't buying his excuse. 'What happened between Warren and me is none of your business.' One of the soldiers entered the room and glanced at Anya. Anya ignored him and lowered her voice. 'And I'd appreciate it if you wouldn't say that stuff in front of my brother.'

Shit. He'd been thoughtless. 'Sorry. I didn't mean to cause trouble for you.'

Anya visibly pulled her anger back; her stiff stance relaxed a fraction. 'It's okay. But please mind your own business in future, Dom.' She paused, releasing a slow, measured breath. 'I want to join the attack training. Julius' team.'

'It's not up to me.'

'But you can talk to Max, tell him I've had training.'

'Max thinks you'd be more valuable out of the fight, and to be honest, I agree.'

Finding the coordinates to the Beyond trumped any training Anya might receive.

Her anger returned. 'You've just said it's not up to you. Put in a word.'

Dom gave it half a second of thought. 'No.'

He would not be bullied.

She screamed in frustration, alarming the soldier in the room, enough that he readied to leave. But then she turned and marched out of the room.

The soldier shouted over, 'What was that all about?'

Dom lay back down and draped his good arm over his eyes. 'None of your business.'

18

Carissa

Carissa left the storage shed and the wolf went with her. She approached the entrance to the courtyard where sweaty soldiers gathered outside. They looked to be taking a break from training. Looks of alarm and panic greeted her.

'What the hell's that thing doing loose?' said one.

The Inventor exited the town hall next to the courtyard. Carissa wondered what business he had in there.

He strode over to the group, holding his hands up. 'The wolf is under my command. You have nothing to fear.'

'I'm telling Max,' said one soldier who looked unconvinced by his answer.

He ran off. Carissa sighed certain Rover's freedom would be short-lived.

If so, she would make the most of her time with

the wolf. Memories of playing with her orb in Praesidium resurfaced. It had been a good distraction, but the ex-Guardian offered more interactive fun.

She ran, away from the soldiers and towards the perimeter fence. She checked behind to see the wolf was hot on her heels. Rover panted, then gave a mechanical whine as he caught up to her. She laughed, her recent conversation with Quintus and this threat to punish the escapees a distant memory. He'd been a voice in her head with no power to do anything. Nothing bad could happen while that remained the case.

Carissa continued her run around the camp. It was big enough in size to wind her. She and Rover paused a moment on one side of the trucks, parked opposite the courtyard that was filled with active soldiers once more. She caught sight of Max closer to the entrance of the camp, next to the building that pressed up against the high wall. He was speaking in a harried tone to three agitated soldiers who had just climbed down from the roof. But seeing the Inventor there, hands on hips and looking worried, sent her part organic heart into overdrive.

Rover whined, as if he sensed her rising panic.

'What's going on there, boy?' she said in a gentle tone that didn't match her mood.

Rover whined again, glancing between her and the Inventor. An angry looking Max was all she saw. That and the Inventor shaking his head. Max looked over suddenly and sent her donor heart plummeting into her black boots. He strode over to where Carissa hid behind one of the trucks, the back end covered in a green tarpaulin. Rover growled low.

The Inventor shuffled after him. 'It's not her fault, Max.'

'It is, Jacob. That thing is here because of her.' He stopped short, his expression as dark as a thundercloud. 'What did you do, Carissa?'

Carissa opened and closed her mouth in shock. 'I... I don't know what you mean.'

But she did.

Max lunged for her, grabbed her arm. The wolf growled and stalked forward, alarming Max.

'Easy, boy,' said the Inventor, but the wolf didn't listen.

He edged close enough to Max, forcing the colonel to release Carissa's arm. She breathed a sigh of relief, still not sure how her conversation with Quintus was an issue. He'd been just a voice.

'I won't ask again, Carissa.'

The loud thumping of her heartbeat drowned out his threats. She pulled at the loose fabric around her neck. 'Jacob! I... I can't breathe.'

The Inventor folded his arms. His lack of help shocked her. 'I'm sorry, Carissa. This is very serious. An orb was spotted just beyond the mouth of the valley. It is looking for this place. What did you do?'

She struggled to draw breath. A step back brought her into direct contact with the immovable wolf. With no place to run, Carissa huffed.

The Inventor uncrossed his arms and stepped towards her. 'Miss, please. This is important. You're not in trouble.'

'She is,' hissed Max.

The Inventor shot him a look and continued, 'Did you try to contact the city? Is that why the orb is here?'

'You know it is,' said Max. 'How else would it know where to look? The anti-magnetic field in the valley camp scrambles signals more complex than our walkie talkies. No machine would be able to get close or get a clear reading on our location. If it's here, it's because someone gave it directions.'

Carissa hated the way the Inventor looked at her, like she was a traitor. It had just been one time... and the one before that.

She looked past both men to the house at the front gate. Jason and Thomas were carrying a gun up to the flat roof.

She flicked her gaze from them to the Inventor. 'I heard voices, but it was only the communications here.'

Max squared off his stance. Rover responded with a low growl.

'Where?' said the Inventor.

Carissa pointed sheepishly to where the spotters were.

'I asked you what you were doing in the old part of the town. Did you climb up there?'

The anger on the Inventor's face turned her

stomach to butterflies. She nodded. There was no point in lying.

'What about these voices?' said Max. 'Quick, child, before the orb gets too close. I need to know if it has our location or if it's guessing.'

That she couldn't answer, but it was too much of a coincidence after speaking with Quintus.

'So it might not be here because of Carissa?' said the Inventor.

Max shrugged. 'It could be on a scouting mission. The second we shoot at it, we reveal our location.' He directed his angry gaze at Carissa. 'I'll ask you again. Is it here because of you, or is this a coincidence?'

Carissa swallowed. 'I heard a second voice while I was up there.' She omitted the part about looking for it the second time. Both the Inventor and Max stared at her. She shook her head violently. 'But I didn't tell Quintus anything.'

'Shit,' said the Inventor.

He dragged his hand down his weathered face.

It was the first time Carissa had heard him curse. *This is bad.*

'I'm sorry! I came down as soon as it happened.'

'But you didn't tell anyone,' said Max.

'I'm sorry.'

Carissa stayed put despite wanting to run away from her mistake.

With a huff, Max stalked off, back to house

nearest the gate with the most intense activity.

The Inventor pointed a finger at her. 'This isn't over, Carissa.'

He followed Max and left Carissa alone with a whining Rover, who must have sensed her pain. At least someone cared about her.

She thought about climbing up to the ledge again, to ask Quintus about the orb, but dismissed that idea.

That's what got you into trouble in the first place, Carissa.

She hadn't meant to seek him out a second time. The first time had happened so fast, and nobody had been as surprised as her to hear his voice. She'd followed the Inventor's command and not connected to the city. This was just one time—and the other. He had to forgive her.

Her betrayal made her hands shake. Her breaths shortened to fine painful points. But unlike the city, there would be no diagnosis of her condition by a concerned Inventor to make sure she was okay.

More soldiers climbed up to the flat roof that gave them a view over the compound wall. The activity piqued her curiosity. She wanted to see what they did. While Rover's company calmed her, his imposing size would make it difficult to sneak up on the operation. Carissa commanded Rover to return to the storage shed. He protested with a sad whine, but did what she asked.

Nobody paid her any mind as she approached

the scene, and if they did, it was fleeting; too much was happening on the flat roof. Carissa squeezed through the commotion and made it inside the house. On the first floor and out on the flat roof, Jason and Thomas stood next to three soldiers. They held a box-shaped gun with a soldered barrel on the front.

Max was there too. He didn't notice her spying on them.

'The orb knows where we are,' said Max to the pair.

'How?' said Jason.

Max shook his head. 'Doesn't matter. We need to disable that thing with the Disruptor gun.'

Carissa had seen this gun in action. Both Jason and Max had used it to gain access through the force field surrounding Arcis. One of the orbs had been recording but Quintus, too busy talking to the participants on the first floor, had not seen the footage. It had disrupted the force field. Then Max had used the same gun to absorb the energy of the field, weakening it.

Thomas pointed in the distance and said, 'There!'

Carissa couldn't see much, not with all the soldiers in the way.

Jason fired a shot from the gun and cursed. 'It's not behaving like the last one. It's too fast.'

'Try again,' Max said.

Through a small gap, she saw Jason steady the gun on his shoulder.

He fired, but cursed again. 'I can't hit my mark. Crap, it's halfway over the top of the magnetic barrier!'

Commotion followed. Soldiers pushed Carissa out of the way to get to the flat roof.

Carissa ran down the stairs, almost tripping a couple of times. Outside, she saw the orb, similar to the one she used to play with. It zipped over the top of the compound wall and flew at speed around the camp.

'Jason. Stop that thing,' shouted Max.

Both men climbed down the side of the property, gun in hand. They chased the orb around. Soldiers fired into the air, but the orb dodged every attempt to be caught.

An idea occurred to Carissa. She didn't know if her command might work. Heart in mouth, she held her hand out, palm facing up. While everyone ignored her, she whistled.

The orb changed position and flew towards her. A slack-jawed Max and shocked soldiers watched as the orb landed on Carissa's hand with a thud.

Her hand shook as she extended it to Jason. 'Shoot it now.'

She closed her eyes, expecting the Disruptor to disable her too. She braced for impact, but felt someone slap the orb out of her hand and push her away. Carissa stumbled back. Her eyes shot open as Jason fired at the orb lying on the ground.

Max blinked at her. 'How did you do that?'

19

Carissa

All eyes were on her, and she didn't understand why. Calling the orb to her was a natural act.

Max shook off his shock and strode over to her. 'I asked you how you commanded that thing.'

Carissa didn't know how to explain. She just could. To her relief, the Inventor was close by.

He said to Max, 'Maybe we should talk somewhere more private.'

Carissa looked around at the sea of surprised faces. She hugged her middle, not liking the attention on her. This felt like the Business District in Praesidium, a place where Originals could run their businesses and Copies visited on occasion. But not too often; a Copy only attracted hateful stares.

'Fine, the workshop. I don't want to let that thing out of my sight.'

Max nodded at Jason and Thomas, prompting Jason to pick up the orb. Max followed the pair back to the workshop.

A fearful Carissa looked up at the Inventor, who pushed her on. 'We need to explain, Carissa. They don't understand you yet.'

She nodded, trusting him, and followed Max. They entered the workshop where Jason and Thomas set the orb down on the workbench crowded with monitors of various sizes at the back of the room.

The workshop felt tight and stuffy with all five of them in the small space.

'Check that thing is inert, and if it was sending a signal back to anywhere,' said Max to the pair.

'On it,' said Thomas.

Max turned round and folded his arms. 'What the hell happened out there?'

The Inventor explained something Carissa could not.

'The machines in Praesidium run on the same frequency. It's how Carissa was able to break us out of the city. She peeled back a seam between two force field points enough for us to escape.'

Max frowned. 'So you're saying she can talk to the machines?'

'Not all of them. She can command the orb. The whistle she used operates on the same command frequency as the orbs. She calls; it has to obey.'

That was news to Carissa. She'd always thought she and the orb had shared a special bond. It disappointed her to learn that, with the right command, anyone could control it.

But Max's brightening expression lightened her mood. 'I'm seeing an opportunity here. Can we replicate the sound to command new orbs that attempt to gain access to the compound?'

'That could work,' said Thomas, looking up from his workstation. 'We could place it in a spot outside the valley and anti-magnetic field. It would draw any orbs to it there.'

Max looked happier at that suggestion. 'How long would they stay inactive?'

The Inventor shrugged. 'As long as the whistle played. The orbs need interaction. Without it, they will stray. But there's one other thing that could make this a short-lived experiment.'

'What?' said Max.

'The Collective can alter the command whenever it likes. Carissa is no longer connected to the city, so she wouldn't have access to the new commands.'

'Well, it's better than nothing.' Max turned to Carissa. 'What will the city send next?'

Carissa had no idea. She thought back to the build for Essention and what Quintus had ordered the Inventor to send out. 'Digging machines.'

'That's what they sent when they broke up Essention,' said Jason with a shake of his head.

The Inventor also shook his head. 'We're talking about building and dismantling urbanos. This will be an attack on us, so while they'll send machines to break down walls, weaponised Guardians and Copies will come too. I guarantee it.'

Max turned to Jason and Thomas. 'What's the verdict on that thing?'

Thomas said, 'It's inactive, thanks to her help.'

He gave Carissa a friendly smile that warmed her heart. Despite the actions that had gotten her into this mess, for the first time she felt useful. But Thomas' next words made her blood run cold.

'But it may have transmitted coordinates back. It got over the barrier and was high up enough to do it.'

Quintus' threat to punish the escapees dominated her thoughts. She stood stiffly.

'So we prepare,' said Max with a tight nod. 'That's all we can do.'

'Can Carissa leave?' said the Inventor.

'No.' Max fixed his hardened stare on her. 'Thomas and Jason need to record her command, to play it through a speaker so we can control new orbs.'

'I can give you that,' said the Inventor. 'You don't need her for this.'

'No!' All faces turned to Carissa. 'It's my fault the orb came. I spoke to Quintus. I need to take responsibility. Let me help.'

Thomas lifted his brows at Max. 'The work would go faster with her here.'

Max hesitated. 'Okay, but Jacob, you stay with her.'

The Inventor nodded.

Carissa walked over to the workbench seeing

the orb open on the table. It hurt to discover her friend
in the city had been nothing more than a machine
programmed to listen to her. Just another piece of
tech to dismantle. Another scout on a mission to
destroy.

And it had come for her.

The Inventor led her away from the table.
Gripping her shoulder tight, he asked, 'What exactly
did Quintus say, miss?'

It hurt too much to keep it in. She looked up
into his watery gaze and blurted out everything.

20

Anya

Anya watched from the entrance to the workshop as Jason and Thomas got to work. Jason handled the basic equipment around him like someone with a passion for this stuff. Her brother's limited experience with Praesidium's hand-me-downs at home in Brookfield had served him well. She watched as he shook off his old life filled with childish hobbies and created a new one where he mattered to those around him.

Jealousy gripped her hard. Her brother was growing with experience and she was stuck in the past. It felt not only as if the last three months had never happened, but that Anya had somehow missed her own awakening.

The Copy sat tentatively in a chair in front of the workshop table where Jason and Thomas both sat. Thomas held a recording device up to Carissa's mouth and instructed her to whistle. She did and

Thomas captured it before telling Max that they could play it through one of the bullhorns.

Max nodded. 'We need to get the teams ready.'

He left the workshop, almost colliding with Anya. His eyes widened in surprise at seeing her.

Worried she might not get another chance to speak to him, she blurted out, 'I want to join one of the teams. I know how to shoot.'

Max blinked. 'Sorry, what?'

'I have attack experience. I want to train with the others again.'

Max shook his head, which annoyed Anya.

'Vanessa needs you more than I do. Despite your lack of recollection, she still maintains you know something, and I think she's right. It's becoming clear to me you might be the only person who knows where the Beyond is located. The only one with access to the coordinates.' He tapped the side of his head.

She had tried to remember the past without Vanessa breathing down her neck, but the drama with Alex coupled with her missing memories had occupied most of her thoughts. And the more she thought about it, the more she wanted to understand the reasons behind Warren's attack; she didn't need the fear of it to cripple her.

'I can help Vanessa and train.'

'No, Anya. I can't risk your life out there. You're too valuable to our efforts.'

'I'm not lying. I really don't remember. Why

174

doesn't anyone believe me?'

Max shook his head as though she had disappointed him. 'I expected better from a Macklin. Your parents were leaders and revered in rebel circles.'

His limited view point irritated her. 'Well, maybe Grace should have taught me to be more like her. You didn't know her. She wasn't an easy person to be around.'

'She was just protecting you.' He glared at her. 'No more delays. I'm ordering you to see Vanessa, now.'

Max walked off, leaving a livid Anya to stew in her anger. Given her current mood, seeing Vanessa was the last thing she wanted to do. Carissa left the workshop next and gave her a glance as she headed down the alley to the storage shed at the end. That must be where they kept the mechanical wolf. She could think of no other place big enough to store it.

A memory flashed in her mind of wolves similar to the one named Rover. A supervisor, in Arcis? Yeah, that was it. Their metal chests used to rise and fall as though the machines could breathe on their own. Their claws, sharp and long, would scrape the tiled floor. Their yellow eyes would track the participants' movements. Her recollection of them was clear; who or what else she'd shared the space with remained vague.

Anya entered the workshop; it contained fewer people now. Jason and Jacob continued to examine the orb while Thomas replayed Carissa's whistle. She waited by the door, hoping to be of some use in here.

Thomas concentrated on a screen she couldn't see, probably showing data from either the recording or the orb. Jacob stood over his shoulder and pointed at something on it. Jason was hunched over the open orb with a scanner in his hand, using it to record data.

Anya took two steps forward. Her movement caught Jason's attention.

He looked up and gave her a half smile. 'Hey. A bit of drama out there.'

'Yeah.' Anya stuffed her hands into her pockets. She stepped closer to the idle orb. 'You seem to know what you're doing.'

'Yeah, me and Thomas caught an orb while we were in Foxrush. We were able to disable it. It looks to be the same design as that one.'

She liked seeing her brother happy. She just wished her own life would sort itself out.

Jason appeared to pick up on her mood. 'What's wrong, Anya?'

She didn't know where to start, but she began with the most pressing issue. 'I feel like a coma patient who's just woken up to find the world has carried on without me. You all know each other, and I know nobody here.'

'You know me,' said Jason. 'And I'm the best person to know around here, better than Thomas.'

'Hey!' said Thomas. He touched a hand to his heart. 'I'm Thomas, in case you haven't figured that out yet.'

Anya grinned.

'And I'm Jacob. But Carissa likes to call me the Inventor,' said the old man.

Anya frowned at the name. 'Why does she call you that?'

'It's what the Copies called me in Praesidium. It was what I did there.'

Anya had seen none of the city while she'd been prisoner. 'You invented things? Like what?'

Jacob shrugged. 'Less inventions, more fixing things. Copies, machines—whatever broke, I guess.'

His admission gave Anya a glimmer of hope. 'I don't suppose you can fix me?'

Jacob laughed; the sound snatched her hope away. 'I'm afraid I can't fix humans, only tech. Like the stuff in young Dom Pavesi. He was sick and I fixed him.'

'So I'm stuck like this, with no idea of what happened for the last three months?'

Jacob flashed her a look of pity, as did Jason and Thomas.

'Give it time, Anya,' said Jason. 'You'll remember again.'

She avoided their lingering gazes. 'But it's not happening fast enough.'

Jacob stepped out from behind the work desk and patted her on the arm. She allowed the gesture, designed to reassure her.

His weathered face drew near to hers. 'I know

it's tough, but the memories are still there. The replication machine, it's a complex piece of equipment. It repressed your memories enough to give you amnesia. But I don't believe your memories are gone. You have to be patient.'

The old man's explanation made Anya's heart thrum faster. The replication machine. She stared at the Inventor. 'Could you build one again? Reverse engineer it to liberate my memories?'

She was clutching at straws, but it was a better idea than none.

Jacob rubbed his chin, giving her a sliver of hope again, but then he shook his head. 'I could try to build one, but I don't have the materials.'

Anya refused to give up on the idea. 'What about Carissa? Or the wolf you made? Do they carry the tech to make one?'

Her suggestion angered the old man. He narrowed his eyes. 'I won't dismantle my wolf or a Copy to give you back something you can live perfectly well without.'

She wasn't certain she *could* live without it. Anya's hope deflated for a second time.

Jacob frowned suddenly. With a wag of his finger, he said, 'But if I had the right parts to build the essence of the machine... We would only need the part capable of affecting your memories.' He released a puff of air. 'It's a long shot and you must understand our priority in here is to protect this compound.'

'Jacob, I need you over here,' said Thomas.

'Leave the idea with me.' He shuffled over to the brown-haired boy, leaving Anya alone.

She left, her painful heart stuffed with more disappointment than it could handle. But she didn't venture far, as another idea hit her. She walked towards the storage shed and entered the space to find the mechanical wolf lying on the floor and Carissa sat next to it. Her legs were curled under her and she was patting the creature.

The beast with the yellow eyes alerted to Anya's presence and growled long and low. Carissa's head snapped round. She clambered to her feet, startled.

'Anya, I didn't hear you come in. Have you been here before?'

'First time.' She smiled at the Copy and clasped her hands to the front, trying to look relaxed in the company of a supervisor from Arcis. To her relief, the wolf lost interest in her and lowered his head onto his spindly, metallic legs. 'I came to check on you.' She nodded behind her. 'That was a lot to deal with out there.'

Carissa nodded, looking close to tears. 'I shouldn't have climbed up to the ledge. It was my fault this happened. I only want to help.'

'And you are,' she said coolly, not there to be a shoulder to cry on. 'Listen, when you found me in the room with Alex, you had my Copy with you.'

With rounded eyes, Carissa nodded again.

'She passed back just one memory to me.'

'I remember. She was being wilful. I tried to make her listen...'

Anya waved her hand at the Copy. 'I'm not angry. It was her choice. But you said that the memories were a part of her.'

Carissa nodded for the third time. 'It happens at the replication stage. The machine imprinted your memories onto the Copy's biogel.'

'Well, that's just it. I need those memories back.'

Carissa shook her head. 'But Canya is dead. It's not possible.'

Anya stepped closer, drawing a growl from the beast. He had raised his head again. Carissa turned and scolded the Guardian. He whimpered and lay his head back down. Anya waited until she had Carissa's full attention before she spoke again.

'Did you see what happened in Arcis?' Carissa nodded. 'How much?'

'All of it.'

'I know it's a long shot, but could you pass the memories back to me in the same way Canya did?'

To Anya's disappointment, the Copy shook her head. 'Canya was able to do that because she was your Copy, right down to a molecular level. You were the same person, in a sense.'

Anya shivered at the memory of her Copy, a rude girl who had turned on them at a pivotal moment in their escape, only to be terminated for her insubordination.

'But could we try?'

Carissa shrugged. 'I guess.'

Anya held out her arm and Carissa grabbed it at the wrist. She did same thing that Canya had done to her—aligning their chips. While Anya had felt an odd sensation travel up her arm the last time, this time she felt nothing. The action didn't pass on any memories or awaken her senses. Something about this felt different.

Then she remembered the chips they'd dug out of their wrists, after their escape from the city. 'Might it work if we had the chips again?'

'I don't think it will help,' said Carissa. 'I'm not your exact Copy. Sorry, I didn't mean to get your hopes up. I just want to be useful.'

Anya strode to the door before turning around. 'So do I, Carissa.'

21

Dom

Due to the drama of the visiting orb, nobody except Dom noticed three trucks approach the mountain pass high above the valley. It was how he and the others had arrived—by truck along a cliffside road that avoided the anti-magnetic barriers covering the valley bed. He'd been too out of it to notice much, but a quick flash of the sheer drop and the crisp, clean air had alerted him to their height.

One by one, the trucks disappeared into the cliff face inside a service elevator big enough to carry the trucks down to the valley. The wall surrounding the camp, as tall as half a house, blocked the view of the exit at the bottom. A flurry of activity told him the trucks had been spotted.

Dom heard one soldier shout, 'Turn off the anti-magnetic field and get Max!'

A minute later, the sound of tyres kicking up gravel followed. Soldiers manning the gate wheeled it back. Max marched out of the town hall, taking long strides to the gate.

He looked relieved as he waved the three trucks in and followed the last one to the grassy verge where the trucks parked.

These must be the rebels Max had been waiting on from another town.

Dom stood back as soldiers not much older than him, dressed in green, camouflage gear and heavy, black boots, got out. Then he saw Kaylie: a girl from his past with whom he'd been intimate once. She had long, blonde hair drawn back into a ponytail and a beauty that rivalled Sheila's.

The male soldiers took a second and third look when she got out of the truck and walked over to a waiting Max. Dom remembered Kaylie as being shallow and vain, a person who had been shocked by his scars when she'd seen them by accident. He hadn't stuck around after their night together to wait for her verdict on them.

She shook Max's outstretched hand with the confidence of someone who commanded her own team of rebels. It was like she was a completely different person.

'We're here to help,' she said to Max. 'Where do you need us?'

'We've just had an orb from the city breach our defences.'

Kaylie nodded, not shocked or disturbed by this news, as Dom would have expected her to be. He stared at this new, confident version of the girl he'd left behind in one of the camps. Maybe he'd pegged her all wrong.

'Things are under control, for now,' said Max. 'Your team should eat something, and after I'll get you up to speed. We're working on a project to prevent more orbs from breaching our defences.'

Kaylie nodded and Max waved Dom forward from where he stood, out of Kaylie's line of sight. 'You remember Dom Pavesi?'

Even with her back to him, Dom caught the stiffening of Kaylie's shoulders. The name had surprised her. She turned slow enough so as to wipe her expression clean.

'Dom,' she said with a friendly smile. 'It's been a long time.'

She shook his hand—it was a slow pump, as though she was working this all out.

'Kaylie, good to see you. We must catch up.'

He let go of her and was turning to leave when Kaylie said, 'I'm free now. Not sure when we're going to get another chance to talk.'

She emphasised the last word. Dom sensed a lecture brewing. Why? He'd been clear about his feelings for her. What was there to talk about?

Kaylie surprised him by linking arms with him. 'Come on. You can show me this place.'

He stood frozen in shock while she waited for him to move. Not sure where to take her, he led her over to the courtyard.

They paused at the entrance. Inside, Dom saw a red-faced and sweating Sheila doing jumping jacks under Imogen's command. Sheila stopped when she saw them. Her eyes widened in surprise. Smiling, she left the session for a moment and walked over to them.

'Kaylie,' she said, out of breath. Her eyes slid between her and Dom. 'What brings you to this place?'

Kaylie let go of Dom's arm and hugged Sheila. Dom caught the tension in Sheila's stiff hug.

'New recruits,' Kaylie said, pulling back. 'I didn't know you were here too.'

Sheila shrugged. 'We come as a package.'

Kaylie laughed. 'You two were always as thick as thieves.'

Sheila matched her laugh. 'Still are. What are you two up to?'

Kaylie slipped her arm into Dom's once more, causing Sheila's brow to lift. 'Dom's going to show me around the camp. Chat later?'

Sheila nodded. 'Looking forward to it. Better get back to it.'

The second Kaylie turned away, Sheila's mouth formed a perfect O. She knew the full story between him and this girl. Kaylie and Sheila had even been friends, before Dom had bolted after sex and never explained why. The reason always came down to his ugly scars. Sheila said Kaylie had asked her about them but when Sheila refused to say, Kaylie had stopped speaking to her.

As if things weren't already interesting enough around here.

He walked her down the road that led past the workshop where Jason, Thomas and Jacob were working.

'They're creating a device to attract the orbs to it.' He pointed down an alley. 'That leads to a storage shed where we have one of the Guardians from Praesidium.'

Kaylie stiffened. 'One of the wolves? Is it safe?'

'As safe as it's ever going to be.'

He felt her shudder right before she released a breath. 'I dunno. If I was running this camp, I would have it destroyed. Not take any chances.'

'It's perfectly harmless,' said Dom.

Kaylie idly massaged his bicep with her fingers. 'Harmless? How can you be sure?'

'Because we have the Inventor from the city here. He created the wolf. It listens to only him.'

She didn't look convinced. 'Well, if you say so.'

Dom bristled at her scepticism. They passed by several streets running perpendicular to the road they were on. The green perimeter fence sectioning the camp from the rest of the town loomed in the distance.

Dom pointed down one of the streets. 'Charlie has a barber shop down there.'

Kaylie's eyes widened and she smiled. 'Charlie's here? I must see him after this.'

Then Dom saw her: Anya. She was leaning against one of the buildings opposite Charlie's place, perhaps waiting to speak with him. She looked over at them, blushed, looked away. Dom pulled his arm out of Kaylie's grasp. Her brow lifted at the move, but she said nothing.

With a small quirk of a smile, she said, 'Show me the rest?'

Dom continued his tour of the camp, which involved them doing a lap of the place. They finished the tour back where they'd started.

Kaylie said, 'I'm starving. How about you and I get reacquainted?'

Dom didn't think that was a good idea. 'I've some things to do.'

Kaylie swapped sides and hooked her right arm with his left. Pain blazed through him. It took all his strength not to flinch.

'I won't take no for an answer. Now, which way is the kitchen?'

He pointed through an open door. She pulled him into the dining hall and he gritted his teeth against the pain. They collected meagre rations of bread and beans, and found a table. Dom massaged the ache in his arm away as they sat down. Seeing Anya had rattled him enough for him to shuck Kaylie's hand off him. But what they had was gone. Why was he still chasing a ghost?

Kaylie made noises that were bordering on erotic as she ate. Other males in the room noticed and elbowed each other. Dom didn't know where to look.

'Are you enjoying your food?'

She looked up in surprise. 'Like you wouldn't believe. I haven't eaten in twelve hours.'

His eyes flicked from her to the men, back to her. 'You're, uh, making a lot of noises... that the soldiers are noticing.'

Kaylie's eyes widened as she looked around her. Then she faced him looking contrite, but Dom didn't buy the act.

She lifted her brow at him. 'Do my noises embarrass you?'

'No, I'm just not sure they're appropriate, that's all.'

She leaned in closer. 'You didn't mind them that one night we got super close.'

How could he forget? He'd acted like an ass walking out like that. But she'd made him feel insecure about his scars.

'That was a long time ago, Kaylie.'

She dropped her gaze to her plate and played with her food. 'What happened, Dom? I seem to remember you enjoying yourself, then you upped and left in the morning.'

Kaylie reminded Dom of Sheila. Both were master manipulators.

'It just didn't work out. I'm sorry but there's nothing more to say.'

Kaylie looked up and swatted the air with her hand. 'Please, I'm over it now. I've moved on. I have a boyfriend back in camp.'

'Really? That's good.'

Maybe they could draw a line under this tension once and for all.

'Want to know his name?'

Not really. 'Sure.'

'Jeremiah.'

'Great.'

'We haven't been going out for that long, only a few months. But it could become something serious.'

'I'm happy for you, Kaylie. I really am.'

Dom tore off a piece of bread and popped it into his mouth.

'But that doesn't mean you and I can't have some fun like the old days.'

Dom choked on his bread. 'What?'

Kaylie laughed and flicked the end of her ponytail back. 'You heard me. We've still got chemistry. I see how you look at me. Wanna know if I've picked up any new tricks?'

Her eyes rounded as she stared at him. Kaylie was a beautiful girl with skin the same honey shade as Sheila's. She had pouty lips and green eyes. And sat in her green uniform, she looked more confident than the girl he used to know.

But he didn't want to lead her on. 'I'm sorry, Kaylie. That's probably not a good idea.'

She tossed her hair again and looked down at

her plate. 'Cool with me. I've got other things going on anyway.'

They sat in awkward silence until Kaylie got up and said, 'I'd better get back to it. Thanks for the tour, Dominic.'

Dom gave her a nod and watched her walk over to the rest of the team. She spoke to them and left the dining hall. When she was gone, the rebels from her team resumed eating. It was clear to him she had earned their respect.

Dom finished up and went outside to the courtyard. There, he found Sheila now running laps— a pastime she claimed to hate because it ruined her figure.

Dom called out to her when she passed. 'Hey, I thought you hated running?'

She slowed, then stopped. 'I do, but ever since my time in Praesidium, I never want to be too weak to fight anyone off.'

It was a solid enough reason.

She grabbed a towel lying next to the room with the boxing bag and wiped her face and neck with it.

He'd asked her recently about her time in there, but she'd kept her answers vague. 'Did anyone hurt you while you were their prisoner?'

Sheila shook her head. 'They tried to force me to breed with a boy. But all he got from me was a punch to the nose.'

Dom smiled at that image but when he caught sadness in Sheila's eyes, he dropped it.

Sheila wiped down her arms. 'So Kaylie, huh? That must be a shock.'

'It was. I knew one day I'd see her again. But she was cool about it.'

'Uh huh. Did she proposition you?'

Dom laughed. 'No, she didn't proposition me.'

Sheila wiped her neck again. 'Liar. I bet she did and you, mister goody two shoes, said, "No, thank you. I'm a priest."'

Dom rolled his eyes. 'Okay. She did, but she was cool about it.'

Sheila made a noise.

'What?' he said.

'Girls are *never* cool with it. She was into you then; she's still into you now.'

Dom dismissed the idea. Kaylie had told him she had a boyfriend. 'Nothing's gonna happen there.'

'Not what *she* said.'

Dom stared at her. 'When did you talk to her?'

'I don't have to actually talk to her, Dom. It's written on her face and in her body language, even though she's trying to hide it.'

Sheila was usually right about women. What the hell did he know?

'Anya saw us together,' he said.

'So?'

Sheila's response surprised him.

He frowned. 'I thought you liked her.'

'I do, Dom, but you're a stranger to her. Stop pining after her. If being with Kaylie will get you over her faster, then maybe you should go for it.'

Dom narrowed his eyes at her. 'Like you are getting over Yasmin?'

Sheila sighed and leaned against the wall. 'Yas and I were an odd couple. We fought a lot. It was great when it was good, but she was hard work. Cold when she wanted to be. It made me realise that I need someone who complements my personality. Someone who won't fight me on everything.'

Dom looked around the yard. It had filled with the new recruits. Imogen was talking to them, hands on hips. Dom looked back at Sheila to see her watching the other group.

Then something clicked. The running, the sudden interest in the courtyard. 'Ah, so this is all for a girl, is it?'

Sheila whipped him with her towel. 'Of course not! I'm not that transparent. I'm doing this for me, after what I went through.'

Dom didn't disagree with that. 'But it's also for Imogen, no?' He glanced back. 'She's a strong soldier. One of Max's best.'

'She is.' He caught the faint smile on Sheila's face. When she caught him looking, she hit his arm. 'Stop distracting me, Dominic. Now go court Kaylie, or whatever you heterosexual lovebirds do these days.'

Sheila began another lap of the track. Imogen flashed a sweet smile at her as she passed.

Dom left the courtyard with a dilemma he

didn't need. Should he move on from the only girl who'd made him feel close to normal, and risk it with a girl who wanted to be with him?

22

Anya

Anya didn't know where to look when Dom showed up at one end of the street with a girl on his arm who looked a lot like Sheila. As tall as Dom, she had the same glow to her skin as him. The sun glinted off her golden hair, tied back in a high ponytail, to give her a halo. But she looked like no angel.

Anya stared down at her own pasty, white skin until they left. Then she followed.

She listened from a position of safety as Dom told her about the camp. She was dressed as a soldier, which meant she was a rebel. She hung on to Dom's arm as though they were familiar with each other. Anya followed them to the storage area with the guns and ammo. Dom paused to explain where everything of importance was kept. On occasion, Kaylie would squeeze Dom's arm and glance up at him when he wasn't looking.

Had Anya met this girl before?

194

She still smarted from her and Carissa's failed experiment to unlock her memories. She'd believed the Copy could pass back her memories to her, as Canya had done partially. Her only hope now was if Jacob could build a partial replication machine capable of reversing her amnesia. Jacob had said her memories were in remission only, not gone completely. She refused to give up hope that she could get them all back.

Jealousy tied her stomach up in knots. Dom and the girl continued to stroll through the compound as if they were an item. The interaction bothered her, even though it shouldn't.

She shook her head and broke off her pursuit. With a new vigour, she would fight to restore the last three months, until all options were exhausted.

'Hey.'

The familiar voice sent an icy shiver through her. She wheeled round.

Warren stood a short distance away. His hands were stuffed in his pockets, his shoulders rounded.

So much for her lack of memories. This was one person she had tried to forget.

'What do you want, Warren?'

She stood tall, even though having him near made her want to crawl into the foetal position.

He nodded at the pair who had disappeared around the corner. 'You two used to be tight in Arcis.'

'Who?' she said, even though she knew.

'He was the reason things went wrong for us.'

Anya couldn't believe her ears. 'Wrong how? So it's his fault that you attacked me?'

Warren slipped his hands out of his pockets. He held them up, his eyes wide. 'No, I didn't mean that. I just meant...' He huffed out a breath, dropping his hands to his side. 'I came to apologise. I know that doesn't mean much now, but I wasn't myself in Arcis.'

Somehow, Anya didn't believe him.

He continued. 'Arcis was like a pressure cooker. We were all under a lot of stress.'

She'd take his word for it because she couldn't remember. But she wouldn't tolerate his excuses.

'A difficult situation didn't give you the right to treat me the way you did. A crisis isn't an excuse to behave like an animal.'

Her words made Warren angry. 'Don't pull that crap with me, Anya. You behaved badly too.'

She squared up to him. 'When?'

'When Tahlia died. You had a hand in her death. You delayed her from reaching her machine and scanning the barcode before the clock ran out. She died from electrocution.'

Tahlia—did the name mean anything? A streak of pink flashed in her mind. A memory?

She folded her arms. 'That doesn't sound like something I'd do.'

'Exactly!' He tugged on clumps of his strawberry blond hair. 'Arcis turned us into people we didn't recognise.'

Having Warren near, chatting to him like the last three months never happened, disturbed her. But her fight was with the city now, not Warren.

She leaned against the wall. When Warren came closer, she put her hand up. 'That's close enough. I still don't trust you.'

He stopped where he was. She pinned her gaze on him. 'Why did you do it?'

It was a simple question, and she expected another excuse. Arcis hadn't turned them into anyone they weren't already. She didn't remember how they'd met, but she knew it was before the attack, and that she'd had her doubts about him even then.

Warren dropped his gaze to the ground, working the tip of his black boot through the gravel. 'Not my finest moment.' He looked up at her; it surprised her to see tears in his eyes. 'I needed to get to the ninth floor. That is the truth. June was impeding my progress on the fourth floor.'

Yes, she remembered. Canya's release of that memory had unlocked some of the events that took place after.

'It was a shitty thing to do to me.'

'It was.' He worked his jaw as if he were trying to hold back the tears. 'And I know that now. I couldn't see past my own problems.'

'What were you looking for on the ninth floor?'

Warren shrugged. 'I didn't find it.'

'Not what I asked.'

Warren sighed. 'My parents spoke about a place that existed beyond the towns and Praesidium's control.' *The Beyond.* 'They abandoned me to go there, left me to deal with this crap alone. I needed to find them and tell them they were wrong about me, that I could handle the truth. I stupidly thought the control centre in Arcis might have the coordinates.'

Anya recalled nothing about Warren's life before her amnesia. Had he told her this story before? She didn't think so. But the common denominator between all their stories was the Beyond.

While she would never trust Warren again, she would try to get past what he did to her—not for his sake, but her own. Right now, the Collective posed a bigger threat to her safety.

'Vanessa thinks I know where the place is, that my parents may have mentioned it in some conversation at home.'

Warren's eyes lit up, enough to confirm his story was real. 'But you don't remember.'

She shook her head and stared at the red-bricked building opposite her. 'I heard a lot of things that didn't make sense. But I don't remember them ever mentioning that place.'

Warren relaxed his stance; it reminded her to keep her own guard up.

'Just because we're talking doesn't mean we're friends.'

Warren's body stiffened again. He wiped away a tear with the back of his fist.

'I meant it when I said I was sorry. I used you to get to the ninth floor. I thought you'd be a good ally. You were, until Dom distracted you and you allied with him instead. I was left with no one.' He turned away and shook his head. 'It's no excuse for what I did.' He turned back. 'All I could think about was how to get off that floor. I didn't think of anyone but me.'

If Warren's story about her helping to kill Tahlia was true, perhaps that made Anya no better than Warren.

'Seems like we both did things we're not proud of.' The statement shocked her to say, but she felt in her gut that she'd behaved badly, even though she couldn't recall her actions. 'How about we try to be better people?'

Warren dried his eyes and nodded. 'I never wanted to hurt you. You were my friend.'

Were. They would never be more than politely civil to each other.

'Well, we're both intact. We made it out of there, even if we lost a part of ourselves doing it.' She couldn't believe what she was about to suggest. She thrust out her hands. 'Truce?'

Warren stared at her hand, then at her. 'Are you sure?'

She nodded. 'As long as you swear never to put anyone through that again.'

'I promise,' said Warren weakly, looking embarrassed.

He shook her hand once. She pulled it back before the feel of him brought her back to that place.

Charlie bolted out of nowhere, grabbed Warren by the shoulder and yanked him back. 'Stay away from her.'

Shocked, Anya stood frozen to the spot. A livid Charlie gripped Warren's arm and dragged the boy along with him.

'Get your hands off me!' said a panicked Warren.

He shot his gaze back to Anya.

Anya raced after them. 'Charlie, what are you doing?'

The old man stopped. She'd never seen him look so angry. 'Did this boy hurt you in Arcis?'

Her mouth opened and closed like a fish. 'Who told you? Was it Dom?'

She would kill him.

'Sheila did. She couldn't stay silent any longer and I'm glad she told me. What were you thinking, Anya?'

He resumed his walk, dragging Warren along. Warren kept up to avoid tripping. He looked fully resigned to his fate.

'That is my business. We were sorting it out.' She stumbled along after them. 'Where are you taking him?'

'To see Max. We can't have a rapist in the camp.'

'I'm not a rapist.' Warren's voice shook. 'It was

a mistake. I didn't mean to hurt anyone. I swear.'

Fat tears dropped from his eyes. Anya almost felt sorry for him. Almost.

Her hands and body shook from the shock.

Jason came out of the workshop, looking startled. 'What's going on?'

Without looking at him, Charlie kept pulling. 'This hooligan attacked your sister in Arcis. I'm taking him to Max.'

Jason's eyes rounded. 'What? When?' He grabbed Anya's shoulder turning her to him. 'Are you okay?'

She shucked him off and ran to catch up with the others. 'Yes.'

She was more than okay. This single event had proven that. Better still, those traumatic events no longer imprisoned her.

Charlie jerked a resigned Warren inside the town hall. Anya kept close to the pair, who moved fast along the corridor. A few soldiers in the town hall frowned as they passed.

Charlie opened the door to the strategy room and pushed Warren inside.

Max looked up in alarm. 'What's this, dad?'

Charlie breathed hard. The mild mannered barber's face scrunched up in anger took Anya aback.

He pointed at a shaking and fearful Warren. 'You tell him.'

'I attacked Anya in Arcis,' he whispered.

Charlie continued. 'Almost raped her, according

to Sheila. And he's wandering around this camp like he did nothing.'

'It's not like that.' His voice rose in protest.

Max slid his angry gaze to Anya. 'Is this true?'

She nodded, caught up in a strange haze. This was her business, nobody else's. If she'd wanted anyone to know she would have told them.

Movement fanned her hair around her face as Jason rushed forward, fist raised. He punched Warren square on the nose.

'Ah!' yelled Warren, scrunching up his eyes.

'Jason, stop it!'

Anya's cheeks burned.

Her brother pointed at a bent-over Warren. 'If you so much as look at her the wrong way, I'll kill you.'

'Enough!' said Max. He focused on Anya. 'I should lock Warren up for this, but I can see Charlie's intervention came as a shock to you.' That was an understatement. 'So, I leave the punishment up to you. What do you want to happen here?'

Warren straightened up, his hand covering his nose. He met her gaze briefly before dropping his to the floor.

She wanted to see him suffer more than he had, but they'd come to an agreement before Charlie had interrupted their discussion. Having more than just her knowing the story gave her a weird sense of calm. A calm she hadn't felt since her Copy had passed the memory back to her.

Eliza Green

Max, Charlie and Jason watched her carefully, waiting for her answer. What would she gain from further punishment in the middle of preparations for an upcoming battle? She had defended herself that night. She was no victim.

Anya pulled in a breath and released it. 'We need everyone ready to fight for when the machines come. You can lock him up if you want, but it doesn't matter. He can't hurt me anymore.'

Warren looked relieved, while the others did not.

'How much of a danger is he to others?' asked Max.

Anya couldn't say; she told him the truth. 'Arcis made us do some crazy things, and while that doesn't excuse Warren's behaviour, he wasn't acting in his right mind. We were under a lot of pressure.'

'We were. I was,' said Warren.

Anya glared at him and he stopped talking.

Her cheeks burned hotter with the attention on her. She was sick of thinking about it. 'Warren's punishment is to live with his guilt. Plus, it's enough that you all know.'

Max folded his arms. 'Are you sure?'

Anya nodded. She was, and grateful to Sheila for doing something she'd been too weak to manage.

She glanced at a relieved Warren, who nodded at her.

Jason growled. 'What did I just tell you?'

Anya placed a hand on his chest and shot him a

warning look.

To Warren she said, 'I didn't do it for you. I'm doing it for me.'

Max gave her a tight nod. 'The lady has spoken. But I want Warren supervised at all times. He won't be left alone with any of the females.'

Jason pointed at him. 'If you look at anyone for too long, I'll personally put you in the hospital.'

Warren, in good sense, didn't reply.

What Anya saw in the almost man was another victim of their tragic circumstances. She hoped he could live with his choices. She had to live with hers.

When this was all over, when they defeated the machines, she vowed to have nothing else to do with him.

There was no room left in her heart for enemies in this camp. Bigger dangers were coming and Anya had to prepare for them, like everyone else. Memories or not, she would help the rebels as much as she could. They had rescued her from Praesidium and, based on her only recollection of Arcis, they had helped her there too. Not to mention they'd kept her brother alive. She owed them.

But turning over a new leaf meant leaving the last three months behind. If she got her memories back, great, but it could no longer be her sole focus. That meant also leaving Dom behind.

From his interaction with the mystery woman, it appeared he'd already moved on.

23

Carissa

Her conversation with Anya had distracted Carissa from her wilful actions for only a short time. She returned to the workshop, hoping for a better diversion. Jason and Thomas continued to work under the Inventor's supervision. It surprised her that he wasn't the one sat in the chair working on the orb. He knew more about Praesidium's machines than either of the Originals.

The Inventor noticed her hovering by the door. If he was still angry with her since she'd told him about Quintus' promises to punish them, he didn't show it.

He hooked a finger at her and pointed to the chair in front of the worktable. 'We need you, miss. We need to record your command frequency again.'

Carissa had recorded her whistle for Thomas, but each time it failed to command the orb. She didn't know why. It sounded the same as the last time.

She sat in the chair and the Inventor pushed a recording device under her nose.

'Whistle into it.'

All eyes were on her as she puckered her lips and blew for the tenth time that day.

The Inventor clicked off the recording and hooked the device up to one of Thomas' machines. It played back her whistle, but the orb, which they had left intact, failed to react.

'Why isn't it working, Jacob?' she said.

'It can happen, miss. We're putting you on the spot. Maybe you're nervous.'

He rubbed his chin and studied the screen that Jason and Thomas monitored.

Jason looked up at the Inventor. 'We have the seven numbers that make up their frequency. Can't we just guess it?'

The Inventor shook his head. 'Too many variables with seven digits. We must hit this one on the head for it to work.'

Carissa understood what they planned to do with the recording of her voice: use it in a playback device that would be buried in the land beyond the anti-magnetic barrier, and attract the orbs to it. The digging machines couldn't pass the barrier, but the orbs could fly over the top of it, as this one had proved already. But why it was still active confused Carissa.

From her seated position, she looked up at the Inventor. 'Why haven't you destroyed this orb?'

The Inventor met her curious gaze. 'We've disabled its connection to Praesidium, miss. Now we want to see if we can reprogram it to listen to our own set of commands.'

'Use it to record like the city does?'

The Inventor nodded at her. 'That's the plan. It will give us eyes on the city. But it won't be much use unless we can get your command frequency to stop more orbs from coming here. The orbs can be reprogrammed if they're isolated from their pack. But when other orbs are around, they go into a hive mind formation. Like worker bees.'

Carissa understood. Similar to how the Copies listened to Quintus and the Collective ten. Independent in thought until his command, delivered through the NMC, called them to the Great Hall.

Similar to how she had behaved while in this camp, searching for a connection like a worker bee hunting for her queen. Feeling lost without her pack.

'Can't you just hook me up to one of your diagnostic machines? Find the code in my security file?'

'I wish.' He shook his head. 'The camps and towns are not equipped with the same tech that you'd find in Praesidium.'

'Why not?'

Both Jason and Thomas glanced up from their work.

'Because the city kept the best tech for themselves. By handing out old, worn tech to the towns, the city could keep the folks there reliant on them.'

The Inventor's criticism of the Collective's ways irritated her. She puffed out her chest. 'Maybe the towns weren't deserving of the technology. Maybe the Collective was worried they might break it. It took a lot of work to put the designs together.'

The Inventor perched his fists on his hips and glared at her. 'And who do you think built those machines, miss? Who do you think built them before that? Everything in that city came from people like me who were taken prisoner and forced to work there. The Collective only designed what it wanted. I and others before me had to build it.'

Carissa recoiled from the Inventor's harsh words. He'd been more subdued in the city. Both Jason and Thomas dropped their heads to hide behind the monitor.

Her own shoulders drooped. 'I just meant the towns weren't ready.'

'That's not the point, miss. You know the Collective was keeping humans prisoner there. You reasoned away your feelings about it by saying we were useful to the city. But we were also expendable.'

Carissa dropped her gaze. 'I'm sorry, Inventor. I'm worried, that's all.'

'At least she has remorse,' muttered Thomas.

She flashed her eyes up to see the Inventor shoot him a look. Thomas slid farther down.

Jacob let his fists fall to his side and huffed out

a breath. 'Why are you worried, miss?'

Her heart raced as she looked up at him. 'What will Quintus do to me when he comes? What will he do to the people in this camp? Will he make me go back?'

The Inventor shook his head, but it didn't put her mind at ease. 'No matter what he promised you, he won't take you back. You've shown independent thought. He won't want you upsetting his or the Collective's plans. Most likely, he will terminate you.'

She shuddered hard at the thought. 'And you, Inventor?'

Quintus had already said he would return the escapees to the city and make them work until they were of no further use.

He nodded. 'And Rover. Everyone in this camp.'

She feared for the beast who had become her friend.

She steadied her nerves and sat up straight. 'I want to try whistling again.'

'Okay.'

He took the recording device from Jason and she whistled into it. He handed it back to Jason, who hooked it up and played a direct feed to the inactive orb. But at a shake of his head, she knew it hadn't worked.

'Miss, you're too nervous. The whistle, the command frequency, it's a part of you. You need to relax, not think about it.' The Inventor glanced at the door. 'I have an idea.'

He pulled her up to stand and took the device from Jason once more. He set it to record. 'Miss, I want you to call Rover.'

Thomas stood up fast, knocking over his chair. 'That thing's coming here? I don't think so.'

Jason pulled him back down.

'Rover is under my command,' said the old man.

Thomas nodded to Carissa. 'And hers apparently.'

The Inventor placated him with open hands. 'Trust me. I wouldn't have brought the Guardian here if I thought he could hurt us.'

Thomas appeared to settle, but his wide eyes said he was still nervous. 'Okay, but I don't have to like it.'

The Inventor turned to Carissa. 'Go.'

Carissa drew in a long breath and blew through pursed lips. It sounded strong and sharp. But no wolf came. She relaxed her mind and tried again. Nothing. She emptied all thoughts of Quintus from her mind and tried again. Nothing.

She blew out a breath and closed her eyes. She searched for her security files, but they were no longer accessible since she had disabled her link to the city. But Quintus could contact her, so did that mean her NMC had fixed the damage done to it? She shook away that thought. If Quintus planned to hurt her friends, he would not get to talk to her again.

She remembered playing with her orb within the city's confines. She imagined playing with Rover instead, him hiding and her calling him. Then she whistled.

A thundering noise broke her out of her thoughts.

Her eyes shot open to see a metallic face with a part organic tongue lolling to the side peering through the door. Rover's eyes were set wide with anticipation. He bounded inside the room, almost knocking Carissa to the floor. She laughed and patted Rover on the nose before commanding him to sit. He did and she looked around her. A shocked Thomas took the recorder from a smiling Inventor, while a chuckling Jason hooked up the new recording to the machine. Rover's mechanical breathing filled the quiet in the room.

Jason played the command silently to the orb. It twisted on the table, then hovered in the air. He turned it off and it dropped to the table once more.

'Well done, you two,' said the Inventor with a clap of his hands. 'We have our command frequency to control the orbs from the city. And now we can set a new command to control this orb.'

24

Dom

Dom punched the boxing bag until the pain in his left arm receded. Recalling what the medics had done to him in Praesidium came out in flurries of anger during moments of confusion. Kaylie being here confused him the most, but he couldn't blame her arrival for why he'd singled Warren out in training. If he was being honest, his actions hadn't been about Anya either, but to claw back a sense of control that continued to elude him in the camp.

He punched the bag harder, imagining the male medic's face there, the one who'd lied to him about his mother being alive. Never would he be a victim again. Half his life had been spent under his father's unrelenting control.

Evening approached and emptied the courtyard of soldiers. Sounds from the dining hall drifted through the open door as the rebels sat down to dinner. This was the time he loved most, when it was just him. No distractions, nobody demanding something from him. He just wished thoughts of his time as a prisoner wouldn't mark these quiet moments.

The second he stopped boxing, the dulled pain intensified suddenly and shot up his left arm into his shoulder. He winced at the constant reminder of what they'd done to him.

A sound at the door alerted him to company. He paused before his next punch.

'What did that bag ever do to you?'

He turned to see June Shaw standing there. She looked paler than before, but he guessed that's what happened when you got food poisoning. According to the camp's lead medic, June was hit with a bad strain of it.

Just her, nobody else.

He wiped a layer of sweat from his brow. 'Just working out my issues.'

She entered the open-sided space, heading towards the stationary bike. Dressed in casual clothes, she carried a towel under her arm.

'I was hoping to do some light training this evening.'

He didn't think she looked well enough to train. 'How are you feeling? What did you eat exactly?'

June shrugged and tightened her ponytail of fine, blonde hair. She walked over to the bike. 'I ate and drank the same as everyone else. It must have reacted with something I was given in Praesidium.'

Dom nodded. That made sense. None of them knew exactly what drugs the Copy medics had fed them. 'Maybe. Keep it light this evening, just in case. We might be heading out tomorrow.'

June's eyes widened. 'Really? I heard Anya's brother was working on something.'

Dom nodded. 'Thomas and Jacob too. A way to control the orbs that might try to pinpoint our location.'

'Well, that's one less problem to worry about.' She climbed onto the stationary bike and began to pedal. 'I'll make sure I'm ready by then.'

'Just take it easy, Shaw. I know how competitive you can get.'

She blew a raspberry. 'No more than you, Pavesi.'

She sped up, ignoring her earlier remarks about doing light training.

Dom returned to the bag and hit it again. The action numbed his left arm for a while. But he couldn't keep hitting the bag just to chase away the pain. The second he stopped, the pain returned to his arm, making it difficult for him to form a fist. He turned his limb one way, then the other. His skin had been fully repaired with no hint of a scar. His arm looked perfectly normal.

June let out a sudden cry. Dom's gaze shot over to her. She had stopped cycling and was doubled over the bike.

He ran over to her and eased her off the seat. 'I

told you to take it easy.'

June looked up at him, panic in her eyes.

In a whisper, she said, 'Take me back to the medical bay. Something's not right.'

She cried out again.

'Shit, okay.'

He looked around for someone to help, but it was just the two of them.

Despite the pain that made his left arm throb, he lifted June up into his arms and carried her back to the makeshift hospital.

Sweat formed on her brow. 'I probably could have walked there.'

'Not on my watch. Besides, I'll get us there faster.'

He felt June jerk in his arms. His grip tightened, which only intensified his pain. The medical facilities were just a short walk from the courtyard, but with June in his arms and an aching limb, it might as well have been miles away. His muscles strained against her weight as he used his back to open the double doors.

The female military medic looked up in surprise.

With a frown, she said, 'I just released her.'

'And now she's back.' He carried her over to the nearest bed, his muscles blazing with the worst fire ever. 'Whatever you did for her, it didn't work.'

He placed a writhing June down on one of the beds.

The medic stared down at her. 'I just gave her saline. She was dehydrated. There's nothing physically wrong with her.'

Dom nodded to June. 'Clearly there is.'

Another pain shot up his left arm and he winced.

'What's wrong with your arm?'

Dom flexed his fingers, which eased the tight feeling a little.

He blinked and said, 'Nothing. Just look after her.'

A second medic, a young man, rushed over and both medics dragged whatever equipment they had, which wasn't much, to her side. IV drips, a skin repair tool, plus other simple items formed the basis of this much needed hospital. What he wouldn't give to have access to the superior equipment in the city.

The female medic inserted a needle into June's arm and fed her something. Morphine possibly.

But it only caused June to buck and writhe more. 'No! Something's wrong. Take it out.'

The medic panicked and yanked out the needle. She rolled up her T-shirt to expose her belly.

Dom jerked back when he saw movement under her skin. 'What the hell's that?'

The female medic stared at it in shock. 'I don't know.'

She reached out her hand slowly, then touched June's belly. June turned her head away. The imprint of a small hand against her skin appeared, then disappeared.

'Is she... pregnant?'

The female medic snatched her hand away. 'Looks like it.'

That didn't make sense. 'But how? She wasn't paired with anyone.'

The soldier looked at her colleague. 'Unless they injected her with something.'

Carissa would know. Dom turned to get her, but the pain in his arm blazed, fading to leave his arm numb.

'Oh shit...' His limb dangled uselessly by his side. 'What's wrong with my arm?'

The male medic steered a shocked Dom over to a spare bed and sat him down. 'It could be the tech they put in you. Your arm was in bad shape when you arrived. It's possible your immune system's rejecting it.'

But that couldn't be it. Jacob had injected fluid from the Guardian wolf so his body would accept the changes.

'Well, whatever it's doing, it can wait.' He pushed the male medic away. 'Get Carissa and Jacob. They'll know what to do for June.'

The medic ran off and returned with the Copy and the man she referred to as the Inventor.

'Holy god,' said a shocked Jacob as June cried out in pain again. 'What happened here?'

Carissa went straight to June's side. 'What's wrong?'

When June wouldn't answer her, Jacob spoke to the medics. 'What's happening, please?'

'June appears to be pregnant.' The female medic shook her head, as if it were impossible. 'And Dom's left arm is paralysed.'

Jacob gave Dom a glance as if to say he'd deal with him later. To Dom's relief, he tended to June first. Jacob spoke to the Copy who looked terrified standing by June's bed. 'Carissa, what did they do to her?'

The wide-eyed Copy stepped back and hugged her middle. 'She was to act as an incubator for a foetus. They may have already implanted her by the time we got her out.'

Jacob visually examined her belly. 'Why is it growing so fast?'

'They sometimes implant a hormone capsule to continue growth while she's out of the growth accelerator machine.'

Jacob nodded and looked at both medics. 'Okay, so we take the foetus out.'

Carissa shook her head. 'It's not possible here. The machine you would need to extract the foetus is in the city. If we take it out, we could end up killing it.'

Dom couldn't believe the Copy was advocating to save the life of an unborn freak over June. 'But it could kill June, if it's growing as fast as you say.'

The female medic agreed with him. 'He's right. Her body isn't built for that kind of rapid change.'

The doors opened and Max and Vanessa burst in.

'What's going on?' said Max, striding over to June's bed.

Jacob explained, 'June was inseminated before we left the city. The foetus is growing too fast for her body to cope with.'

'I was afraid of this.' Vanessa shook her head. 'We found her on a bed. She had IVs stuck in her arms. Carissa, do something to help her.'

'What can I do?' said the Copy.

Dom watched from his bed as they decided June's fate. As his lifeless arm lay dead by his side, something occurred to him from his time under the knife. 'The Copies, they don't age. Could Carissa have something inside her to stop the growth?'

Jacob's eyes widened. Both Max and Vanessa looked relieved at the suggestion.

Vanessa said to Max, 'If we can stop it from growing too fast, it will give her body time to adjust.'

'Adjust?' said a terrified June. 'I don't want to be pregnant. I don't want this... thing inside me.'

'Then what?' said Max, ignoring June's protestations. 'She sees out the next nine months with god knows what growing in her belly?'

'I said I don't want this,' June repeated.

Dom reached over and grabbed June's hand. She shot him an alarmed look.

'It will be okay. I won't let anything happen to you.'

Still holding her hand, he spoke to Jacob. 'Does Carissa have any growth repressors that might work?'

Jacob nodded slowly. 'The Copies store them in their biogel to keep their bodies and organs at the same size. If I take a biogel sample from her, I could inject it straight into June's womb. The inert biogel would be harmless to June. To separate out the repressors from the gel would take a lab, plus time and equipment we don't have.'

June crushed Dom's good hand.

'It's the fastest way,' he said to reassure her. 'The alternative is this thing bursts out of your belly.'

June relaxed her grip and nodded at Jacob.

The city's inventor pursed his lips. 'Okay, I'll need to take a sample from you, Carissa.'

Carissa already had her sleeve rolled up. Jacob took a needle from one of the medics while a worried Max and Vanessa looked on.

Dom stared down at his dead limb. This had to work. June was a part of their rebel family—a part of his and Sheila's family.

Jacob drew clear fluid from Carissa's arm and wasted no time in injecting it straight into June's belly. The hand imprint appeared, as if searching for a way out. June gasped as it probed her belly. But then it disappeared and everything went calm. June sighed with relief, but the fear in her eyes remained.

'That's it?' said Dom.

Jacob nodded. 'It should stop the foetus from developing more, and might even calm it down.'

'But it's only a temporary solution?' said Max.

Jacob nodded. 'As Carissa said, this baby will need to come out. That will mean returning to the city. This just buys us time.'

Max nodded, then walked over to Dom. He glanced down at his left arm. 'What happened to you? Why are you in a bed?'

As if June's problem was all but forgotten, everyone focused on Dom.

'His arm is paralysed,' said the male medic. 'We think his body is rejecting the tech.'

Jacob walked over and sat down beside him. 'That's impossible.'

He picked up Dom's dead arm and rotated it. It felt like it belonged to someone else.

'I'm going to have to open it up. We may need to consider surgery.'

Dom's eyes widened. 'Surgery? No way.'

'Well, it's either that or you lose the use of this arm,' said Jacob, placing it back down on his lap. 'Your body wasn't designed to house this much technology.'

Yet, it hadn't stopped the Collective from operating on him. In fact, he'd been due to have all his organs replaced.

'My arm feels fine. In fact, I can feel it again.'

He wasn't lying. A tingle started in his fingers that gave him hope. He moved the tip of one finger.

Jacob stared at it. 'Well, I never. It must be creating new nerve pathways. It's possible your nerves weren't up for the job of controlling the arm so the tech killed them, or switched them off temporarily.'

Encouraged by that suggestion, Dom flexed his hand. 'I feel the strength returning.'

New feeling shot up his arm. It no longer blazed with a deadly heat. He assumed the worst of it had been due to the Collective's technology severing his nerves.

He lifted his arm up from the bed and sighed with relief.

But Jacob didn't look happy. He rubbed his chin and frowned. 'Still, I'd like to open you up, make sure it hasn't done any damage.'

No more surgeries.

Jacob picked up a laser scalpel and came at Dom.

Panic swelled in his chest and he shuffled back. 'No! Keep that thing away from me.'

'Hold him down,' said Jacob to the medics.

They grabbed an arm each. Max held his feet.

To Dom, Jacob said, 'I'm sorry, but I need to take a look. I need to see what this tech is doing to your organic matter.'

The restraints on his body brought it all back. The same panic flared inside him at his new lack of freedom, similar to when he'd been strapped down on the Collective's operating table.

Dom squeezed his eyes shut and dragged new air through his teeth. 'I said no!'

He shoved against the restraint. His left arm, held down by the male medic, flew up and knocked the medic back. He hit the ground and stared up at him, stunned.

Dom scooted back on the bed and out of Jacob's reach. The Inventor paused with the scalpel in his hand, a look of shock on his face.

'I'm sorry,' said Dom to the medic on the ground.

Jacob regained his composure. 'I guess we can rule out an issue with your arm.' He frowned. 'Looks like you've been infused with Copy super strength.'

25

Dom

In his dorm bed, Dom flexed his arm. It felt strong, no longer riddled with the pain that had almost driven him to cut off his limb. Had his nerves really been rewiring themselves?

The military medic had given him the all clear to leave the medical bay and he'd slept like a brick last night. That morning, however, the thought that Praesidium's tech had been altering his DNA somehow propelled him out of bed. Maybe he should let Jacob open him up to make sure he wasn't turning into a machine.

While the medic had given him the all clear to leave, June had not been granted the same permission. He walked back to the medical bay to find her sitting up in bed and eating food. Alex sat beside her on the bed. Her skin had returned to a healthier colour.

'Morning,' he said as he approached her.

June and Alex held hands. Alex was clutching

hers so tight one might think he was the patient.

'Hey,' June replied with a smile. 'Thanks for helping me last night. I don't know what I would have done.'

'You should have come found me,' Alex growled at her. 'I wasn't far.'

June nodded and lowered her eyes. 'I'm sorry. I didn't think.'

Dom stepped closer to the bed. 'How are you feeling?'

June grazed her belly with the fingers of her free hand. 'I'd feel better if I didn't have whatever this is growing inside me. I don't want it, Dom. I'm too young to do this.'

'One step at a time,' said Dom, hoping his words would reassure her.

He remembered his own rising, desperate panic when Praesidium's machines had fitted his new forearm bones. He couldn't imagine what it would be like to have a living being inside him.

Alex looked close to tears. It was clear to Dom he cared for June.

He was a Breeder. Would he know anything about the thing growing inside of June?

'Alex,' he said. The blond-haired boy looked up. 'We haven't been properly introduced. I'm Dom.'

He extended his hand and the young man shook it.

With a nod, Alex said, 'We met in the city's medical facility, but you were too out of it to remember.'

Dom could barely remember his own name back then. 'I guess that's what a heavy infection will do to a person.' He folded his arms. 'Do you know what the city did to June?'

'Probably more than anyone else here. I told the medics here what I could about the procedure.' He let go of June's hand and stood up. With a sigh, he said, 'A crude way to describe it, but there were two types of "vessels". Girls like Anya were paired with a boy like me. The plan was for me to impregnate her.' Dom hid his shudder. 'The Collective would expect her to carry the foetus for three months, then June would act as an incubator, to carry the baby for the rest of the time.'

'Would they have let Anya go after they took out her foetus?'

Alex shook his head. 'She would have continued a new cycle and another, until they had no further use for her. A young woman was only as useful as her reproductive system. If the babies produced from our pairing didn't measure up to the Collective's requirements to make hybrids, she would have been terminated.'

June sat up straight. 'So girls—women—were expendable?'

Alex nodded. 'Pretty much. The Collective thinks like a machine. It doesn't understand or care about psychological or physical torture. Its Copies learn that behaviour from them.'

Dom could attest to that. The Copies who did the Collective's bidding had been cold and unfeeling, except for one. And Quintus had wanted to turn Dom into a machine without his consent.

'So Anya and others like her would have been kept prisoners indefinitely?'

Alex pursed his lips as if there was more to it. 'For the last two years, that was the way it had been done. Then the rebels infiltrated Arcis and the Collective began to speed up its testing, taking the foetus out earlier and using the growth acceleration machine on the carriers to bring it, and the resulting babies, to maturation faster.'

Dom remembered something he'd seen in Arcis on the seventh floor. His group had been expected to care for babies, but he and Anya had discovered a second area behind a curtained off section. Children ranging in ages from four to six played alone. They had scars like him.

He relayed the story to them both. June looked shocked; her memories, like Anya's, were gone.

But Alex just nodded. 'The babies were the product of my and other Breeders' work. The children are... were hybrids, fitted with Fifth Gen tech to create hardier versions of the children born by conception alone.'

June rubbed her belly. 'So this thing inside me is normal?'

'Most likely.'

'Most likely?' repeated June.

'We can't be sure what drugs the Copy medics gave you, or what effect it had on the foetus.'

June pulled back the covers and went to stand up, prompting a nervous Alex to stick his arm out. 'Where do you think you're going?'

She looked at both Dom and Alex. 'I'm leaving. The medic said I could.'

Dom stared at her. 'But you're pregnant. You should be on bed rest.'

'Listen to the caveman over here.' June rolled her eyes at the pair. 'Women have been getting on while pregnant for centuries. We potentially have a deluge of machines on their way to our location and I refuse to sit here and do nothing. I can do something less strenuous, like help to train the non-soldiers.'

Dom relaxed at that suggestion. He'd pictured June running straight into the fight. He could live with her carrying out a static task.

With a nod, he said, 'In that case, I've got the newbies to train. Can you show them how to shoot?'

June smiled. 'That I can do.' With Alex's help, she stood. Then she said to him, 'You wanna learn how to fire a gun?'

Alex smiled and nodded. 'Hell yeah.'

They walked outside, where Dom parted ways with June and Alex, but not before he left her with strict instructions to keep an eye on Warren.

'Will do,' she said, even though she probably didn't remember why Dom hated him.

He returned to the courtyard. The extra rebels

that travelled with Kaylie had started drill training, under Julius and Imogen's watchful eye.

Kaylie stood back from the session, watching the progress. Dom stopped next to her.

'Hey, handsome,' she said glancing up at his profile. 'Where did you get to last night? I looked for you after dinner but you were gone.'

Dom rubbed his arm. 'I had to do something.'

In his peripheral vision, Kaylie watched him.

'Mysterious,' she said before sliding her eyes to the front. 'They're ready to do something more than exercise.'

So was Dom. But camp was the safest place to be without a plan. 'Jacob and his team are working on something. We should hear back soon.'

For an hour, Dom watched the action until all drills set by Julius and Imogen had been completed. Sheila was switching between running laps and watching Imogen work. Julius pushed his team the hardest and shouted commands at the weaker ones in the group. On occasion, he would glance over at Dom.

Dom flexed his muscles, needing to work off his excess energy with the punching bag. A sudden commotion outside the courtyard entrance cut through his plans.

His heart beat sped up when Jason and Thomas strode towards the town hall. Jason held a bullhorn in his hand with a small, black device taped to the side. When he saw Jacob following with the orb in his hand, Dom excused himself and cut through the dining hall to intercept them. Kaylie, Julius and Sheila followed him down the corridor to the battle strategy room at the end.

'What's happening?' Sheila asked him.

'I don't know.'

He entered the room to see Max examining the device that Jason held. Julius pushed past him to make it to Max. Max's second in command had a sense of urgency and arrogance that Dom didn't like. Imogen made her way to the top, more politely than Julius. The Inventor stood off to the side, holding the orb like it was an offering.

'Have we got something we can use?' said Dom.

Max smiled and nodded. 'They isolated Carissa's command frequency to play through the bullhorn and also reprogrammed the orb to listen to a new command.'

'How will we use the orb?' said Sheila.

Jacob answered, 'In theory, to scout out the area and see what direction they will approach from. Assuming they don't catch it, I'm hoping it will act as our eyes out there.'

Dom examined the device in Jason's hand. 'So we bury the bullhorn and the recorder. Will the device work remotely?'

Jason shook his head. 'The anti-magnetic field will screw up any signal we try to send out. We need someone to be on the other side of the barrier. That creates a problem for cover. There's nothing but stony landscape out there.'

'We have another way,' said Jacob. Everyone looked at him. 'Carissa went high and got past the barrier. If we put someone on the mountain, the signal might work.'

'And if it doesn't?' said Julius.

Jacob shrugged. 'Then we're sitting ducks in here. The machines won't stop until they get what they want. Quintus—the Collective—will see to that. Our best bet is the orb.' He held it up. 'If we can capture more of them, we might be able to reprogram the orbs and use them to defend this place.'

Julius blew out a long breath. 'That's a long shot.'

Max nodded in agreement. 'We can't be sure this one will return when it scouts out the area.'

'Well, there's only one way to test it out: to get out there,' said Jacob.

'Going high is not an option,' said Jason. 'The bullhorn doesn't have enough range. We need to bury it beyond our anti-magnetic field, stop the orbs before they hit the valley.'

A soldier not much older than Dom burst into the room. 'Max, there's another orb flying over the camp. Shall I get the Copy?'

'No, leave her out of it,' said Jacob. He dropped the orb into Dom's hand and said to Jason, 'Let's test out our device, shall we?'

Jason led the way with Thomas and Jacob close

behind. Dom kept to the rear with Max, Julius, Sheila and Kaylie, still holding onto the orb that had attempted to transmit data back to the city. It felt cold in his hand and he hated touching it. Julius kept close to him as if he didn't trust him to look after an object from the city. But Dom was as much a part of Praesidium as this orb and Carissa. He'd been violated and turned into something else. What that was, he still didn't know.

Outside, he spotted the rogue orb flying high overhead. Soldiers pointed guns at the object, which darted every which way. One of the soldiers held the Disruptor gun, the same one they'd used to shoot the first one down. Their efforts had attracted quite the crowd.

Jason pointed the bullhorn into the air while Thomas pressed a button on a screen he held that probably controlled the recording. A whistle sounded through the horn, but the orb continued to dart overhead. The orb in Dom's hand remained inactive. He didn't see how much use this one would be.

Jacob cursed. 'Maybe it can't hear it from up there.'

Carissa rushed over to the Inventor's side from the direction of the alleyway. Her wide eyes flitted between Jacob and the orb. 'What can I do?'

'Carissa,' Jacob said, beckoning her close. 'How close was the orb to you when you called it last time?'

She narrowed her gaze as she took in the

proximity of the flying orb. She looked back at him. 'Closer than this. I can whistle for it again?'

Jacob patted her on the shoulder. 'No, we need it to respond to the device.' To the boys he said, 'Increase the volume. It might hear it better from up there.'

Jason cranked up the volume dial on the bullhorn to maximum and darted over to the courtyard wall. With a couple of soldiers offering their hands as footholds, he climbed onto the top of the wall. Wobbling on the narrow, flat surface, he lifted the bullhorn up higher.

'Everybody quiet,' hissed Max.

Thomas hit a button on his screen and the recorded whistle bounced around the mountainsides in a strange echo. The sound sent an eerie chill through Dom.

The orb stopped darting and swooped in for a closer look.

'Again!' demanded Jacob.

Thomas replayed the noise and the orb came to hover in front of the bullhorn in Jason's outstretched hand. He climbed down carefully from the wall and, to Dom's relief, the orb followed him. He separated himself from the new orb long enough for the soldier with the Disruptor gun to stun it. Then the soldier used the gun to drain it of its power. The orb dropped to the ground with a thud.

Surprisingly, the orb in Dom's hand never moved.

Max said, 'If one is here, more are on the way.' He strode up to the gate. 'Let's set things up outside before they get here.'

26

Anya

Anya had been watching June show Jerome, Alex and, reluctantly, Warren how to shoot when the commotion with the orb drew them away from their practice. She arrived at the courtyard to see her brother climbing down from the wall with the orb in tow.

When the soldier shot the orb, June passed the revolver to Anya. 'You know how to shoot, right?'

Anya nodded. 'But I think you're supposed to stay here.'

June had relayed her condition to Anya. At least the rapid growth had been stemmed for now.

June smirked at her. 'Can't help it. I'm a soldier first. I promise I'll only watch.' She paused, her smirk dropping away. 'Will you be okay with the guys?'

Anya nodded, appreciating her concern. Warren no longer felt like the threat he once was.

An angry Alex protested. 'June, I won't let you

leave.'

It was clear he cared for June, but from what Anya had gathered about the feisty, blonde-haired rebel, being told what to do never ended well.

Not surprisingly, a wide-eyed June rounded on him. 'Won't let me? You don't own me. This *thing* inside me doesn't own me. I do what I want when I want.'

She stormed off to follow the others.

'Harsh,' said Jerome.

Warren chuckled but stopped when Anya flashed him a hard look.

'Sorry,' he muttered.

Alex looked ready to follow June, but Anya stopped him with a hand on his arm. 'Give her space. She's dealing with a lot of things. We humans aren't used to people controlling our every move.'

His gaze followed June. 'But I just want to keep her safe.'

She patted his arm, drawing his attention to her. 'And you're being a good friend by caring. But from what I remember of June, the more you push, the harder she pushes back.'

'I can vouch for that,' said Warren.

'Me too,' said Jerome. Both of them bypassed the memory-stealing machine on the ninth floor. 'She used to be the most competitive among us. She and Frank, a friend of ours, would bet each other over the stupidest things.' Jerome smiled sadly, as if remembering. 'If you want to keep her on side, leave her be.'

Warren made a noise. 'Didn't help where I was concerned.'

Anya glared at him. 'I think you deserved everything you got, don't you?'

Warren lowered his eyes, his lips pressed together.

He referred to his and June's pairing on the fourth floor—that much Anya remembered. June had been scuppering his chance to rotate. It was what had led Warren to attack Anya.

Jerome elbowed Warren. 'What's that about? You two were acting weird enough with each other in Arcis. I thought you'd be over it by now.'

'We are,' said Anya, not wanting to get into the details.

Warren straightened up, cleared his throat. 'So are we going to stand around and gossip like women, or can we shoot something?'

That was the best idea Anya had heard all day.

'The others will look to us to defend this place, if needed, so we must learn fast,' she said.

Alex nodded, as did the others.

She stood back from the paper target that June had pinned to the wall of an unoccupied property. She set the gun, supported her hand and fired once. 'Never rest your finger on the trigger. Only touch it when you're ready to fire. And use the pad of your first finger, not the crook.'

She handed the gun to Alex next, who did a

good job of copying her technique. She gave them six rounds each.

Warren was next, then Jerome. After June's lesson and the one with Dom before, they were getting more comfortable with using the guns.

Jerome handed the gun back to Anya. She checked the chamber, then slipped it into the waistband of her combats.

'Won't we be using different guns against the machines?' he asked.

Anya shook her head. 'You might not be using anything.'

The non-soldiers would only be called up as a last resort. But Anya had training and she planned to be front and centre when the machines came. She needed to do it for her family, and for what the city had taken from her.

'But yes, you're right,' she continued. 'There are better guns, some that can change the molecular structure of the machines and draw power from them, to render them inactive.'

Jerome's eyes widened suddenly. 'Do they work on biogel?'

Anya shrugged, not seeing how that mattered. 'I guess so.'

Alex explained. 'Jerome wants to know if the guns will work on him. He's a newborn, and no different to a Copy, except he was never connected to the Collective.'

Anya cursed her own insensitivity. 'I'm sorry,

Jerome. I keep forgetting what you are. I never really thought of you as anything other than human.'

Alex laughed and shook his head. The others stared at him, including Anya.

'What's so funny?'

'All that time I was stuck in my room and fed a bunch of drugs, all so I could help to create a controllable being that could pass as human?' He gestured to Jerome. 'Well, here he is.'

Jerome grew angry. 'Nobody controls me.'

'No,' said Alex, 'But you were created. You are a child of the city.'

Anya had never thought of it like that before. She remembered her own newborn, the one called Canya. 'So what went wrong, with their experiment, I mean?'

Alex folded his arms. 'I'd say, they got it right. Their mistake? Controlling the Copies so much that they wiped all natural emotions from them. Take your Copy, for instance. Raw and unmanageable.' Anya didn't disagree. 'But as soon as she reached maturity, she would have calmed down. That's the point at which the newborns lose all their memories, and are essentially wiped of their human traits before they're given their NMC. But Jerome here, he's what happens when you allow nature to take its course. His teachers? Humans. The newborns are like sponges.'

Anya was beginning to understand. And she didn't like the lesson. 'So, if the Collective had created newborns and allowed them to keep their memories, they would be indistinguishable from humans?'

'Except for their eyes, yes,' said Alex.

'So we could tell them apart using that feature?'

'Did you figure out Jerome? Sometimes the eyes aren't different enough. And if they are, they could be explained by quirky genetics if the newborns' mannerisms presented as human-like.'

The others stayed quiet.

'But we know and like Jerome. What makes him so different from other Copies?'

Alex smiled. 'He is exactly who the Collective tried to create: a Copy indistinguishable from a human. If we can learn from him, we might learn the machines' weaknesses and take down the city.'

27

Dom

Carrying the Disruptor in his hand and a pair of binoculars around his neck, Dom followed Max out of the camp. His leader held on to the Atomiser while soldiers followed with electricity shooting weapons.

The Atomiser had a crude, boxy design with a short, fat barrel soldered to the front of the homemade weapon. It looked more like a school project than a major weapon built to fight Praesidium's technology. But despite its appearance, the Disruptor had allowed Max's team to infiltrate Arcis and rescue the participants who never made it to the portal on the ninth floor.

The feeling in his left arm had returned to normal, despite the new strength that Dom had yet to test out properly. It made sense, he supposed, that an arm containing Fifth Gen metal bones would prove useful. Maybe the Collective wasn't just looking for their Copy, Breeder and Guardian. Maybe their search included Dom too.

He tried not to think about how his upgrades might have increased his worth to the Collective.

Jason, Thomas and Jacob followed the lead group. Jason carried the bullhorn while Thomas gripped the screen with the remote control for the recorder. Jacob held on tight to the reprogrammed orb that, to Dom's relief, was still inactive. Bringing up the rear of their group were three more armed soldiers who also carried shovels.

They entered the valley to the front of the camp, which was nestled back far enough to be invisible to those passing the neck of the Ferrous mountain range. Dom looked up as they approached the anti-magnetic field. The mid-morning sun glinted off the guns belonging to the spotters.

The air thickened suddenly, creating resistance against his arms and torso. Both the gun in his hand and the binoculars around his neck lifted up as if they had a life of their own. He fought the resistance, not only to the metal he carried, but to the metal inside him. The invisible barrier squeezed him tighter the more progress he made.

The Disruptor in his hand had weighed little before, but now it weighed a tonne. It resisted the space between him and the field, as the anti-magnetic field repelled the metal atoms.

Jason struggled to move too with the bullhorn in his hand. In fact, the anti-magnetic field had slowed everyone's movements down to an almost crawl.

'This won't work,' huffed Max. With great difficulty, he removed a walkie talkie from his belt and pressed the button on the side. 'Dad, it's no good; we can't pass it. I'll need you to turn off the barrier.'

Max waited a moment. The load in Dom's arm lightened suddenly.

The colonel slipped the walkie talkie back into the pouch on his belt. A collective sigh of relief came from the soldiers. Everyone carried on under the watchful eye of the spotters. But the service elevator to their right limited how far the spotters could travel along the shelf. Scopes would provide them with the extra visual distance they needed.

'How far out do we need to go?' asked Dom.

Jacob replied from behind him. 'Far enough so we can get a visual on the orbs.'

Thoughts of a swarm of orbs descending on his location terrified Dom. He hoped the city wasn't as armed as he imagined it would be. From his time as prisoner, he hadn't seen much, except for what medical equipment they used. And he'd been in too much pain to remember much detail about his escape. But Quintus, who had ordered his heart to be replaced on the next surgery, wasn't someone likely to forget about them.

They trekked through the rocky terrain of the valley bed, surrounded by walls of sheer rock on either side. The valley floor was dotted with large chunks of rock, dislodged from above. His pulse hammered the closer they got to the mouth of the valley, to the area that would put them all at risk. Revealing their location would hand an advantage to the city. Max went first, followed by Jacob and half of the soldiers.

Dom gripped the Disruptor tight and steadied his pulse as he stayed back with Jason and Thomas, and the remaining three soldiers.

He waited for Max to give the signal.

Max waved his arm once, a sign that it was safe to proceed. Dom emerged from the sheltered valley onto the open plain. The city was too far to see from this distance. So too were the towns. A sigh of relief passed his lips when he saw nothing between them and the next patch of civilisation. If the machines brought the fight to them, there would be no place to hide, except in the camp. It would also be impossible to sneak out of the camp without being seen. The camp provided good camouflage, but it had also trapped them.

He pressed the binoculars to his eyes and checked for any sign that new orbs were on their way. The one in Jacob's hand remained idle.

Jason moved out in front with the bullhorn. Thomas followed with the screen.

'Does the screen act as a remote controller?' asked Dom, removing the binoculars.

'Among other things,' replied Thomas.

'How much range does it have?'

Thomas checked it by walking back from Jason

and the bullhorn. 'I'd say about twenty feet from this rock, if we're lucky.'

He patted the rock face that marked the entrance point to the valley.

Jason counted out twenty feet from where Thomas stood, then stopped. Thomas checked his screen and waved him closer, finally putting his hand up.

He met Jason where he stood and pointed down. 'Seventeen feet. The signal drops off any farther out than that.' He tapped his foot once on the hard, flat ground. 'We should bury it here.'

Max checked the landscape through a set of his own binoculars and said, 'There's nothing out there, but it doesn't mean anything.' He brought them down. 'These things can move fast. Best get digging.'

He nodded at the three soldiers who carried shovels as well as weapons. They handed their weapons to Max and got to digging.

When they'd gone deep enough, Jason told them to stop. He set the device in the bone-dry soil, making sure the amplifier of the bullhorn lined up with the surface. Jason and Thomas dropped to their knees and covered both the bullhorn and the recorder attached to its side.

'It should be invisible to the naked eye,' Jacob said to the pair. 'The orbs are also recording devices, so we don't want them to see it's out here. But the amplifier needs to be close enough to the surface that it's not distorted by the clay above it.'

When the two men finished covering it with a thin layer of soil, Thomas picked up his screen and stood, then pressed a button on it. A muffled whistle played once through the soil. Dom hoped it would be loud enough for the orbs to hear when they came. Two had already arrived, the last one probably on a mission to find the first one. It would only be a matter of time before more came. The orb in Jacob's hand remained inactive.

Max checked the landscape through his binoculars again

He cursed. 'Activity in the area. We need to hurry.'

Jacob tossed the orb into the air and caught it. 'We have a weapon. It's not much, but it might distract them if it's seen flying in the opposite direction. They have a hive-like mind.'

While Max and Jacob discussed tactics, Dom checked the landscape for himself. His heart raced double-time upon seeing dozens of orbs headed straight for their location. That confirmed one of two things: either the first scout had transmitted its location, or Carissa's brief conversation with Quintus had given up the coordinates.

And they hadn't come alone.

Plumes of dust obscured some of the orbs from sight. Two larger machines hovered above the flat landscape, kicking up the dry dust. Dom readied the Disruptor, which shook with the power it had stolen from the reprogrammed orb earlier. It worked to disrupt the flight pattern of smaller objects like the orbs, then steal their energy to render them inert. But a blast of power to a giant digging machine would do little to slow it down. He kept his shaky finger off the trigger, not wanting to fire too early. The irony that he was as much machine as the looming threat, and as much at risk from the gun he held, wasn't lost on him.

The larger machines approached at a fast clip, but not as fast as the swarm of orbs.

Jacob cursed and fussed with the reprogrammed orb. Thomas and Jason disagreed over which command was the right one to initiate it. In the end, Max's bark to hurry up made up their mind.

'Okay, here goes nothing,' said Thomas, selecting an option on his screen.

'Everyone get back from view,' said Max. The soldiers slipped inside the valley. 'That goes for you too, Jacob.'

The old man protested. 'Not until I know this damn orb works.'

Dom refused to move either, mirroring the old man's concern. Thomas played a whistle at a different pitch through the screen's speakers. The orb stirred in Jacob's hand then zipped up into the air. It took flight and sped off towards the approaching machines.

'Everyone fall back, now!' said Max.

They dropped back to cover.

'How close do the orbs need to get, Thomas?' said Max.

'Probably within ten feet of the burial site. It

will be tight.'

Not much room to get this right.

Dom gripped the Disruptor in one hand and checked progress through his binoculars. The orbs sent from the city were heading straight for them, but the reprogrammed scout was running rings around the two digging machines. It confused them enough to bring them to a halt. But still the orbs came. Dom abandoned his binoculars for his gun. He lifted it and set against the crook of his shoulder.

They were hidden from sight, but the anti-magnetic field was down. The orbs would have free passage through the valley if the sound from the bullhorn didn't work. Thomas poised his finger over his screen. Then, when the orbs were just twenty feet out from the burial site, he played the sound. It repeated on a loop.

The orbs kept flying as though they hadn't heard it.

Dom prepared to shoot at the swarm. His hands shook when his finger touched the trigger. Shooting them had to be a last resort. To do so would alert the recording orbs to their presence and show the Collective who dared to fight its machines.

But his hopes lifted when, one by one, the orbs nosedived and hovered over the buried bullhorn. While they were distracted, the soldiers fired bolts of electricity from their guns at them. The distracted orbs dropped like stones. Dom prepared to fire to deal with the last ones, but Jacob put a hand on his arm.

'I need that for something else. Don't fire.'

The soldiers incapacitated the remaining orbs and Max prepared to leave. But Jacob pulled on Dom's sleeve, dragging him out of cover and closer to the orbs.

'What are you doing?' said a shocked Max.

'I need one of those machines,' said Jacob. 'There's a young woman with amnesia and I said I could fix her. One of those machines could have the parts I need to reverse her memory loss.'

Anya.

Dom nodded at Jacob. 'Whatever you need.'

He focused on the machines, still far enough away for him to prepare.

'Hold on,' said Max. 'Who's in command here?'

Jacob turned and faced him. 'You are. But Anya's having trouble recalling regular memories and I think the amnesia is to blame. If we unlock her repressed memories, we could trigger other ones she may have, like the coordinates to the Beyond. One of those machines will go a long way to getting us out of here faster.'

Max conceded with a sharp nod. 'Wait a second.'

He marched out from cover with his Atomiser and checked the scene with his binoculars. Dom mirrored his action. He saw one of the machines had broken off and was following the erratic orb. The second was coming for the valley.

'Looks like we don't have a choice.' Max dropped the binoculars and gripped the Atomiser with both hands. 'All soldiers to the front.' He contacted base. 'Dad, erect the anti-magnetic field.'

Dom heard Charlie reply, 'But you're not back inside.'

'Just do it.'

Dom heard a hum and felt a push as the field was re-established.

The soldiers with electrical guns created an arc to the front.

Dom stood next to Max as he explained again how to use the Disruptor.

Thomas added, 'The Disruptor won't do much against a machine that size. Max needs to shoot first to de-atomise the outer structure, then you can use the stored power from the Disruptor to blast the inner sanctum and do damage.'

'Try not to damage too much of it,' said Jacob quickly. 'I need as much of it intact as possible.'

They passed by the inactive orbs and continued towards the machine. It was picking up speed.

'We'll need to act fast,' said Max. 'Even with the anti-magnetic barrier, this thing could steamroll through it in minutes. Everyone fan out. Let's surround this thing.' Max handed the Atomiser to Thomas. 'Thomas and Dom, you two together.'

Dom frowned at Max. 'What are you going to do?'

'Become a distraction.'

Dom and Thomas went left while the soldiers headed right. Max stepped into the path of the machine. The rumble became a roar as the machine's massive height and width bore down on them.

The machine didn't appear to be sentient, unlike the Copies. It had a mission, and that was to break through the barrier. The closer it got to the mouth of the mountain pass, the slower its speed became. The anti-magnetic field was doing its job.

Dom arced out wider, hoping to find a weak spot in the side of the machine's design. Thomas kept close. On the other side, the soldiers fired bolts of electricity from their guns, while Max stood in the machine's path, not wavering from his spot. The machine pitched right when the soldiers' electricity found its target, then righted itself before coming at Max again. Thomas tapped Dom on the shoulder, pointing at a box visible on the underside of the hovering machine. It appeared to be the location of the control mechanism for the machine.

'That's right—hit its underbelly,' shouted Jacob.

Thomas fired at the box once; it shimmered as it became translucent. Dom fired the Disruptor's stored energy at the box, steadying against the recoil the gun made. He quickly absorbed the power from the control mechanism. The machine dropped out of its hover and ground to a halt, feet away from a sweating Max.

A smiling Jacob ran up to the machine and

yanked some wires loose. 'That should render it inactive. Good job, everyone.'

Max, who had recovered from his shock, said, 'How the hell will we get this thing back?'

Jacob said, 'In pieces.'

They spent the next half an hour dismantling the parts that Jacob wanted, then buried the rest. The city's orbs were still inactive. The second digger had disappeared, as too had the reprogrammed orb.

This was just one non-sentient machine. Dom hated to think what would happen if the Copies came next.

'Collect the orbs. Maybe we can reprogram these too,' said Max to the soldiers.

'No, leave them,' said Jacob, when some soldiers picked up a handful.

'Why?' said Max.

'Because the city will notice if they don't return. When they wake, they'll reset and return to the city. The Collective will see they approached the valley and got distracted by a piece of land. They'll just assume they're defective and send more. If we take them, they'll know we have them and hit harder.'

'But what about the digging machine?'

'They're designed to be expendable. The Collective would expect to lose some in a battle like this.'

Max relented with a nod. 'Everybody back to the camp.' He pressed the button on the side of his walkie talkie. 'Dad, we're heading back. Drop the field.'

Charlie asked, 'Did everything go okay?'

'As well as can be expected. Give us three minutes to get back, then put the barrier up.'

They moved as fast as they could while carrying machine parts, to make it back before Charlie erected the field. When Dom was just ten feet away, a sudden force smacked him against the rock face of the valley wall. It pinned his left arm to the wall. He let go of the sheets of metal, hoping to release the field's hold on him. But it only slammed them against the wall too.

Max popped out the other side. He dropped his parts and gun and waded through the field to Dom.

He pulled on his arm. 'Sorry, we can't take the risk of lowering it again.'

With some effort, he freed Dom and dragged him and the pieces of metal to the safe side. Dom felt his human limbs lighten, though the force still repelled his machine body.

Safely through the gates, Dom got to his feet, wondering if his physical adjustments would be a help or a hindrance in a fight against the city.

'I hope you're right about those orbs resetting themselves and returning home, Jacob,' said Max.

'Trust me,' said the old man. 'I've been working on those machines for a year. I picked up a few things about their mannerisms and likely behaviour.'

'And what about your reprogrammed orb?'

'The signal won't reach it, wherever it's gone, but I programmed it to reset itself in a day. When that happens, it will return here to ground zero.'

Max released a sigh. 'It's a start, but a bullhorn won't stop those things from coming. We must prepare for the second wave.'

28

Carissa

Carissa watched from the street opposite the alley as Dom and Max carried the remnants of a digging machine to the storage shed. She moved closer but remained outside of the space where Rover had been locked up again. The Inventor entered the space next, followed by Thomas and Jason. An excitable Rover whined for attention.

'We'll let you get on,' said Max to the Inventor. 'Let me know if you hear back from your reprogrammed orb.'

The Inventor nodded and Max left. Carissa slid inside the space as Jason and Thomas started to dismantle a section of the giant machine. The Inventor looked on, fists on his hips. Despite the lack of tools and equipment in this camp, he appeared to enjoy his work here more than the work he'd left behind in the city.

Dom stared at the pieces of metal. They

contained what Carissa recognised to be a control mechanism for the digging machine. She caught him glancing down at his arm before looking at the Inventor.

'How will this machine help Anya?' he asked.

The old man wagged his finger at him. 'Not only Anya, but June too. I'm just not sure yet.'

A tense-looking Dom formed a fist with his left hand then relaxed it.

It must be hard to remember a person who thinks of you only as a stranger.

That had been Carissa's relationship with the Inventor. They'd first met when she was a newborn, but a memory wipe at the moment of her connection to the Collective had robbed her of that week. She'd become a blank slate from that point on, but the Inventor had recalled Carissa's wild newborn streak and her strong dislike of his wife, Mags.

She shuffled closer to the machine parts, hoping the Inventor would ask her to help. Her connection to Quintus had brought the orbs closer. She had to make it right.

Dom's gaze never left the machine parts. 'How long before you can build something?'

The Inventor shook his head. 'I wish I knew. I only ever saw the inside of the replication machine once, so I'm not sure I can. But the digging machines have a power source, so I'm hoping to build a connection point to allow Anya to get her memories back.' He patted Dom on the back. 'Don't worry. If there's a way, I'll find it.'

'And if it doesn't work?' asked Thomas, looking up from his sorting. 'Are there any replication machines in Praesidium?'

The Inventor shrugged. 'The only working one I knew of was in Arcis. Once they take the urbano apart, they dismantle the machines.'

Dom frowned as if he remembered something. He looked up at the Inventor. 'They used one to copy me.'

'Where?'

'In the medical facility, after they swapped out my tech. The process failed in Arcis, so they wanted to try again.'

The Inventor smiled, but it didn't last. 'There's no way to access it without going back. If we can do this here, I'd like to try.'

Dom nodded. 'Anything I can do to help—'

'You'll be the first I ask.'

Dom's shoulders rounded as he left the workshop. Carissa watched him go, knowing how he felt. Without a solid plan, everything they attempted felt shaky at best. Carissa disliked variables she couldn't control. She was like Quintus in that way.

Stepping closer to the dismantled pieces of the machine, she said, 'I can help, Jacob.'

The Inventor looked at her a moment then waved off Jason and Thomas. 'Carissa can help me sort through this. Get back to the workshop and see if you can locate the reprogrammed orb. We'll need as much detail as possible about what's going on out there.'

Both men departed, leaving just the Inventor and Carissa, much to Rover's delight. His bum wiggled as he attempted to reach her, but his chain yanked him back. She walked over to him and patted him on his smooth exoskeleton shell.

'I'm here, boy. Settle down.'

The beast lay down on the floor and rested its head on its metal legs. It closed its eyes, as if content.

Carissa turned her attention to the pile of metal and rolled up her sleeves. 'What can I do?'

The Inventor separated a cover from a main component. The power source sparked; he yanked his hand back. 'The control unit is a bit battered, but I was hoping we could remove its power source.' He stood and stepped back. 'It's set to your frequency, Carissa. See if you can touch it.'

Carissa edged closer to what appeared to be a damaged power node. Rover whined suddenly as though he sensed the danger. She thought of Quintus' actions against both Anya and June, and drew in a deep breath. She grabbed the node, which sparked in her hand, and yanked it free.

A flurry of breaths escaped her lips. She held it out to the Inventor. But he pointed to the floor.

'Place it down there, gently. It's possible the machine already sent back coordinates and details of the active anti-magnetic field. If that happened, the power node could be set to self-destruct.'

Carissa froze at the thought, but battled her fear to set the object down without compromising it. She wanted Anya to get her memories back as much as Anya did.

She shuffled back from it and looked at the Inventor. 'What now?'

He perched his fists on his hips and examined the remaining collection of useless, metal components.

'We need a new casing for our power node and its insulating compound. If I can design a crude mould fast, we should be able to melt the outer shell to fit both parts.'

Carissa thought back to the times they'd spent together in his workshop. It warmed her part-organic heart that they could still do this. The difference this time was that the Inventor worked because he wanted to, not because Quintus ordered him to.

Carissa realised the same situation applied to her. She was free to choose. She hadn't been given that option in the city.

She pulled apart more of the machine, separating usable parts from scrap metal.

Locating the insulated wires that connected the power node to the digging machine, she held them up. 'Will these help to connect to Anya?'

The Inventor nodded. 'I'll need to buffer the energy surge between it and Anya, but it might. Salvage what you can. We can go through everything after.'

They spent the next hour carefully picking through the remainder of the machine. Carissa was certain Quintus would notice it had not returned.

'Should we return the unused parts to the entrance of the valley, Jacob?'

The Inventor frowned. 'What's the likelihood they'll look for their machine?'

She shrugged. 'My sense is Quintus and the Collective have become precious about their commodities since our escape.'

Including her.

The Inventor patted her on one shoulder. 'Don't worry, Carissa. I won't let anything bad happen to you.'

'Nor I you, Jacob.'

If the Collective sent more machines, she hoped she could keep that promise.

Max surprised her by showing up at the door, unannounced. 'How long before Anya gets her memories back, Jacob?'

Carissa prepared to answer him, but the colonel refused to look at her. He still didn't trust her.

'It will take as long as it takes,' said the Inventor.

Max entered the space. The wolf growled at him, jerking him to a stop. 'I hate that thing.'

Carissa attempted to allay his fears. 'He won't hurt you. He's just protecting his space.'

But Max ignored her and spoke to the old man. 'When you restore them, I want to speak with her immediately.'

'I'll work faster without you standing over my shoulder.'

'You don't seem to appreciate the urgency.'

The Inventor looked up. 'Indeed I do, Max, but if you're not helping, you're slowing me down.'

Max held his hands up. 'Fair enough.'

'Have you asked young Anya about the Beyond?' said the Inventor.

Max nodded. 'Anya says she doesn't know anything. Vanessa has been trying to pin her down for a proper chat. But with everything else going on, it's been difficult. It would help if we could skip a lengthy discussion and get straight to the information we need. This is the closest we've come to finding the coordinates. But my gut says they're in the one place we haven't looked.'

The Inventor frowned at him. 'You think they're in the city?'

Max folded his arms. 'The search party turned up nothing close to this location. If the border was that easy to find, the machines would have found something already. Vanessa and I were chatting and we think it's possible one of our members, someone who was preparing to cross, got caught and may have hidden them there. I'm hoping Anya will confirm who the last person was that her parents spoke to.'

'It's one possibility,' said the Inventor. 'It all depends on what young Anya remembers. Your theory of them being in the city might amount to nothing. Without Anya's memories, we could be following a hunch that turns out to be a dead end.'

'I know, but we must consider it,' said Max with a nod. 'Either way, we'll have to go there. Whatever happens next, our fate lies in that city.'

The thought of returning both excited and terrified Carissa.

29

Dom

Attacking the machine had released some of Dom's stress. Exacting revenge on the city was exactly what he needed. But the depleting adrenaline left him with too much energy to burn and seeking a new distraction. He joined Julius' training session. As afternoon slipped into evening, he battled against the temptation to look in on Jacob and the others. Even if Anya did get her memories back, it didn't mean she would feel the same way about him as before.

When Max called Kaylie and Julius in to meet with him, Dom took over training both of their teams. He pushed them through a punishing set of drills to purge all thoughts of Anya from his mind. Imogen worked with another group, while nearer the back perimeter fence, Dom heard the newbies practising their shooting.

The soldiers dropped from exhaustion forcing Dom to call time on the session. Just in time, too.

Kaylie and Julius returned to the yard. He observed Imogen and Sheila chatting with each other. They stood close together, Imogen leaning in to catch Sheila's words, both smiling. It warmed his heart to finally see Sheila happy. He hadn't taken to hard-edged Yasmin all that much.

Kaylie chatted with her team, glancing over at Dom on occasion. She waved at him, and he responded with a short wave back. Why hadn't he given it a chance between him and Kaylie? While their time together had only happened a year ago, they'd been nothing more than a couple of kids. A year had transformed Dom from boy to man. He now saw things with greater clarity.

Dom's muscles ached from the rough treatment the anti-magnetic field had given him. But it felt good to be useful, even better, to be in control of his destiny, no matter what the outcome. Without any new announcement from the workshop team about the reprogrammed orb or the possible invention for Anya, Dom called it a night.

He picked up his bottle, filled with a supply of collected rainwater. With no running water in the camp, he washed up in the bathroom using a basin of the same water from the limited supply. He settled down in one of the spare rooms Max kept aside for the commanders, which he knew hadn't been used since his arrival. The noisy dorm made it impossible for Dom to think through their next steps in their fight with the city.

The cool and dark room was exactly what he needed. He lay down on the bed and draped his hand over his eyes. Someone opened the door.

'Occupied,' he said without opening his eyes.

The door closed and he settled back down to sleep. But a sudden weight on the bed displaced him. He shot his eyes open to see Kaylie sitting there.

Dom propped himself up on his elbow. 'What are you doing here?'

Kaylie had coloured her lips with a light red stain. 'I wanted to say goodnight.'

She had also changed from her army green uniform into a T-shirt with a floral pattern and a pair of black combats. He caught a hint of perfume from her. The smell of it, freesia and roses, brought back a flood of memories of their one night together.

She smiled, scooting closer to him. 'Well? Aren't you going to say goodnight to me?'

Dom sat up and gave her a curt nod. 'Goodnight, Kaylie.'

But she didn't leave. Instead, she took his hand and wove her fingers through his.

He frowned at their joined hands, then at her. 'Kaylie, what are you doing?'

She smiled. 'Reconnecting with an old friend.'

Sheila would roll her eyes at his stupidity for not catching Kaylie's interest in him. In fact, she'd called it earlier.

'What about your boyfriend?'

Kaylie bit her soft, stained lip. Her blonde hair

partially covered her face. 'I might have lied about that.'

He reclaimed his hand. 'Lied? Why?'

Kaylie huffed and folded her arms. 'Men really are dense. Because you were being weird about me arriving here, so I made it up. I wanted things to go back to the way they were before we, you know, hooked up.'

Dom hadn't noticed her back then. It had taken Sheila to point her out before he did.

'I'm sorry. I wasn't trying to make things awkward or make you uncomfortable. I was surprised to see you, that's all.'

'Me too.' Kaylie shifted closer. 'I thought seeing you again would bring it all back. I mean, we slept together and you didn't talk to me again. I was humiliated. But seeing you again has only strengthened my feelings for you.'

He'd stopped talking to her because of her reaction to his scars. It had nothing to do with the other stuff.

She placed her hands on either side of him. He didn't need Sheila's wisdom to know what Kaylie wanted. How had he been so blind to her attraction to him?

His thoughts shot to Anya, but only for a brief moment. He couldn't keep chasing hope that everything would return to normal once her memories returned. If they returned.

Kaylie leaned forward, catching Dom unawares.

He didn't move as she neared her mouth to his. He didn't stop her when her lips grazed his. And for a second, he kissed her back. He even liked it when she moaned a little and climbed onto his lap. But something didn't feel right. His body wanted this, not his head.

He eased her off him.

Kaylie sat up, her cheeks reddening. 'Did I do something wrong?'

He shook his head. 'It's me. I know it's a cliché line that's been used a million times, but it's true. I'm not in a place where this can happen with anyone.'

Kaylie slid back to sit on the end of the bed.

'I can wait,' she whispered.

It wouldn't be fair to her. He grabbed her hands and squeezed. 'It has been great seeing you and if things were different, we would probably pick up where we left off, but the last few months have changed me.'

He wanted to say it was because of Anya. But that was only partially true. He'd also learned about his mother's death and had been put through multiple surgeries that had not only hardened his body, but his mind too. If he was being truthful, he'd changed too much to be with anyone.

Kaylie eased her hands out of his, nodding. 'I knew it was too good to be true, seeing you again.'

'I'm sorry, Kaylie.'

She stood up and walked to the door. 'Be happy, Dom.'

He watched her go and let the best advice he'd heard in a long time sink in. It was time to move on.

From Anya.

From all of it.

30

Carissa

With the Inventor's help, Carissa managed to separate enough smaller operational parts from the scrap metal for him to make an attempt at inventing something.

They returned to the workshop. There, he melted and remoulded scrap metal to create new housing for the power node and its insulating compound. Next, he soldered the wires from the digging machine to the node itself. Jason melted more metal to make new connection circles that he then stuck to the inside of an old swimming cap, from the salvaged supplies of the towns. The Inventor then fed the wires through the cap and soldered them to the circles until all eight wires from the node were connected. A single wire from the power node connected to one of the monitoring machines on the workbench.

The Inventor said the cap would help to stimulate cortical responses.

Carissa nervously watched his attempts to improve the design. It was the reason why Quintus had kept him around for so long: his attention to detail.

But the perfection stage lasted longer than she could stand. She got to her feet and strode over to where the Inventor sat hunched over the chip, with a magnifying eyepiece on his head. He looked up at her, his eye suddenly magnified to comical proportions.

'Must you stand over me like that, Carissa? I'm trying to work.'

She pulled his hand away from the chip, eliciting a huff from the old man.

'We should test it out.'

The Inventor huffed again and returned to his work. 'When I know it's perfect and will wake up the encoded memories. I don't want to get young Anya's hopes up.'

Jason, she noticed, looked as impatient as her. He rolled his eyes at her, then his hand at the Inventor. She grinned at his joke, but her irritation at how slow he worked pushed her to take action.

'Test it out on me.'

The Inventor looked up at her. 'You, miss?'

'Yes. I don't remember my first week as a newborn.' She lifted her chin. 'Try to unlock my memories of that time.'

The Inventor frowned and slipped the magnifying eye off his head. 'Your memories were wiped, miss. I don't think this will work.'

'So were Anya's,' said Jason. 'What's to say the Collective didn't use the same type of machine on Carissa?'

The Inventor stood up slowly and rested a finger on his lip. The cap remained on the table next to an interested Thomas. It frustrated Carissa how slowly the Inventor processed thoughts; all the Originals were the same. Would this be her life now, slowing her thoughts down just so she could fit in? Without the Collective's constant intrusion and guidance, she'd experienced a shift in her own thinking. Now her ideas, including her plan to contact Quintus, were her own. Despite her evolution, however, she hadn't lost her speed.

'Hurry up,' she squealed, briefly squeezing her eyes shut.

Dropping his finger, the Inventor flashed her a look. 'I see not all of the newborn is lost, miss. Hold your horses while I think a moment longer.'

She tapped her foot in time to the slow wheel that appeared to turn the Inventor's thoughts. It was so easy. Just put the cap on her and away they'd go. If he didn't speed up, she'd do it herself.

The Inventor stirred from his deep thought. It gave Carissa hope.

He turned to Jason and Thomas. 'I'm worried the power surge from the node might overload her circuitry.'

The what?

Thomas slid the cap closer to him. 'I can add a circuit to limit the input and output.'

'Do it,' said the Inventor, before turning to Carissa. 'Now, miss, if I'd put this thing on you, it might have killed you. Patience is never a bad thing.'

Carissa's mechanical heart beat to a near frenzy. She swallowed hard. Thomas made an adjustment that took another half an hour, but this time Carissa could wait.

When the cap was ready, the Inventor ordered her to sit in a chair closer to the workbench where the power node sat. She did, but what came next made her hands shake. What if it didn't work? Worse, what if it killed her?

She looked up at the Inventor for some reassurance. He smiled down at her like this was no big deal. 'You look like you're about to bolt from the room. I'm just glad Rover's in the storage shed otherwise he might not let me do this. Relax, child.'

Carissa took a deep breath and faced forward. She closed her eyes, feeling the cap slide over her hair. She heard someone fiddle with some knobs, then the Inventor say, 'Crank it up slowly. Let's start with a low energy burst.'

A what? Before Carissa could ask, the cap delivered a jolt to her synapses. They fired wildly inside her head, making her skin tingle.

'Oh!' The word rushed out of her.

The Inventor's hand on her shoulder soothed her. 'Are you okay, miss?'

She opened her eyes and nodded at him.

With a smile, she said, 'More. I can take it.'

Thomas turned the dial on the monitoring machine up another notch.

Then he pressed a button. She gripped the arms of the chair. The new jolt caused her head to shake. She steadied herself against the power.

'More.'

She sucked in a breath and steeled herself against the next hit.

But the Inventor touched her arm. 'Slow down, miss. Now, try to think back to before you became a Copy, to your time as a newborn. What do you remember?'

Carissa released her breath and concentrated on any memories that preceded her first one as a Copy: when she'd found herself on a table in the medical facility in Praesidium. A medic had looked down at her. She'd felt her voice inside her head. A second voice, belonging to a male named Quintus, had congratulated her on her Copy status. While she hadn't seen him, it had felt like she already knew him and the other nine just like him.

Carissa tried to think further back, but the memories lacked clarity and she struggled to make a connection. She shook her head.

The Inventor patted her arm. 'One more, Thomas.'

Thomas clicked one more notch on the dial. This time, the energy burst shook her bones, right down to her ankles. She gritted her teeth against the pain and exhaled. Not waiting for the Inventor's command, Carissa thought back to those loose memories from before. One drifted away from the pack and called to her.

It was of Mags, the Inventor's wife. Carissa had just broken her favourite figurine. Amid her telling off, Carissa remembered feeling more smug than sorry at having broken it. Mags hadn't been as easy-going as the Inventor. But the repercussions of her actions had hit home when an upset and angry Inventor had returned.

She opened her eyes and stared up at the Inventor.

'Well?' he said, his eyes round.

She swiped at her tears and fought against the lump in her throat. More memories of that time hit her, all of her giving Mags a hard time. All reminding her of how selfishly Canya—Anya's double—had behaved. How badly Carissa had behaved to someone the Inventor had loved.

'What's wrong, miss? Did the shock hurt you?'

Still wearing the cap, she stood up and wrapped her arms around the Inventor's middle. 'I'm so sorry.'

Tears stained the Inventor's overalls.

He stroked her head. 'Sorry about what? That it didn't work? Don't worry. Jason, Thomas and I won't give up.'

She pulled away and sniffed. 'Not that. About how I treated Mags. I... I was... horrible.'

She bawled louder than she'd ever done before. The sound surprised her, as all of her newborn's emotions as well as the memories hit her. Carissa buried her face in the Inventor's belly.

He shook her gently and said, 'Come on, now. That was a long time ago. Mags didn't hold grudges.'

Carissa sniffed her latest tears away and looked up. 'Really?'

'Yes. But you know what?'

'What?'

The Inventor grinned and cupped her face. 'We've just found a way to reverse the memory wipe.'

31

Anya

Anya felt lost that morning, wondering how she might help the rebels' efforts against the city. Vanessa had finally cornered her last night and forced her to talk about her time at home. She needn't have bothered. She still couldn't pinpoint any specific mention her parents might have made of the coordinates to the Beyond, or a person holding that same information. She had apologised to the woman who'd been a friend to her parents. She wanted to do this for her—for all of them.

'Maybe the memory wipe has affected your recollection of certain things,' Vanessa had suggested.

Anya had shrugged. 'Maybe.'

She couldn't bring herself to tell her it was possible her parents had never discussed the issue. Max and the others were counting on her. If she revealed her doubts, it could crush everyone's hopes.

The responsibility on her shoulders weighed her down. But last night had been difficult for another reason. She'd seen Dom, a young man she didn't remember but whom her subconscious refused to let go. She'd also seen Kaylie, a woman as beautiful as Sheila, watch him throughout training. Something primal had stirred in her belly at the attention she gave him.

To focus on something else, she'd shown Warren, Alex and Jerome how to shoot again. But she was distracted by the fact Jacob, Jason and Thomas were busy building a machine that might or might not access her wiped memories.

Given the failure of her attempts with Carissa, she didn't hold out much hope for that.

But Kaylie's attention bothered Anya for reasons her mind refused to explain to her. That morning in the dining hall as she sat down with her food, her suspicions about their connection intensified. She overheard Kaylie telling Sheila she'd been in Dom's room last night.

'I don't know,' Kaylie said to Sheila. 'I think he just needs time. If I leave him alone, I think he'll come around to the idea of the two of us.'

Sheila shrugged. 'I don't know, Kaylie. What happened in the city was traumatic for all of us. I don't know what he's feeling anymore.'

Kaylie nodded and played with her food. 'That's why I'm giving him space. He didn't say there was anyone else, so that means I still have a chance.'

Anya's food lost all taste after hearing that.

Sheila caught her eye for a brief second. Anya blushed and concentrated on her food. To her relief, their conversation switched from boys to training.

Her out-of-control emotions should make her hate Kaylie, but she didn't. The young woman hadn't spread rumours or tried to ruin Anya's good name. But then, she didn't know about the three months spent in Essention with Arcis at its centre, or the vague memories of Dom that had surfaced to remind Anya he might have been someone to her.

She dropped her tray back and took a walk outside. Aside from being excluded from most discussions, she didn't want to bump into Dom. That would only open up a new discussion about things she couldn't recall.

Carissa startled her by racing out of the alleyway. She was headed straight for her.

Jacob ran after her, puffing and out of breath. 'Slow down, miss. Don't frighten her.'

The girl ran up to Anya, eyes wide and a big smile on her face. Anya had never seen the Copy so animated before.

She tucked her hands behind her. 'We have something for you.'

Had Jacob been successful? She lifted her cautious gaze to him. When he gave her a nod, tears welled in her eyes.

Jason came running up next. 'Okay, sis. Time to

see if our experiment works on you too.'

The Copy grabbed her hand and led her to the workshop. Anya looked around, worried that either Vanessa or Max would see and drill her for more information about the Beyond. But to her relief, the streets were empty and the dining hall was full.

'I don't want anyone to know about this until we're sure it works,' she said to Jason.

'Our secret for now.'

Carissa's hand felt cold in hers as she dragged her along. 'Come on, it only hurts a bit.'

Anya glanced at Jason in worry. 'What hurts a bit?'

Jason laughed while Jacob clucked his tongue at Carissa.

'Not hurt, I meant pinch,' said Carissa in an attempt to undo her mistake.

But Anya didn't care. She would take whatever pain the machine offered, if it meant regaining a lost part of her.

Carissa pulled her into the workshop. A chair sat next to a trestle table with three monitors on it. On the table, a swimming cap with protruding wires appeared to be connected to a round, black energy source. Anya looked around for the replication machine that she'd expected Jacob to build.

'Where is it? Is it in the shed next door?'

Maybe it was too big to wheel into this space.

Jason shook his head while Jacob picked up the cap.

He shook it gently. 'This is it.'

Anya stared at the simple mechanism, not seeing how it would do anything. The machine in Arcis had been huge and imposing, according to anyone who'd seen it. How could a tiny cap undo its work?

'Sit, please,' said Jacob.

'Okay...'

She slid into the seat amid four pairs of eager eyes, and waited for Jacob to explain.

'I gave up on the idea of building a replication machine in favour of this. It's a neural stimulator and the idea is that it jolts the active neurons in your brain to get them firing. Some part of your brain is on memory lockdown, and that means hibernation or possibly retrograde amnesia. So, with a burst of power, we hope to do for you what we did for Carissa.'

Anya looked at the excited Copy.

'The Inventor, I mean Jacob, tried it on me. I remember my time as a newborn.'

Anya stared at her. Would it be that easy?

Jacob slipped the cap over her head and ordered Thomas, who sat at the workbench, to turn the dial up one notch. Anya waited nervously, remembering Carissa's outburst about this hurting. A small jolt was delivered through the discs that connected to her head. It felt no worse than a static shock. She tried to remember something from Arcis, but nothing came to her.

'Anything?' said Jacob.

Anya shook her head.

He nodded. 'Okay, we'll take this slow. I don't want to hurt you.'

There was that word again. Anya gripped the chair as Thomas clicked the dial up by one. He hit something and a zap pierced her skin.

'Ow!' she said.

'Try again, Anya,' said Jacob. 'I don't know how far we need to crank this dial up.'

She focused on the block of time that had eluded her thus far. Other than the couple of memories, including Warren's attack on her and Dom's haircut, she couldn't remember anything. She shook her head a second time, trying to temper her own expectations.

'Again.'

Jacob nodded to Thomas, who twisted the dial.

She braced for the next hit, which delivered a short, sharp prick of pain.

'Shit...' she muttered, gritting against the jolt that she hoped wouldn't do any permanent damage. 'Are you sure this is safe?'

Jacob patted her on the shoulder. 'Nothing in this world is safe anymore. But we need to try this.'

She agreed and tried to recall something from her past. Nothing came to her.

'Are you okay?' said Jason.

Anya nodded. 'No worse than the times Arcis shocked me, I guess.' She settled into her chair and braced for the next hit. 'Let's try this again.'

But when Thomas didn't turn the dial and the others stared at her, she blinked in surprise. 'What?'

'What did you just say?' said Carissa.

She didn't understand. 'I said I got shocked.'

'By Arcis,' said the Copy.

'Yeah, so?'

She didn't see what the big deal was.

'That happened in Arcis,' said a smiling Carissa.

The time it had first happened hit her. The shooting pain she'd experienced due to her failure to keep to a timed schedule.

'Did I just remember something from Arcis?'

Jacob grinned. 'I think you did, young lady. What else do you remember?'

Anya closed her eyes and concentrated, but that one memory masked any others. She opened her eyes. 'That's the only thing.'

'Then what say you to another blast?'

Elation warmed her as she agreed to more torture.

Thomas clicked the dial one higher and this time Anya welcomed the pain. It shuddered and shook her so hard, she almost bit her tongue. A new memory trickled through. This one was of the ground floor and the wolves. Then another of the food fight on the first floor. Tahlia's death on the same floor hit her hard, then Frank's on the third. Warren's competitiveness from the ground floor and his insistence they become allies preceded Dom's confession to her that he was a rebel. June, another rebel, had been her friend throughout. Sheila's brashness, which Anya had seen as bitchy, had been a front for something else.

Then her connection with Dom. It was a whisper at first that transformed into a loud roar in her ear. In Praesidium, when she and Alex had gotten closer, she had recalled someone with scars. That person had been Dom. While she hadn't remembered him, her subconscious had never forgotten.

She bolted up from the chair, alarming Jacob. 'Are you alright?'

'Yeah,' she muttered. 'I've got to go.'

She made it to the door and Carissa asked, 'Did it work?'

Anya paused and turned to Jacob, Carissa, Jason and Thomas. All four waited for her answer.

She smiled and left the room.

32

Anya

Anya rushed out the door of the workshop, her hands shaking as a torrent of new memories, feelings and emotions invaded her mind. Her time in Essention and Arcis knitted together like the pieces of a puzzle.

Tahlia's death hit her the hardest. She'd been to blame for that, scuppering her chances to reach the terminal on the first floor so the rest of them could improve their chances to rotate. Frank's death, while gruesome, had not been her fault. She'd done everything she could to save him. She remembered Jerome now, Frank's closest friend. He had forgiven her.

Her feet stumbled over the stony ground in her search for one person. She entered the courtyard, pulse pounding hard in her veins. The yard was full of soldiers but she couldn't see him. She almost didn't hear someone calling her name.

'Anya!'

In a daze, Anya looked round. A concerned Sheila approached her. 'Are you okay? I was calling you. You look like you've seen a ghost.' Her eyes widened and she drew in a sharp breath. 'You have them back?'

Sheila: intuitive and sharp as always.

Anya managed a quick nod, which drew a giggle from Sheila.

'Holy hell! So how up to speed are you?'

Anya couldn't think straight as the memories muddled her thoughts. She was still processing. Three months' worth of information. Three months of hell. And elation.

She pressed her fingers to her head. 'I'm getting there.'

Sheila folded her arms and flashed her a cool look. 'Well, I guess you remember we hated each other.'

Anya smiled. 'Yeah, I remember.'

Sheila's face softened into a smile and she punched her on the arm. 'Now, go find him.'

Anya had no idea where to look next. 'I thought he'd be here.'

She pointed to the opposite side of the camp. 'He went to get guns. He's there with Kaylie.'

The mention of Kaylie made Anya's blood run cold. 'Are they an item?'

Sheila rolled her eyes. 'So what if they are? You gonna let that stop you?'

No. Not after this long.

Anya flashed Sheila a grin. She ran back down the street she'd just come from, taking a right turn at the street that housed Charlie's barber shop. She slowed as she passed, seeing Charlie inside cutting one of the female soldier's hair. He looked up and frowned at her. She responded with a grin, to which he smiled and nodded.

Anya approached the end of the street and took a left towards the perimeter fence. She passed several ransacked properties with open-sided entrances that made them perfect for storage and not much else. The last one had people in it. She stopped when she saw Kaylie leaning against a half broken wall, smiling at someone she couldn't see. Anya walked up to the open entrance, breaking Kaylie's attention away from Dom, who was bending down to pick up boxes from the floor.

'Oh hey, Anya. What brings you here?' she said.

Dom jerked up too fast, banging his head on the lip of the table.

'I just needed to talk to Dom for a second. Do you mind?'

Kaylie looked between Dom and her, clearly unsure what to do. 'We were just going through the gun supplies.'

Dom turned around slowly, his expression cool. 'What's up, Anya? We're kind of busy. Can it wait?'

His attitude surprised her. Had Kaylie's arrival, a person clearly from his past, changed things between them?

It didn't matter. She hadn't gone through what she did to give up now.

'It worked.'

Dom frowned and folded his arms. 'What did?'

She said nothing, waiting for him to catch up.

His eyes widened. 'How?'

But his body still held tension.

'Jacob built a device to give me back what I lost.'

Anya's heart thundered in her chest. She had expected more excitement from him at this turn of events.

'What device?' said Kaylie, more alert.

Anya pinned Dom with her gaze, hoping she wouldn't have to explain it to Kaylie.

To her relief, Dom said, 'Kaylie, let's do this later.'

'But Max needs it done now.'

Dom's eyes never left Anya. 'He'll make an exception for this.'

Kaylie huffed, while Anya tried not to make a big deal out of it.

When she was gone, Dom said, 'How much do you remember?'

'All of it,' she whispered.

Dom uncrossed his arms; she caught the hesitation, the lack of surety in his stance.

His hands flexed by his sides, as though this moment confused him. She made it easy for him. In two strides her toes met his. She reached up and grabbed his face, pulling it down to hers, and kissed him.

He jerked beneath her touch, as though it had released a lifetime of pain. His hands gripped her head, pulling her closer, kissing her harder, deeper. A groan escaped from his lips and his hands got even busier. She tried to rein in her own joy but it overflowed from her like a bubbling pot of water. Her fingers worked through his curls, long at the top. A flashback of her time with Alex reminded her of her confusion, her expectation that a different man should be in her arms. It was Dom. It always had been. Somehow, she never forgot.

Dom pulled back. His soft gaze examined every inch of her face. 'Anya, I don't know what to say.'

She felt the same way.

'I had given up on you.'

She pulled back in surprise. 'When?'

'Last night. I was done with it all.'

She loosened her grip on him. A pain radiated from her chest to her limbs, making everything weak.

She gripped the wall for support. 'Okay, I understand.'

But he surprised her by grabbing her hand and pulling her close. 'Do you think I'm letting you go again? I was miserable without you.'

Her heart blossomed with the love she felt for this man. 'Me too, even though I didn't remember it. But my subconscious never forgot.'

Eliza Green

She wanted to ask something, afraid of the answer. 'My newborn, Canya.'

Dom nodded slowly.

'Did anything happen between you two?'

When his hand loosened on hers, she had her answer. 'Yes and no. I thought she was you for a while. I was in so much pain that I didn't see what she was. But whatever happened, it didn't mean anything.'

Anya buried the jealousy for her newborn, who had not only experienced Anya's time with Dom, but created new memories too. While Anya and Dom hadn't had sex, their time spent together had been a private, intimate experience.

When Dom looked worried, she smiled and said, 'That was then. Let's start a new chapter.'

He smiled and nodded. 'Agreed. Come on.'

He pulled her from the supply room.

'Where are we going?'

'I assume you haven't told Max yet, so unless Jacob has, I think he'd like to hear it.'

Anya agreed. 'There's someone else who needs to know first.'

Dom frowned. 'Who?'

She led him to the medical bay where a bored looking June lay fully clothed on one of the beds. Her stomach pains had gone away for now, but she was under strict monitoring. June's eyes widened when she saw her approach.

'Come on,' said Anya, pulling her up from the

bed.

'Where are we going?'

'You'll see.'

June frowned at Dom, who just shrugged innocently. Anya loved him for not ruining the surprise.

She led June to the workshop, where Jacob was checking the connections in the cap and Thomas and Jason were reading something on the monitor.

Jacob looked up, clearly relieved. 'There you are, Anya. We were worried about you when you just ran—'

He smiled when he saw June and Dom.

Anya led a confused June into the room and sat her in the chair, still set up from her session. 'I need you to work your magic on June. She doesn't remember either.'

Jacob picked up the cap. 'Gladly.'

June peered up at Anya. 'Your memories?'

Anya nodded. 'And soon to be your memories.'

An eager June rested her hands on her lap. 'Then hit me with what you've got.'

She closed her eyes when Jacob slid the cap over her head. Thomas hit her with the lowest pain setting. The jolt had barely hurt Anya, but it doubled June over. She clutched at her belly.

'Ow.' She straightened up in the chair. To Jacob, she said, 'I don't think Junior likes the pain.'

The Inventor pulled the cap off her head. 'We'll have to wait until Junior's gone.'

Anya touched June's shoulder, feeling bad for getting her hopes up. 'I'm sorry.'

June stood.

With a smile, she said, 'Don't be. Knowing I can get them back gives me something to look forward to.'

Dom grabbed Anya's hand, surprising her. 'Max, now.'

Anya nodded and turned from the others, who were visibly excited by her newfound status.

She walked hand in hand with Dom, something that felt so right and natural. They entered Max's office without knocking to find him in deep discussion with Julius, Imogen and Vanessa.

They looked up, obviously surprised to see them.

'She has her memories back,' blurted out Dom. Anya glared at him, but he shrugged. 'Sorry. I'm too excited.'

So was she.

Vanessa grabbed her hands. 'Thank God. What do you remember, Anya?'

'All of it.'

A relieved Vanessa led her over to a chair. Anya sat in it while Vanessa sat in the one beside her. Her eyes went to Julius and Imogen, both of whom she didn't know.

Max must have sensed her concern, because he said, 'I trust both of them.'

She nodded and concentrated on Vanessa. Dom

hovered in the background and chewed on his thumb.

Vanessa grabbed her hands. 'Your memories might have unlocked latent ones from before Arcis. Think back to any conversations your parents might have had.'

Anya closed her eyes and pictured her home life. Her parents were talking with someone called... what was her name? Janet.

She opened her eyes. 'Does someone called Janet mean anything to you?'

Vanessa became animated. Her eyes slid to a shocked Max. 'Yes, she was one of the original rebel recruiters. She was taken by the Collective.' She concentrated on Anya once more. 'Think about that conversation.'

Dom lingered behind Imogen and Julius. The latter appeared to be most interested in what she had to say next. When she looked over at Dom, he winked at her. But the presence of the other two bothered her. She closed her eyes and concentrated on the conversation instead. Her mother, Grace, had been talking to Janet about her upcoming attempt to cross over. She replayed their secret chat in her mind.

Her mother said, 'Please be careful out there, Janet.' She handed her a diary. 'If the machines get their hands on this, all of it will be for nothing. We found it in one of the camps, hidden by a rebel who we think crossed over. It contains the presumed coordinates to the Beyond. You'll need it if you are to cross, but don't take it with you.'

Anya opened her eyes and relayed the conversation back to everyone.

Vanessa stood up and joined a stern looking Max. 'We find Janet, we find the diary.'

Max shook his head, deflating Anya's hope. 'Janet was captured by the Collective.'

Vanessa glanced at the others. 'I don't remember her being in the city.'

'Doesn't mean she wasn't there,' said Anya. 'You and I didn't meet until the end.'

'If she had the diary on her and got caught, chances are the Collective has it now,' said Vanessa.

Anya wasn't so sure. 'If they did, why would they put us through the hell of Arcis? If their ultimate goal was to escape to the Beyond, why delay their exit by keeping us prisoner to learn more about humanity?'

Dom stepped forward. 'They asked me about the Beyond while I was their prisoner. I don't think they know where it is.'

A frowning Max stared at the floor. 'So, maybe she ditched it somewhere before her capture.'

'Maybe,' said Vanessa. 'Or it could be hidden inside the city.'

Max seemed to ponder this. 'Rumours are an underground city existed before the machines built over it to create Praesidium.'

Vanessa nodded, apparently in agreement. 'There are dozens of underground tunnels beneath that city that appear to lead nowhere. The Copies hate the dark, so it always struck me as odd that the Collective would have built them.'

Dom said, 'It's possible Janet would have figured that out and hid the diary in one of the tunnels, so the Copies wouldn't find it.'

Max dragged a hand down his face. 'Assuming the coordinates are even there, now we need to locate a map of the tunnels where those coordinates might be hidden? Great.'

A thought struck Anya. Her gaze flitted around the room. 'Carissa may still have access to the schematics of the tunnels. She helped us to escape.'

Max slid his gaze to Vanessa, looking more confident. 'We should ask her. We'll need to go there anyway to rescue the others. I'm not leaving this region until I know the Collective is decommissioned, or whatever ends its tyrannical life.'

Vanessa smiled at Anya. 'You did good, Miss Macklin. Your parents would have been proud.'

A soldier burst into the room, breaking apart their short-lived joy. 'Colonel Roberts, you're needed outside. We have a problem.'

33

Dom

Dom followed the soldier outside to see what was causing the trouble. Close behind him were Anya, Max, Vanessa, Julius and Imogen. He looked up to see a dozen orbs zipping over the top of the compound. That meant only one thing: the Collective must have found the bullhorn and changed the command frequency code controlling their orbs.

Max pushed past him as one of the flying spheres nosedived for a better look. Max swatted it away when it looked like it was on a collision course.

'Get Jacob, now!' he snapped at Julius, who was already racing towards the alley and the workshop.

His second in command didn't get far before Jacob came running out of the alley, followed by Jason and Thomas.

Max strode forward to meet him. 'What happened, Jacob?'

'The recording, it's no longer playing the command. Something may have broken it.'

One of the machines, perhaps? Dom had watched Jason and Thomas bury the device well enough for the orbs not to see it. Something must have known it was there. His thoughts turned to Jacob's reprogrammed orb, which was supposed to listen only to his commands. Maybe it had reset itself and returned to the city to warn the Collective.

Max turned to Thomas, pointing up. 'Can we recalibrate the anti-magnetic field to reach higher?'

Thomas shook his head. 'We'd need time to shift the position of each generator so the field projects a sharper upwards arc. It would cover the space higher up in the valley, but would leave a large portion of the valley bed unprotected.'

Max cursed. 'We don't have time for that. We have to pack up and leave. Now.' He turned to Dom. 'Assemble the soldiers and arm them. Everyone gets a gun, even those without full training.'

Anya touched his arm, surprising him. In the commotion, he'd almost forgotten she was there. But she wasn't looking at him.

'I've been teaching Warren, Alex and Jerome how to shoot,' she said to Max.

When had she done that?

Max nodded. 'That leaves Carissa and the Guardian.' He slid his gaze to Jacob. 'You know how to shoot?' Jacob nodded. 'Any news on your reprogrammed orb?'

'Still out there. We can track it better when we get past the anti-magnetic field.'

'Do you think it had something to do with this attack?'

Max ducked suddenly when one of the buzzing orbs zipped closer to his head.

Dom protected his and Anya's heads as it weaved in and around their group.

'No,' said Jacob. 'I programmed it to lead the machines away, not towards us.'

Max seemed happy with that explanation, but Dom was not. They knew nothing about the true nature of the orbs. How little had the Collective allowed Jacob to see and understand as a prisoner in the city?

'Okay,' said Max, pointing to the mountain shelf above the camp. 'I want soldiers up top as soon as we turn off the anti-magnetic field. We leave in half an hour.'

'What about the orbs?' said Dom, as another dashed around the space above.

Max shook his head. 'Let them look all they want. We're not coming back here and I'm not wasting my time or ammo attacking them. If something worse is coming, these things were sent to distract us.'

Dom grabbed Anya's hand and together they raced to the storage supply room to sort through the guns. The greyish, metal ones, sleek and smooth, shot electricity, similar to the Electro Guns. Others, more crude constructions, shot homemade projectiles like tiny, metal balls. Anya took four of the spare, and rarely used, revolvers to arm her lesser trained group. He needed the electricity shooting weapons in the hands of the more experienced soldiers.

With two handfuls of guns, she said, 'I'll take responsibility for the newbies. Don't worry; we'll fire only if we have to.'

'I'm not happy about Warren being in your group.'

She shook her head. 'Don't worry about him. He won't cause any trouble.'

Dom nodded, grateful that she understood combat better than some of the soldiers he'd trained with. He gathered up as many weapons as he could. New soldiers came to collect more. He handed them out until everyone had a weapon and the store was empty.

He returned to the town hall amid a dozen orbs invading everyone's personal space. Max was right. It didn't matter what they saw now. Not if they were all leaving the camp.

Max, Charlie, Jacob and Vanessa had gathered at the entrance to the camp along with Julius, Imogen and Kaylie, plus their teams. Carissa stayed close to the beast while the ex-Guardian whined and clawed at the rock-hard ground with its long, spindly nails. Dom shuddered as he recalled the Guardians that had supervised them on the ground floor of Arcis. Their menacing presence had put everyone on edge, but it was who they answered to, an unseen presence, that had put Dom on the highest alert. Rover appeared to be more docile than the ones he remembered. Not only that, but Rover had helped them to escape the city.

Dom assembled his troops, including June, who looked ready to fight, despite her condition. He saw her wince and knead a fist to the small of her back. But when she caught Dom looking, she straightened up and shook her head at him, as if to indicate she was fine. He needed her experience. Even Warren's. Nobody could be idle.

'Can you command them, Carissa?' said Max, pointing up at the orbs.

She whistled but the orbs didn't respond.

Jason came running up with a hand-sized screen, showing the activity of both the recording and the bullhorn buried in the dirt. 'It's still running.'

He showed the screen to Max.

Max's mouth pressed into a thin line. 'That means the Collective knows about the device and these orbs are running on a different command frequency.' Just as Dom had suspected. 'Who knows what's waiting for us out there?'

The rest of the camp gathered by the entrance. Charlie clutched what looked to be a remote controller for the anti-magnetic field. Dom frowned at it.

'It's a mobile version,' Charlie said.

Dom glanced up at the orbs. They were longer

flying erratically, but were doing systematic sweeps of the space below them. His team, which included Imogen and Sheila, lined up behind him, and readied for combat. Next to them was a hard-faced Kaylie and her team. Next to her stood Julius and his team, which included the two medics from camp. Anya was behind the main groups with Jerome, Warren and Alex, who, Dom noticed, all held their guns correctly. Her training had paid off. Behind them were spare soldiers sitting in the trucks. Dom expected they would struggle with the rough valley terrain. No matter, they had to take the risk.

Max spoke. 'Listen up, everyone. The second Charlie turns off the anti-magnetic field in the valley, we need to move fast. We've got limited cover from above.' He pointed up to the shelf above the camp where more soldiers with guns waited. 'But the orbs might be communicating in real time back to the city. We don't know what's out there. One thing's for certain: we stay, they trap us.'

The mechanical beast growled up at the orbs that continued their systematic catalogue of the camp.

'Once we go, don't stop.'

Dom looked up at the mountain pass they'd used to reach the camp. The service elevator was located in a section of the mountain rock, a short distance from the entrance to the camp. He didn't understand why they were escaping through the valley terrain. The trucks and soldiers could be up and out with a few runs.

'Why aren't we using the mountain pass?' he asked Max.

'Because it's one way in and out that doesn't provide us with cover. Chances are the orbs have found our special way in. We can't take any chances.'

Two soldiers opened the gates. Dom heard the hum of the field and felt a strong kick back that stopped him from moving forward. Charlie fiddled with the anti-magnetic controller, sucking away the repelling force.

The valley ahead was riddled with rocks, making the trucks their last resort rather than their first line of defence. Dom led the way with Kaylie. She gave him a sharp nod as the soldiers followed their respective team leaders. Max dropped back with Vanessa while Charlie, Jacob and Carissa climbed aboard the beast. Julius and his team travelled behind the beast, while Sheila joined Anya and her newbies at the back. It pleased Dom to know Anya had help.

Their journey into the unprotected valley agitated the visiting orbs. They swarmed faster in the space above them, tracking them all the way to the entrance. Dom arrived at the mouth of the valley first and looked out. He heard the bullhorn playing Carissa's whistle over and over. The orbs ignored it, which confirmed the city had changed the frequency command code.

He stuck his head out as the orbs rushed into the open landscape like a swarm of bees. Then he saw something that destroyed his last shred of hope.

Three, maybe four diggers were coming at them. But that's not what shocked him most. Behind were half a dozen Guardian beasts, each carrying two Copies on their backs.

'Shit.' He pulled back. 'There's a whole load of Copies and Guardians heading this way.'

They were too far gone to turn back now; the valley without its anti-magnetic protection would trap them, not protect them. Dom hoped the trucks bringing up the rear would make it through to serve as a battering ram. He glanced back to see one of them had already gotten stuck on an impassable fragment of rock. If they had more time, they could clear the valley. His hope deflated as Max pushed ahead of him and cursed.

'We can't turn back now,' said Max.

'So what do we do?' said Dom.

'We have no choice. We must fight.'

Dom sucked in a deep breath and swapped the safety of the valley for the open landscape. His team followed him out in the lead, while Kaylie's team set up a defensive arc around them. He released a tight breath and kept an even walking pace, despite the thrumming of his heartbeat, willing him to run back. His left hand, part of the most recent experiments on him, gripped the Disruptor tight. Max beside him held the Atomiser. They'd already used both guns to take down the giant digger, but they had to get closer than this to use them.

He got set to run towards the diggers, but what

he saw changed his mind. The machines were slowing their approach.

Dom glanced back at Max. 'What are they doing?'

Max also frowned as the machines came to a stop about a quarter of a mile out. 'I don't know. I'm not sure what they're waiting for.'

Dom took a guess. 'Maybe they didn't expect us to show up. Maybe they expected us to be in the trucks.'

Max chewed on his lip. Charlie and Jacob pushed through to the front, surprising him.

'Dad, Jacob, get back to where it's safe!'

Jacob held up a hand to Max. 'Please, let me explain. It's a standoff. They're protecting something. They're not here to fight.'

'What are they protecting?' said Max.

Dom wondered that too as he checked the approaching group for a glimpse of their true intentions.

'My guess would be something has happened in the city,' said Jacob. 'They are pre-empting our return there. I won't know for sure what's happened until the reprogrammed orb returns, but I should be able to call for it now that the anti-magnetic field is off.'

Max jerked his head back to Rover, stood with his head low. His glare was fixed on the beasts similar to him, hidden behind the digging machines. 'Okay, but could you do that from back there?'

Both men nodded and retreated to stand by the

waiting wolf.

Dom turned back to the standoff. 'So what should we do?'

Max said, 'If we go back, they could block off the entrance to the valley and trap us. At least out here, we can keep them at a distance. And if they approach, we can scatter.'

As soon as Max walked towards the stationary diggers, Dom signalled for his team to follow. Together, they neared the waiting machines. They jerked to a stop when the machines started up again. But instead of hovering forward, they shifted to the side to create a path. One of the Guardian beasts carrying two Copies on its back walked through the gap. Dom watched as one of the Copies jumped down from the beast and stood next to it.

Dom didn't understand what was happening. 'Does he want to talk?'

Max shrugged. 'Only one way to find out.'

They continued their approach to the lone Copy, who came closer to their position while his beast followed at a short distance. Max signalled for Dom to stop. His team halted their progress.

'We should meet him alone,' said Max, glancing down at his gun.

Dom agreed. Together, they could take out one Copy.

In a neutral space between their two groups, Max and Dom faced off with the Copy. He was dressed as a guard, but Dom didn't recognise him from his time in Praesidium's medical facility.

'Is he familiar to you?' whispered Max.

Dom shook his head.

The Copy stopped, forcing Max and Dom hold their position.

He spoke. 'I am here on behalf of the Collective. It wishes you no harm.'

Max pointed to the machines behind him. 'If so, why didn't you come alone?'

The Copy guard nodded at the team gathered a short distance behind Dom and Max. 'Because you didn't. The Collective asks that you return its property now.'

Property?

'We don't have anything belonging to your Collective,' said Max.

'Copy, designation 173-C; Guardian, designation unknown; Breeder, designation 33-X; Newborn, designation unknown; Inventor; and the Librarian. You will return all assets to the city immediately.'

'Or what?' said Max.

'Or we will take them by force,' said the guard. 'But the Collective believes you can be reasoned with.'

From Dom's limited experience of the Collective, if it wanted something it would take it by force. The city had another game plan, he was sure of it.

Max smiled at the stony-faced guard. 'They are

guests of mine. If they want to return, I won't stop them. But I won't force them to leave.'

The guard stood tall while his beast dipped his head low and menacing. 'You will return them to their rightful owners. The Copy, the Guardian, the Breeder, the newborn, the Inventor and the Librarian.'

'The last two do not belong to you,' snarled Max.

Dom tightened his grip on his gun. He failed to see how they would reach an agreement.

'The Inventor and Librarian have been in the city for a year. That gives the Collective automatic rights over their fate.'

Max held his gun down by his side. Dom knew his commander well enough to know it was just for show. He would act fast, if needed.

'I said no.'

The Copy pressed a button set into his temple and spoke to a voice unheard and a person unseen.

While he did, Max whispered, 'They're nervous about something. They don't look armed. We could take them down.'

Dom checked the other Copies perched on the backs of the Guardians, hidden from sight behind the digging machines. 'We can't say that for certain.'

Max shrugged lightly. 'What's the alternative? They don't want to fight. We do. I don't know about you, but I'm curious about what's going on in the city.'

This group meeting also piqued Dom's

curiosity about the state of the city.

The Copy guard ended his one-sided conversation. 'What is your answer, Original?'

'Go to hell,' replied Max.

The Copy guard looked back as a second beast walked through the gap between the digging machines.

He looked to the front and pinned his glare on Max. 'The Collective hoped you would say that.'

34

Dom

So much for negotiating.

The machines widened their gap farther as five more Guardians, a Copy on each back, charged through the space. Dom had been right about their firepower. Pointed at them were several weapons. He recognised them to be Electro Guns.

'Electricity,' said Dom to Max.

Max nodded as though they looked familiar. Maybe he'd seen them, when he and the others had infiltrated Arcis. These weapons had been on the fifth floor. The good news was the weapons had a limited charge. The bad news was their guns did too.

The lead Copy guard, without a weapon, dropped back while his armed counterparts raced towards their group.

'Scatter!' shouted Max.

Dom looked back to see the three main groups belonging to Imogen, Kaylie and Julius divide, but without breaking apart their formation. Carissa, perched on Rover's back, looked terrified as she clung on with both hands. Rover growled as Jacob and Charlie stood defiantly beside him.

The Copies were under instructions to take back their property that included Rover and Carissa. The other beasts were headed straight for them. Dom looked back to see Imogen and Kaylie creating separate arcs not only to protect the pair, but the two old men in the vicinity. Vanessa, who had one of Anya's revolvers, helped her group to protect the entrance to the valley. Julius and his team were retreating to help them.

Where the hell were the trucks?

He caught Anya glancing back inside the valley, then to the front. She didn't look happy.

Dom checked his Disruptor. It served two functions: to disrupt the air and the orbs' flight pattern, and to steal a machine's energy to use it against them. He cursed to find his gun, with a full store of energy when he'd left camp, was now empty. The anti-magnetic field must have disrupted the magnetisation of the gun and drained it.

With Max by his side, he sized up the danger. Three Guardians carrying mounted Copies charged at Imogen and Kaylie. Both stood to the front of their teams protecting Rover, Carissa, Jacob and Charlie. A hail of electrical charges discharged from their guns, designed to disable the machines' mechanisms. The air crackled with electricity as the Copies returned fire with their Electro Guns. Orbs zipped overhead, but Dom ignored the devices without weaponry.

His empty Disruptor was of no use. He aimed the barrel up and attempted to draw power from the electrical discharges around him, but the energy had dispersed too much for the gun to latch on to anything. Max ran at the beasts and fired his Atomiser. His attempts weakened their outer shell momentarily and revealed their innards. But without a follow-up disabling shot of power, it did little more than aggravate them. One turned and swiped at him with his metal paw. Max flew backwards. Dom's heart pumped too hard and too fast; he thought he might pass out. But then Max got to his feet and he breathed out a sigh of relief.

A panting Max scrambled back to his side. 'The Atomiser's useless without a follow up blast from the Disruptor.'

Imogen and Kaylie's team continued to fire their weapons at the approaching Copies. Their efforts kept them from getting close to Rover, Carissa or Jacob. The beasts yelped when new blasts hit their sides. Copies dismounted and tried to attack from a new position.

Dom wanted to help them, but that would mean walking into the Collective's trap and abandoning their strategy. Against his better reason and with an empty gun, he held his position. That's when he saw the lead Copy guard charging at him, a weapon raised at his side. He was pointing it at Dom.

The beast galloped towards him. In a panic, he grappled with his empty gun.

'You can arm your weapon with a blast from theirs,' said Max.

The beast turned sharply to the right. A shot discharged from the Copy's weapon. Dom dodged the blast and raised his Disruptor in response. Setting the trigger to pull not release, he braced the gun against his chest. The Copy fired his weapon again. The Disruptor shook him as it absorbed the new energy into his gun. The Guardian galloped past, then charged at him again. This time, Dom was ready.

'The Atomiser will work best if we slow them down,' said Max. 'Don't shoot too early.'

Dom watched his attacker come at him. He flicked the trigger to release but hesitated, unsure which entity to hit: the Guardian or the Copy. Both had the power to hurt him, kill him, even.

The Guardian was almost upon him, the Copy almost in firing range. He raised his weapon higher and fired.

The discharge of electricity popped out of his gun and propelled towards its target. The Copy guard attempted to fire at him first. But Dom's blast hit him before he had a chance to release the energy. The force knocked the gun out of the Copy's hand and him off his seat. Both hit the ground with a thud. The Guardian, clearly shaken, kept running.

'Crap.'

Dom dodged its attack as it galloped at him. It

stayed on its path until Dom heard a new whistle that turned the Guardian around and brought it tearing past Dom and Max. It returned to a safe spot behind the diggers.

Max ran up to the stunned Copy on the ground. He shot him with the Atomiser. A giant hole appeared in the Copy's side. Dom pointed the Disruptor at the gaping hole, flicked the dial back to "capture", and drew energy from him.

The Copy screamed in pain before his eyes went blank and he entered a sort of shutdown mode. Dom thought he heard a tinny sounding voice shout, 'Pull back.'

He watched in confusion as the Guardians retreated to safety, their Copies doing little more than steer them. He looked back at the Copy on the ground, his eyes frozen open in shock.

His gaze landed on a frowning Max next. 'What are they doing?' The digging machines stayed put in the distance. The last Guardian and Copy disappeared behind them. 'Why have they dropped back?'

Max looked up at the orbs, which hadn't left them alone for a second, and hazarded a guess. 'They wanted to see what weapons we have and how they work. And we just showed them.'

It was one theory. Dom heard a scream that sounded like it came from Anya.

He turned sharply to see Julius' group stepping away from Anya's group. Two of Julius' soldiers had grabbed Jerome and Alex by the necks and were pulling them out of their line of defence. They had relieved them of their revolvers and were pressing them to their temples. Julius protected his two team members as the other soldiers shuffled the Breeder and the newborn along, past the other groups.

'Stay back!' shouted Charlie to the soldiers protecting Rover and Jacob, who were closer to Anya's team than Max's.

Dom stepped forward, but Max pulled him back.

'That means you too,' he warned.

But Dom shucked him off. Holding his weapon tight to his chest, he ran over to where Julius was herding members of their rebel group towards the digging machines.

He slowed his approach when he saw how jittery Julius looked. He'd sensed something was off about Max's second in command. He hadn't imagined this.

'Julius, what are you doing?'

The soldiers who threatened Jerome and Alex both had a vacant look to their eyes. Julius was in control, but Dom feared he listened to another.

'Stay back, Dom. This has nothing to do with you,' shouted Julius.

Dom let the Disruptor fall to the ground. It had one charge, not enough to stop three. 'Let's talk about this.'

Julius shook his head and kept his Electro Gun on Dom. He must have stolen it from one of the

Copies.

'I don't need to talk. This was always the plan.'

Dom didn't understand. 'What plan? To do what?'

'To infiltrate your camp. Jerome wasn't the only newborn.' He tapped the side of his head. 'Difference is I've got a chip in my head. I listen to only one voice.'

The Collective.

35

Carissa

Rover hadn't stopped moving from the second they left the camp. But his nervous shifting unsettled Carissa, sat on his back. If it wasn't for Jacob stood next to him, she was sure the beast would have bolted by now.

Carissa couldn't tell what had made Rover restless. He whined as the Guardian beasts commanded by the Copies tried to get to her.

Jacob patted the wolf's neck and said, 'Hush now.'

The wolf wasn't connected. He didn't listen to the Collective's commands. So why was he reacting like this?

'He's moving too much. I want to get down.'

The distance to the ground scared Carissa. If she tried without the Inventor's help, she'd surely fall.

'Rover's just excited by the presence of the other Guardians,' said the Inventor. 'You're safe up there.'

She didn't agree, firming up her grip on the hand hold to keep still on Rover's squirming back. She watched the Copy guards approach, guns pointed at the rebel soldiers who had created an arc in front. To protect not just her and Rover, but the Inventor and Charlie too.

The Guardians charged at the group, but a few well-placed pops at their heads put them off. Much to the Copies' irritation, the wolves veered off to the left and right, away from the fight.

Orbs darted overhead. Carissa whistled at them, but they ignored her and continued their flight. Were they acting as Quintus' eyes and ears?

She didn't have to wait long to find out. A loud whistle sounded from an area behind the diggers that called the Guardians back. Rover tried to go with them, nearly knocking Carissa off his back.

'Settle down, Rover,' said Jacob.

Carissa sensed the old man's alarm at his wolf's eagerness to run after its replicas.

The second the last Guardian had returned to safety, a voice came through Carissa's supposedly broken NMC.

'173-C, come back to the city. We need all our children to return.'

The voice frightened her; she almost slid off Rover's back.

Quintus said, 'Your chip is self-repairing. All you did was damage it, not destroy it. You cannot break your connection to the Collective, 173.C. You belong with us.'

Commotion to her left drew her focus as two soldiers from Julius' group attacked Jerome and Alex and took them hostage. Julius provided cover as they steered their hostages over to the Collective's side.

'He is one of ours,' said Quintus in her head. 'A loyal newborn with all his emotions intact, and an NMC. The other two listen to him. We didn't realise the power emotions held in the Original's world until we saw how you as a newborn interacted with the Inventor.'

'How?' she whispered.

Jacob below didn't react to her one-sided conversation. He was too busy tracking the movement of Julius and his two rogue soldiers.

Quintus said, 'The Originals respond to emotions. I noticed that early on, but the other nine didn't agree. So we carried out more tests on the emotions of the participants. In Arcis, with the last set, a little loyalty appeared to go a long way to earning trust.'

Carissa stared at Julius, a newborn like Jerome, but who listened to the Collective. The whistle to return the wolves and Copies to safety must have accelerated his own plans for action.

Dom had dropped his gun on the ground and was trying to reason with Julius. But Carissa knew the newborn served only one. In the city, Julius' experiences with the rebels would be picked apart and used to strengthen the Collective's position in this battle.

Julius could not be allowed to leave.

'Convince the rebel leader to call this off and surrender our property.' Quintus' voice sounded harried and stressed. 'That includes you, 173-C. We do not need sustenance out here. We can last longer than the humans.'

She spoke low so as not to attract attention. 'What's wrong, Quintus?'

'Nothing, why?'

'You're eager to have us return yet you can survive without us. You can make more Copies.'

'Yes, but we need the experiences of the Copies that have lived among the rebels. We must learn how to cross over to the Beyond. Time is running out for us.'

Running out?

'What's happened to the city, Quintus?'

Rover jerked forward suddenly, forcing Carissa to grip the handhold tighter.

She saw Julius was making progress, more than she liked. She glanced down to see Jacob was no longer paying attention to her. She slid off Rover's back and hit the ground with a thud. As soon as she did, Rover took off towards the digging machines where the other beasts were.

Jacob spun round in shock. 'Carissa!' He pulled her to her feet. She brushed the dirt off her trousers. 'What are you doing?'

Her voice came out as a squeak. 'My NMC is working again, Inventor. Quintus is talking to me.'

Quintus said in her head, 'Convince the Inventor to return to the city.'

Jacob's gaze hardened. 'What is he asking you to do?'

She told him the truth. 'He wants us back. But he wants Julius more because he's had experience with the rebels. We have to stop him.'

Jacob glanced around uneasily.

He grabbed Carissa's arm suddenly. 'Remember where your files are?'

'What is his answer, 173-C?' said Quintus.

Her security files; the Inventor had shown her how to access them. She nodded, relieved Quintus could only hear her, not the Inventor.

'Grab what you can before he terminates access, and save them to your backup.'

Carissa concentrated on the connection to the city, made possible again by Quintus' efforts to contact her. She opened the database that gave her access to maps and security codes. Though she was sure the Collective would revoke it after her attempts. She found over-ground maps and underground ones with incomplete sections. She grabbed maps of the city's medical facility and designs for the Guardians and Copies. And any medical data she could.

'I can sense you, 173-C,' said Quintus. 'Whatever you are looking for won't matter if your friends are all dead. Stop what you're doing, and I promise not to hurt them.'

Carissa froze.

The Inventor looked down at her. 'What is it?'

'He's threatening to hurt you all.'

The old man's mouth pressed into a thin, white line. 'Access the command frequency code, Carissa. Do it now, before he can change it.'

Carissa found it in her security files. They had been updated, but her access had not been revoked. 'I have it.'

The Inventor nodded. 'Now use it.'

He ran over to Max, who was watching Dom, and spoke to him. Max looked over at her.

She whistled hard. The ground shook suddenly as three Guardians, including Rover, thundered towards their group. The startled Copies who rode the beasts fell to the ground. The orbs flying erratically overhead circled above Carissa's head now. She ignored them and saw Max raise his weapon while the Inventor grabbed Dom's discarded Disruptor. He handed the more lethal weapon to Max and took control of the Atomiser. Dom continued to keep Julius in his sights. Other soldiers had joined his efforts.

Carissa watched the three beasts come. Rover, she noticed, stuck to one in particular.

Max aimed for the other one, but the Inventor stopped him and pointed at the one Rover followed. 'That one.'

'Hurry!' she said, guessing Quintus would

change the code and call his Guardians back.

Charlie grabbed a spare Electro Gun and joined Max. The Disruptor in Max's hand shook with the power stolen from the frozen Copy on the ground. Charlie pointed his Electro Gun at the Guardian that Rover followed and hit it. The beast came to a shuddering halt while the second Guardian slowed in confusion. Rover slowed too and part whined part growled at Charlie.

The Inventor fired the Atomiser at a section of the fallen Guardian. Max followed up with a blast from the Disruptor to disable it. The old man tossed the weapon aside and accessed the control panel through a de-atomised hole, then disconnected the beast's central command. The wolf went into full shutdown mode.

'It's just temporary,' said the Inventor. 'When he reboots, he'll listen to the first voice he hears.'

A new whistle sounded in Carissa's head and almost deafened her. She covered her ears to drown out the noise. Quintus had changed the command frequency code.

The beast they'd failed to stop shook away its confusion at losing its directive then looked around at the group. Its yellow gaze sharpened in tandem with a snapping, snarling threat directed at the people before him. Rover lay down and rested his head on top of the deactivated Guardian.

'You've made a huge mistake, 173-C,' said Quintus. 'One you will pay for dearly.'

36

Dom

Dom hadn't noticed the activity happening behind him. If he had, he'd have grabbed one of the soldier's weapons and run over to help. It was their shocked faces that alerted him to the impending danger. He spun round, Julius forgotten, to see one of the beasts knock Max to the ground. The impact dislodged the Disruptor from his hand. It skittered across the dirt. Dom ran over to the fight and grabbed the gun from where it had landed. He checked the charge to find it was empty.

With a huff, he exchanged the Disruptor for the Atomiser that had been discarded nearby. He aimed the weapon at the Guardian that was stalking towards Max and Jacob. The blast found its mark but did little more than de-atomise a section of the hardened exoskeleton. Without a blast from the Disruptor, the structure would repair itself.

Kaylie and Imogen rushed forward and fired

their electrical weapons at the hole Dom had made, but it had already closed up.

Dom set the Atomiser to fire again but the rogue Guardian lunged at Max and snapped him up in his teeth, shaking him from side to side. Max's screams punctured the air, setting Dom's teeth on edge. He grappled with the gun and released another blast. Kaylie and Imogen fired at the hole faster this time. The Guardian yelped and released Max. But the damage was done. Dom swallowed hard as the sound of Max's bones breaking filled the air.

The injured Guardian refocused on its new aggressors: Kaylie and Imogen. They coaxed the wolf away from Max, giving Dom space to check on him.

His face was a bloodied mess, but worse, his eyes were closed. Dom pressed two fingers to his neck. No pulse.

Rage bubbled up in his throat. He released it in a loud yell. Dom snatched up the Disruptor gun and strode over to the soldiers in the middle of the battlefield, frozen in shock and staring at their dead colonel.

He stopped before them. 'Protect the others.'

Anya and her team, including Vanessa, were being attacked by diving orbs.

The soldiers ran off to help them.

He assessed the chaotic scene as Max's death forced him into a new role. A shocked Jacob stared at him. Two soldiers restrained Charlie as he attempted to get to Max. Imogen and Kaylie continued to lead the rogue Guardian away. Sheila glanced at Dom, looking for guidance.

Hell, he had no clue. Dom ran a shaky hand through his hair and assessed the rest of the scene.

Julius. He turned to see the Collective's mole and his two newborns had almost reached the digging machines, with Jerome and Alex their prisoners. But with a vicious Guardian loose and two more headed this way, he couldn't think about them right now.

Several armed Copies followed the pair of Guardians, this time on foot. Dom knew to win this everyone had to work together.

He only had a few seconds to get this right, or as close to right as he could.

He looked over at Anya, armed and ready for combat, as were Jason, Warren and Vanessa. The orbs were a nuisance, but Anya, he saw, understood the real danger lay elsewhere. While the soldiers fired at the orbs, she had a fast talk with them, then pointed at the approaching Guardians and Copies.

Dom's gaze flicked back to the danger. 'I need everyone to listen to me. We don't have much time. These things are coming. Real bullets will injure the Copies, not immobilise them, but we need to slow them down. So get Anya's team out from defence and swap your guns for theirs. I need everyone else to create a distraction for the Guardians. Don't get too close to them.'

His stomach lurched as soon as he suggested it. The team with the least experience would have to fight alongside the soldiers.

Anya and her team stepped up and swapped their revolvers for guns that shot electricity. Not as effective as the Electro guns, but they would deal damage. When one of the soldiers tried to swap with Anya, she held on and raced towards Imogen's group.

The valley was left unprotected. The soldiers in the trucks, stuck in the dangerous terrain and the camp's only mode of transport, were on their own now.

Two Guardians under the Collective's control ran rings around the main group surrounding Carissa, Charlie and the Inventor. Intermittent blasts of electricity nipped at them and kept them away. After what had just happened to Max, Dom was tempted to hand Jacob and Carissa over. But if it hadn't been for the Inventor or the young Copy, they wouldn't be here right now.

The one other thing that kept the Guardians at bay surprised him more: June.

She was following the attackers' arc around the group. Whenever she lunged at them, they startled and took a step back. Dom wondered if what she carried might save her life—all their lives.

The Copies scattered and fired Electro shots into their group. A couple of soldiers were hit and dropped to the ground. Dom knew the Electro Guns weren't enough to kill, but if the Collective had modified them, he couldn't assume anything. The two hit soldiers writhed in pain on the ground.

Out of action. But still alive.

While the Copies grappled with the soldiers protecting Jacob and Carissa, Dom turned his attention to the first of the beasts. A dejected looking Rover still sat beside the decommissioned beast. Dom called him over. Rover looked up and trotted over tentatively, glancing back at the Guardian he'd left behind on the ground. But the second Dom stalked closer to one of the Collective's Guardians, Rover perked up and fell into step. He heard him growl behind him. The sound comforted him; he would not be doing this alone.

On his sweeping arc around the team that now also protected Vanessa, he tapped June's arm. 'The wolves are avoiding you. Come with us?'

She replied with a nod and kept her steely gaze on the two Guardians running laps around the team. Rover kept pace with Dom. As he'd already seen, the beasts refused to get close to June. The Collective must have warned them not to hurt her.

June had one of the Electro Guns. But his Disruptor was out of charge.

He held it up. 'This thing needs power. I need you to fire at one of the Guardians.' June flashed him an unsure look. 'Trust me, the beast won't harm you.'

She raised her weapon and nestled it into the crook of her shoulder. She fired and her shot crackled in the air. Dom steadied his weapon as the energy blast filled and shook his gun. The beast looked over, head low, looking ready to charge. Dom swapped the

Disruptor for the Atomiser and aimed it at the beast's belly while Rover chased the second Guardian around. He fired once; it exposed the delicate innards of the beast with his shot. He swapped the guns over and shot the juiced-up Disruptor at the open wound. The wolf went limp and dropped to the dirt.

'Jacob, I need you!' shouted Dom.

He had to risk the Inventor's life for the next part.

Two soldiers shadowed the old man as he ran to the site of the fallen Guardian. He slid down to the ground and worked fast to disconnect the beast's power supply.

Dom looked up to see the second Guardian running straight for him. It had shaken Rover's pursuit. The Collective's Guardian lunged at him, like it had with Max, knocking both guns out of his hand and Dom to the ground. June couldn't get there fast enough to counteract the beast's command. As it winched open its jaw, Dom caught a flash of jagged, metal teeth glistening with saliva. A breath rushed out of him and he raised his left arm, just as a set of teeth clamped down on it. He squeezed his eyes shut and braced for the pain, but nothing more than a sting hit him. Opening his eyes, he checked the damage. The beast had punctured his flesh only; his teeth had hit the new arm the Collective had given him.

He looked up in surprise at his super arm. The beast shook Dom to get loose. He gritted his teeth through the new pain. Jacob, he saw, had finished with the other Guardian.

'Jacob,' he said nodding at the Atomiser. 'The gun.'

The Inventor grabbed it and pointed it at the beast. He fired once. But without a second blast from the Disruptor, the beast continued to move.

'You have to do it now.'

Dom controlled the thrashing beast as best as he could. Jacob cursed as he tried to locate the wriggling Guardian's control panel. June's presence, along with two soldiers who protected Jacob, appeared to unsettle the beast even more.

Dom stared into the yellow eyes of the wolf that, if it weren't for his surgery, would have ripped his arm right off. A strength he'd only seen a flash of kept the wolf under control.

Jacob did enough to take the wolf off line.

The creature released its hold on him, allowing a shaken Dom to ease his arm out of its jaw.

His arm was slick with blood, but Dom ignored it and surveyed the rest of the scene. The soldiers fought with a dozen Copies. From the chaotic scene, he couldn't tell who was winning. A Copy went down and a sharp whistle sounded. The Copies scuffled back amid peppered gunfire, returning to the digging machines that Dom now knew were only there as cover.

The rebel soldiers relaxed their tense posture around a terrified Carissa, Vanessa and an angry Charlie. Charlie broke free from his protection to go to Max.

Dom searched for Anya to find her staring in shock at something on the ground.

What the hell?

And that's when he saw the familiar faces. Dead.

37

Dom

He stared at the carnage around him. Bodies from both sides lay dead on the ground. The Copies had beaten a hasty retreat back to their position of safety. Dom assumed the whistle had come from the Collective.

The defeated Guardians lay broken and abandoned. A panting Jacob straightened up after decommissioning the latest one. Rover sniffed around the decommissioned wolves, whining in confusion and looking at Jacob.

Everyone had been shocked into a similar state of numbness. But with Max gone, Dom had no time to grieve the dead. He walked over to Charlie, who had bent over the body of his dead son.

He hunkered down beside him. 'I'm really sorry, Charlie.'

Charlie nodded but kept his eyes on Max.

Dom swallowed back the lump in his throat as

he stood and checked out the opposing scene. The diggers were in a state of retreat, kicking up plumes of dust into the air. The Copies had rallied around Julius and his two rogue soldiers, helping to corral Jerome and Alex away. A few Guardians that hadn't been sent into battle carried extra passengers on their backs.

Dom waited to make sure they weren't coming back. The orbs that had acted like pests followed after the fleet, but one flew in the opposite direction. Dom tracked its movement overhead to see it heading for Jacob's open hand. The old man lifted his hand up and the orb he had reprogrammed landed in it. Dom wondered what information the device had captured.

But a more serious situation surrounded him: the troops who'd been stunned into silent submission. They could do no more out here. The camp would serve as their haven for a while longer, long enough to regroup and figure out a way to rescue Jerome and Alex.

June cried out in pain.

And to find out what lived inside of June.

Half the soldiers looked to Dom; the other half had rallied around some fallen soldiers. His eyes went to Anya red eyed and crying, staring down at someone. Sheila tried to lead her away, but Anya pushed her off.

Dom's heart thumped in his throat on his walk over to her. His breaths shortened to a fine, painful point. Who else was dead?

He shoved soldiers aside in his attempts to reach Anya. His bloody arm drew more than a few curious glances. She didn't look up from the ground. He saw who had caught her attention.

Jason.

Lying on top of him was Warren. He must have thrown himself on top of Anya's brother.

Sheila looked up at Dom, her eyes an equal shade of red to Anya's.

'A Copy fired at Jason. Warren tried to protect him, but he was too late. The Copy caught him with a second blast, to the back.'

Dom's mouth opened but no words came out. He'd hardly known Jason. And Warren? At least he'd died doing something worth a damn.

'Anya, I'm so sorry...'

She looked up at him, wiping away another fat tear with her hand. But she said nothing.

Dom glanced around. Kaylie was watching their interaction. She lowered her eyes and turned away.

He needed to comfort her, to do something. Taking a step closer to her, he paused when she put a shaky hand up.

'Please stop. If you don't I might never stop crying.'

Dom obeyed her command. He'd do anything for her.

Her gaze shifted from her brother to the ground. Dom saw the life in her eyes fade.

He did the only thing he could.

Setting his shoulders back, he said, 'Everyone back to the camp. I don't think the Collective will come after us straight away, but we'll need to leave for the city soon to rescue Jerome and Alex.' His gaze went to a struggling June. 'And to get help for Shaw.' He nodded at the shocked soldiers. 'Collect our fallen. We will bury them in the camp.'

Imogen and Kaylie organised their teams to pick up the bodies. They included three young soldiers, as well as Jason and Warren. Judging from Thomas' bloodshot eyes, Jason's death had hit him hard.

Anya ran off towards the camp.

'Anya...' he called after her.

Sheila put a hand on his arm. 'Let her go. She needs time.'

His energy slumped to an all-time low. All he wanted to do was collapse to the ground. But with too many people watching him, he responded with a nod. If that's what she needed, that's what he'd give her.

Dom turned back to see Vanessa by Max's side, her hand on Charlie's arm, talking to him, giving him comfort.

It took every ounce of strength to watch Charlie grieve for the man who'd been more of a father to Dom than his own had been. How could he command these people in Max's absence? He was no leader.

Despite his inner doubts, he joined Charlie and Vanessa and his former mentor. 'I think we should head back. It's not safe out here.'

Vanessa looked up at him and nodded. 'Just give us a minute.'

Dom stood back from them, wanting to shout at the injustice of it all. Itching to drive a digger-shaped hole through the Collective's plans of reaching the Beyond. He'd make sure they never escaped this region, a place they controlled with the most advanced technology he'd ever seen. Its absence in the towns had forced people to survive in an unfair society, run solely by machine minds. For the first time, he believed this world was not the real one.

Dom ordered three soldiers to wait with Vanessa and Charlie, to help carry their leader home.

June's cry alerted him to her continuing distress. He ran over to her. An alarmed Jacob propped her up and an anxious Carissa had a hand on her belly.

The Copy looked up at Jacob. 'We need to help her.'

Jacob nodded. 'Not out here. We need to get her back to the compound.'

Whatever Jacob could do for June would be beyond Dom's skills. Carissa and Jacob slipped an arm each around June's waist and helped her to walk, while Rover dragged one of the decommissioned wolves behind him. Two dead Guardians remained in the battlefield. Dom wondered if the Collective would return for their fallen.

'Can you manage without me?' said Dom to Jacob, nodding at the stragglers who had yet to leave the battlefield.

Jacob nodded. 'Max was your friend. We can manage.'

Dom waited until Jacob reached the safety of the valley before turning back to where Max's body lay. The soldiers were lifting Max up under a distressed Charlie's watchful eye. They carried him back to the valley, Charlie barking commands to support his head. Dom followed behind with Vanessa.

She shook her head. 'It's up to you now, Dom. You need to get us out of here.'

Why him? He watched his feet. 'I don't know what I'm doing.'

'The soldiers, they listen to you. I know Max would want you as his replacement. Julius betrayed his trust. He always respected you.'

But Max's posthumous approval of him wasn't enough. Dom had to believe he could do the job.

They entered the valley, where the two trucks that had followed had gotten stuck. The other trucks must have retreated back to the camp after seeing their attempts. They would need to dig them out of there later.

'What if I can't do it?'

Vanessa patted his arm. 'You have to. There's nobody else.'

38

Carissa

Carissa helped the Inventor to walk June back to the camp. It was her fault this had happened. Quintus had warned of this exact outcome if she didn't give herself up. She hadn't listened to him, and now people she knew were dead. And June, a person Carissa had sworn to protect after her Original had died, struggled to cope with the changes to her body. She would not lose anyone else.

Carissa supported June's side while the soldiers carried the dead back to camp. She glanced down at June's belly, which had swelled out since earlier that day. The growth repressor that Jacob had injected into June's belly must have stopped working. They needed a more permanent solution to stop Praesidium's creation from growing. But without the city's intervention, Carissa was at a loss as to how they could do that.

An out-of-breath Inventor helped June through

the gates and to the medical bay. The bloodied medics wearing soldier uniforms swapped their guns for gauze and antiseptic as they tended to the wounded. The soldiers carrying the dead lay Jason and Warren beside the three dead soldiers and fetched sheets from the medical bay to cover them.

Carissa looked around for Anya. There was no sign of her.

June yowled with pain. Carissa shook away her distractions, determined to do something good today.

Together, she and the Inventor got June to a bed and placed her down gently. The old man collapsed on a spare bed. Carissa glanced between him, June and the female medic who had come round to the side of the bed.

'Help her, Jacob.'

She had just watched him singlehandedly decommission three of the Collective's beasts. He could do this.

He ruffled his grey hair, but Carissa couldn't tell if her demands had worked. Vanessa rushed into the room and came to one side of the bed.

Her expression was dark, like a thundercloud. 'This is a disaster, Jacob.' She waved her hand at June. 'Let something good come out of this.'

With sad eyes, the Inventor looked up at her. 'I'm trying my best.'

Carissa's nervous energy set her pacing the area in front of June's bed. The Inventor's lack of ideas worried her.

'There must be something, Inventor.' She stopped pacing. 'We need to use more of my growth repressors.'

He nodded slowly. 'I was hoping for a more permanent solution.'

She would do anything to help June. She stuck her arm out. 'Take what you need.'

'The foetus has grown and there's not much space in there, but it's all we can do.' The Inventor turned to the medic. 'I need a sterilised syringe, and the ultrasound wand.'

The medic nodded and hurried away. She returned with both items and handed the needle to Jacob. Jacob swabbed Carissa's arm and pricked it with the needle. She flinched at the pain. He drew out a sample of clear biogel from her arm, as he'd done once before. Then the Inventor swabbed June's distended belly and used the glitchy ultrasound to locate the creation inside her. He poked the needle through the skin and injected the biogel into the cavity around the foetus.

The activity in June's belly died down. With a deep sigh, June curled up on her side and went to sleep.

Jacob sat back and huffed out a breath. 'We're on borrowed time with this solution. We'll need to get her to the city as soon as possible. The repressors aren't lasting long enough.'

'Is that the only way we can help her?' said Vanessa.

338

Jacob nodded. 'The equipment we need to remove the baby is there.'

Carissa sat on the bed next to June while the others discussed her future. She got a cloth and dried the sweat on June's brow. When June stirred suddenly, Carissa snatched the cloth away. Her Original's sister looked up at her, her fine, blonde hair stuck to her face.

'Thank you,' she said with a sleepy smile.

Carissa didn't want thanks. 'I'm the cause of all of this. I let this happen to you. Jason, Warren and Max are dead because of me.'

A hand on her arm alarmed her. She spun round to see it was Vanessa.

'Don't blame yourself for the Collective's actions.'

How could she not? They'd attacked the rebels because they wanted her.

She looked up into her dark brown eyes. 'I should have given Quintus what he wanted. He told me to return home. If I had, none of this would have happened.'

'And if you had, we couldn't have halted the baby's growth with your growth repressors.' Vanessa shook her arm. 'Remember your value here today when you doubt yourself again.'

The Inventor pulled the orb from his pocket. 'Also, if you hadn't been here, I wouldn't have this.'

He threw it up into the air and caught it.

'What do you think is on it?' said a tired June.

'An aerial shot of the city, I hope,' he said. 'A snapshot of their activities since we left. They've lost key personnel. I'm praying that will give us an advantage.'

Vanessa frowned at the orb in the old man's hand. 'No better time than the present to check out what's on it.'

The Inventor cast a glance June's way.

With a nod she said, 'Go. I need to sleep for a bit. Find a way to get Jerome and Alex back.'

Vanessa and the Inventor left the medical bay. A curious Carissa followed after them. Without Jerome and Alex, she was the only one left to decipher the plans of the Collective.

They arrived at the workshop, which had a different feel to it without Jason. Thomas was there, plodding aimlessly around the space. He jerked his head up when they burst into the room.

'What's wrong?' he said, looking close to tears, like he couldn't bear any more bad news.

Jacob showed him the reprogrammed orb. 'I need to see what this thing has recorded.'

Thomas looked relieved to have a job. He took a seat at the table. Carissa sat next to him; she had more experience with the orbs than he did. Although, he better understood how his equipment worked.

'The recordings are stored in the grey sphere,' she said, clicking the orb open at the connection point to reveal two halves. 'Normally, the orb plugs into a special charging station that transmits the data to the receiver. But in this instance, you can use any energy source to make the transfer.'

Thomas hooked the orb up to the machine. The orb's last twenty-four hours passed to his machine in the format of a file. He clicked on the file and pulled up the recording. He played it for all four of them.

The orb had zipped across a stony landscape for a while before it came across the city. It flew overhead and recorded the chaos their escape had created. Copies were hastily being gathered into armies. The courtyard to the front of the Learning Centre was a mess, littered with bricks from the entrance to the underground where the Inventor's workshop had been. Carissa assumed rolling diggers had damaged the construction to reveal the workshop buried below. The orb had flown over the heads of the army before joining a litany of other orbs that awaited further instructions. Unlike the ordered Copies and beasts, the orbs zipped about in a nervous pattern.

The Inventor jabbed at the screen. 'Do you see that?'

Carissa followed the Inventor's finger, resting on the edge of the business district where they'd barely escaped with their lives.

She saw one of the beasts, two of its spindly legs planted inside the city. The other two were outside in the stony landscape.

Carissa looked up at him and whispered, 'The city's force field is down.'

39

Dom

A hectic afternoon turned into a subdued evening, leaving Dom with too much on his mind. The mood in the camp remained bleak, filled with dazed and shocked soldiers. He sat in the dining hall amid a slew of supplies they'd unpacked after hastily packing them that morning in preparation for their departure. The report from the military medics was that June was stable again, for now.

He stared down at his food, appetite gone. Rebel soldiers milled around him but he didn't see them. Someone sat opposite him.

He looked up to see it was Sheila. She had that look in her eye, the one that said someone would pay.

'Jesus,' she muttered.

She stuffed a bread roll filled with potted meat into her mouth. Restrictions would be paramount now. Dom had to look at what they had left and balance it with what they'd need for their journey to the city. But not tonight. He had no stomach for leadership.

'It's a fustercluck,' she continued with an outward breath.

He didn't disagree.

She looked up at him, her eyes glistening with unshed tears and an anger to which he could relate. 'Warren and Jason are dead. One of the soldiers from Kaylie's team, a young woman I'd never spoken to, two men from ours. And Max. Double cluck.'

Dom stared at her. 'I was there, Sheila. What's your point?'

She met his glare, her pupils contracting to two fine points. 'No need to get snippy with me. I'm just summarising.'

He was on edge; he didn't mean to take it out on her. 'I'm sorry. I just... Everyone's looking to me to fix this. What the hell do I know about battles?'

Sheila made a noise. 'Uh, everything? Haven't you been in one since age seven? Not to mention your experience with the Collective in the city. What they did to you was horrible.'

He didn't disagree, but it hadn't felt like he'd won that battle. And he'd allowed his father to ruin his life, until the fateful day he'd stumbled, hit his head and died.

Dom held up his arm, the one with the tech in it, bruised and dotted with puncture marks. His miracle limb had stopped him from becoming a Guardian's chew toy.

'I suppose one good thing came out of my surgeries.'

He flexed his hand, which hadn't suffered any damage.

Sheila nodded, her eyes fixed on his limb. 'Maybe we'd all be better off with robotic arms, at least until we find the Beyond.'

He kept his thoughts to himself that finding it was a long shot. Anya's recollection had only produced a vague idea of where the coordinates might be. Nothing concrete.

'Maybe.'

All around him, soldiers whispered about the events that had just occurred in the flatlands. His skin crawled at the furtive glances sent his way, looking at him like he was their last hope. Dom was no Saviour.

Vanessa walked into the dining hall with Jacob and Charlie. From Charlie's despondent mood and his red, raw eyes, it was clear he had been crying. When the old man neared, Dom stood and wrapped his arms around his friend.

'I'm so sorry,' he whispered into his ear.

Charlie nodded. Vanessa and Jacob sat down next to Sheila. Sheila stood up and followed with a hug of her own. Charlie patted her on the back, but pushed her away when she lingered too long.

Dom returned to his seat amid the scrutinising gazes of his peers.

Their attention on him made his skin itch. 'What?'

Vanessa leaned forward, her expression serious. 'In Max's absence, you're the leader now. Get used to people looking at you.'

'Who says?'

Vanessa had already told him there was no one else. He didn't believe that.

Charlie patted his hand once. 'My son would have wanted it this way.'

Jacob added, 'It's more imperative than ever that we find the coordinates to the Beyond. We don't have enough supplies to survive in this region.'

'What makes you think it exists?' said Dom.

'Because we all need hope,' said Jacob. 'Without it, the Collective has won.'

His brain couldn't handle the pressure. Maybe tomorrow, after a good night's sleep...

'Can I at least have tonight off? I'm not ready to be anyone's leader.'

He knew they would return to the city soon to rescue Jerome and Alex, and fix June.

Vanessa looked at the others, who nodded. 'Of course, but first we should bury our dead.'

He caught Charlie's shudder.

'Of course, I wasn't thinking...'

Charlie pinned his watery gaze on him. 'My son would be proud of you, Dominic Pavesi. So would your mother.'

A lump rose in Dom's throat. He hoped so, because right now, he felt like a fraud.

Ω

There wasn't a dry eye in the camp as the brawny soldiers dug six shallow graves in the soft, grassy patch where the trucks were parked. Some of the dead were younger than Dom. The soldiers had used bed sheets from the hospital to cover their dead. He could barely watch as Max was lowered into the ground, amid sniffles from a distraught Charlie. He was reminded of his own father's death, an event that had given him mixed feelings. He and his mother had buried him in the woods away from prying eyes. He'd even shed a few tears, although Dom was sure it had been relief he'd felt.

This was ten times worse than burying his father. Max had been his family.

He looked around at the gathered soldiers' faces when the bodies of their comrades were lowered into the graves. Warren was next. Dom hadn't thought much of him during Arcis, and even less after, but in the end he'd done something worthwhile. If Dom ever met his parents, he'd be sure to tell them that. Everyone needed someone to care about them in this world.

His gaze found Anya next. Sheila stood beside her. He'd wanted to be the one to comfort her, but his new rise into the ranks separated them again. All he could do was watch from the other side of the grave as her last family member was lowered into the ground.

Anya wore a despondent expression and her eyes remained dry as a bone. In contrast, Dom battled against a lump in his throat. Kaylie and Imogen watched him, both leaders of their respective teams. Their stance hinted at unwavering loyalty, a pair who would do whatever he asked. But what if he got everyone killed? He wasn't ready for this role, despite what both Vanessa and Charlie believed.

Jason, Anya's brother, who'd helped the rebels to fight against the Collective, was lowered into his grave next to Max. Jason, who'd helped Max rescue their group from Arcis, was dead. Dom owed him his life. If Anya let him, Dom would repay Jason by protecting her for the rest of his life.

Vanessa said a prayer and everyone respectfully bowed their heads. Soldiers carrying shovels began to toss loose dirt over the graves until the bodies were no longer visible. Everyone else peeled off from the scene, including Anya, before the last shovel of dirt was delivered, but Dom stayed until the bittersweet end. It marked the end of a harrowing day, but the beginning of a new one where revenge would be exacted. The sight of the six graves made him want leave, but as leader, he could no longer turn his back when things got too tough. He broke out of his trance when Vanessa touched him on the shoulder.

'Get some rest, Dom. We'll be safe for tonight. I'll make sure the spotters resume their posts in the mountain.'

He nodded. The Collective had a prize from

their fight that day: phantom scalps from their dead, but also prisoners.

Feeling bone weary, Dom ambled back to the main hall. Inside the private officer's room he'd claimed as his own, he removed his heavy boots and let them drop them to the floor. He unbuttoned his trousers, covered in a layer of brown dust, and peeled them off each leg. His T-shirt hit the floor last, as dusty as the rest of him. Someone had left a bowl of water by his bed. He used it to wash his face and neck, then the blood off his left arm.

Dom examined his wet arm with the bones of steel. The puncture wounds from the beast were still visible, but had begun to heal. The artificial antibiotics that Jacob had taken from Rover were teeming with self-repairing nanobots, and had the ability to heal his flesh.

One less thing to worry about, I suppose.

He crawled under the covers and draped his metal arm over his eyes. When the door opened, he didn't stir.

'Not now, Sheila. I'm too tired to talk.'

'Uh, it's not Sheila,' said a timid voice.

He dropped his arm and bolted upright in the bed at hearing Anya's voice.

She clasped her hands to the front. 'I hope it's okay to come here. I didn't want to be alone tonight.'

'Of course.'

He shuffled back up the bed and made room for her to sit, but she ignored his offer and crawled under the covers.

Her skin felt hot to the touch, her eyes were red raw, like she'd been crying.

Dom shuffled back down to a lying position. He touched her face gently, not wanting to scare her off. 'Are you okay?'

She looked up at him through pained eyes. 'No, but I will be. I just need time.' She paused; he sensed she wanted to say more. 'I wanted to thank you for what you did today.'

He hadn't done anything. 'What did I do?'

'You took control of a situation that was out of control. You tried to help Jerome and Alex when Julius was taking them prisoner.'

He dropped his gaze to the bed. 'But people died. Max—'

Anya turned his chin until his gaze met hers. 'None of that was your fault.'

It was kind of her to say, but as leader he must accept his losses as well as his victories.

'Get some sleep,' he said.

He tucked her into the spot where she belonged, under his arm, head nestled into his shoulder, her hand on his chest. God, he'd missed her. Just having her close halved his anxiety.

But when she refused to settle, he worried she wasn't going to stay. Her next move surprised him. She travelled up his body to kiss his mouth. Her lips on his shocked him so much that he let out a groan. Their tongues explored each other's mouths like they'd been starved of anything this good for a while. Dom's hands wove into her hair as she settled on top of him, igniting feelings in every part of him.

'Anya,' he muttered. 'It's probably not a good idea if you stay. Things might happen.'

She pulled back. 'What if I want them to?'

His eyes widened at her admission, but he wouldn't take advantage of her while she was feeling low.

He shook his head. 'It's not a good idea...'

She silenced him with a finger to his lips. 'I'm not asking for your advice. I've never been surer about anything in my life. Being here with you after what happened... I was out there feeling really crap, but as soon as I walked in here I knew this was where I needed to be.'

She kissed him again. The feel of her warm body against his melted his fears away. A desire stronger than he could fight filled the void.

Dom flipped her onto her back, which drew a small laugh from her.

He smiled down at her, but only briefly. His next question couldn't be more serious.

'Are you sure?'

Anya looked up at him. He searched her eyes for the desperation he'd expected to find after her loss, the need to do something to forget. But all he found was fire and love, and a certainty that matched his in that moment.

She pulled his face down to hers and kissed him

hard. Her kiss chased away the fears, the doubt, the pain of losing her to the Collective. It freed his mind to concentrate on the wide-eyed person below him, nervously anticipating his next move. He would take his time and make sure she was okay, because he needed her like he needed air.

A thin layer of clothing separated them, but with a few fumbling tugs that was gone.

No more barriers.

Dom joined with Anya, giving her an intimacy he desperately craved—something that would only strengthen what he already felt for her. His joy filled him up. A new elation he'd never thought possible made life good again.

40

Anya

Anya stirred in the bed beside Dom. Despite her aching neck from sleeping against his shoulder all night, she nestled in closer to him. Another part of her hurt from their exploration of each other last night, but she'd wanted it all. She'd wanted him. Not because of Jason, but because she was sick of being someone she wasn't. She and Dom had a connection, but he would not be her saviour or protector. The recent events had changed her, transformed her into a new person.

Dom stirred beside her. He eased his arm out from under her neck.

'Holy hell,' he cried out. 'Cramp. Muscles.'

She giggled at him, then stretched her own aching limbs. 'Okay, maybe sleeping like that all night wasn't a good idea.'

'You think?'

He wore a stupid grin on his face, despite his

discomfort.

She liked seeing him happy. She vowed to give him the life he deserved, not one filled with pain and disappointment, but one where he had to worry about nothing.

Anya sat up and stretched again, then got dressed.

Dom gave her a sad face as he watched her. 'Do we have to go out there?'

She nodded, even though the idea of staying in Dom's room for the day appealed to her. She picked up his dusty clothes and shook them out, feeling angry and sad at the reminder of where they'd just been, and tossed them to him.

His curious gaze lingered on her as he dressed. 'Are you okay?'

She nodded. 'I will be.'

They left the room together hand in hand and passed by the dining hall. Their joined limbs attracted stares and whispers, but Anya didn't care. She was past caring what others thought of her. Sheila sat at a table with Imogen, deep in conversation about something. She looked up when Dom paused at the door. She got to her feet. Imogen followed suit when Sheila poked her in the arm.

Anya caught the awkward glance Kaylie gave Dom, then her, before she looked away. How could she feel bad for something that felt so right?

She and Dom walked on to Max's office. Was it Dom's office now? He opened the door to reveal

Vanessa, Charlie, Jacob, Thomas and Carissa waiting inside. They turned as he entered the room. Anya followed with Sheila and Imogen close on her heels.

They stood together in the space known as the strategy room.

'Dom, good to see you,' said Vanessa. 'I hope you're ready to discuss ways to get back inside the city?'

He nodded, his lips thin and white. Anya rested a hand on his back. She felt the tension he held there instantly lessen.

Jacob shared details of the footage from the orb that showed the city was defenceless. Anya repeated her memory of her mother's conversation with Janet, and the diary with the coordinates. Carissa then shared her experience out on the battlefield. Quintus had contacted her, but she'd grabbed the schematics of the city before he disconnected her again.

Anya barely listened to the rest. She couldn't wait to get back to the city, to confront the Collective and tear it apart like it had done her family. First her parents, then her brother. She was done being their experiment.

Her memories were back. She would make full use of her knowledge to expose the Collective's one weakness: its desire to be free. When she was done with the Ten, she would lock them up in a special prison designed just for them.

The Collective had dealt her a blow, but it had not destroyed her spirit. If anything, the Ten had made her stronger.

They had unknowingly turned her into a vengeful phoenix. Now, she would rise from the ashes of her dead innocence.

And hit the city with everything she had.

Ω

Thank you for reading THE HAVEN. I hope you enjoyed it. The story continues in THE BEYOND. Coming in 2020.

Sign up to my newsletter at www.elizagreenbooks.com to hear about new releases in this series and receive a free gift!

Other books in the Breeder Files Series

The Facility (Book 1)
The Collective (Book 2)
The Rebels (Book 1.5) is *The Facility* retold from Dom and Warren's perspective.

The Haven

Other Eliza Green Books
Genesis Series

First an alien species emerged from the shadows.
Then his wife disappeared...

Bill Taggart is done following rules. After losing his wife and his last shred of happiness on humanity's new home, he focuses his attention on the hostile alien race living there. Sent to observe them before a population transfer from Earth, Bill hopes to find a clue to explain his wife's disappearance. But when his study of the non-aggressive natives clashes with official reports, the investigator suspects there's more to this relocation.

Starts with *Genesis Code*

Available in Digital and Paperback

www.elizagreenbooks.com/genesis-code

Genesis (Book 0) Get this teaser story for free only when you sign up to my mailing list. Check out **www.elizagreenbooks.com** for more information.

Kate Gellar Books

Eliza also writes paranormal romance under the pen name Kate Gellar.

Dark witches and guardians are mortal enemies? Tell that to Abby and her four hot demon fighting men.

Rogue Magic (free when you sign up to my mailing list. Check out **www.kategellarbooks.com** for more information)

Word from the Author

The third book is here! I hope you enjoyed catching up with Anya, Dom and the gang. All is right with the world. Anya has her memories back. She and Dom are back together. And what the actual hell is this Beyond place anyway? Find out in the next book.

Another amazing cover from Deranged Doctor Design. I really wish *Deranged Doctor* was my author name. So flippin' cool.

Thanks to Sara for editing this baby. Much love to my launch team for jumping on every new release and reviewing without me having to poke them with a stick. (I don't do that, I swear... *grins*). I roped in a couple of late betas to read the story, because I like to road test the idea before it hits the shelves. Tom and Iffet, thank you. One of you was on holidays at the time. Damn! I don't feel guilty about that at all. (Yes, yes I do. Irish Catholic guilt strikes again.)

Reviews are a privilege but if you decide to leave one, thank you. It's the best way to let other readers know if a book is for them. A one liner is all you need.

Drop me a line if you want to chat about the books, or if you just like stalking people. I'd be super excited to hear from you. Except if you're a real stalker. Then I'll be super excited to stalk you back...

Reviews

Word of mouth is crucial for authors. If you enjoyed this book, please consider leaving a review where you purchased it; make it as long or as short as you like. I know review writing can be a hassle, but it's the most effective way to let others know what you thought. Plus, it helps me reach new readers instantly!

You can also find me on:

www.twitter.com/elizagreenbooks
www.facebook.com/elizagreenbooks
www.instagram.com/elizagreenbooks
www.wattpad.com/elizagreenbooks
Goodreads – search for Eliza Green

Printed in Great Britain
by Amazon